HIGH
JOVE HO

MW00414936

"In all of the Homespuns I've read and reviewed
I've been very taken with the loving renderings of
colorful small-town people doing small-town things
and bringing 5 STAR and GOLD 5 STAR rankings
to readers. This series should be selling off the
bookshelves within hours! Never have I given a
series an overall review, but I feel this one, thus,
far, deserves it! Continue the excellent choices in
authors and editors! It's working for this re-
viewer!"

—*Heartland Critiques*

We at Jove Books are thrilled by the enthusiastic critical
acclaim that the Homespun Romances are receiving. We
would like to thank you, the readers and fans of this wonderful series, for making it the success that it is. It is our
pleasure to bring you the highest quality of romance writing in these breathtaking tales of love and family in the
heartland of America.

And now, sit back and enjoy this delightful new Homespun Romance . . .

HOME AGAIN
by Linda Shertzer

Titles by Linda Shertzer

HOME AGAIN

LINDA SHERTZER

J

JOVE BOOKS, NEW YORK

HOME AGAIN

A Jove Book / published by arrangement with
the author

PRINTING HISTORY
Jove edition / June 1996

The Putnam Berkley World Wide Web site address is
http://www.berkley.com

ISBN: 0-515-11881-8

A JOVE BOOK®
Jove Books are published by The Berkley Publishing Group,
200 Madison Avenue, New York, New York 10016.
JOVE and the "J" design are trademarks
belonging to Jove Publications, Inc.

PRINTED IN THE UNITED STATES OF AMERICA

10 9 8 7 6 5 4 3 2 1

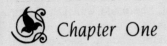 Chapter One

"Sam?"

Bertha Hamilton rose from the rocking chair and, with trembling fingers, clutched the front porch rail for support. The man coming up the front walk couldn't possibly be her husband. Sam was dead.

"Sam?" she called again.

"Bertha!" He pulled his ragged-brimmed hat from his head, revealing his auburn hair. With a whoop of joy, he tossed the hat skyward and took off at a run.

"Oh, Sam! It really is you!"

Here was the man she'd worried about, prayed for, longed for; and when she hadn't heard a single word from him in seven years, she had reluctantly given him up for dead.

"Just stop right there!" she cried angrily, raising her hands palm out.

He skidded to a halt at the bottom of the steps.

"Seven years!" she shouted. "Seven years without one single, solitary, gosh-darned word!"

"Bertha, sweetheart!" His dark brown eyes were wide with surprise and puzzlement. "I thought you'd be glad to see me."

"I'd have been plumb delighted to see you six—even five—years ago!" She stood erect, hands on hips, and glared at him. "But it's been *seven* long, lonely years. Do you think I can just let them all pass by unnoticed?"

"But I'm home now. The waiting's over." Placing one

1

foot on the bottom step, he stretched out his arms, ready to embrace her.

Her heart ached to allow her to run to him and feel his arms around her again. But she'd been without him this long, she stubbornly insisted. She could wait just a little longer until they'd settled this.

And then what? Not see him again for another seven years? Or maybe never?

"I've missed you, sweetheart."

"Missed me? Thunderation! Three letters in four months and then nothing! That's how much you missed me?"

He shrugged. "You know I never was much for writing long stuff, but—"

"I wasn't asking for *The Complete Works of William Shakespeare,*" she interrupted. "A letter, a telegram, a message from a Pony Express rider. You could've tied a note to a pigeon's leg and sent it flying."

"But—"

"Two words, Sam!" She jammed two fingers up in the air in front of his face. "All it would've taken was two measly words, scribbled on a torn piece of paper with a stick of charcoal. Two words—'I'm alive.'"

"I wrote—a lot more than you seem to think. But you never wrote back." He turned her accusations around on her.

"Do you know why? Because you forgot to tell me where you were, you big dummy!"

He took his foot off the bottom step. His long legs stood astride now as he confronted her. "Well, shoot, you knew I was going to Nevada."

"Nevada—oh, that tells me a lot!" she countered. "Do you know how big Nevada is?"

"I know a darn sight better than you do."

He crossed his arms over his broad chest and reared his tall figure back to glare at her. Even though she was standing on the porch and he was on the ground, she still felt as if he was glaring down at her.

"Hellfire, woman. I don't know what you're so riled up

about. It's not like I sneaked off in the middle of the night or something. I left a letter in every town I passed through that had a general store."

"How could I write to you in one town when you were going to be someplace else the next week?"

"I did the best I could. There isn't a whole lot of chance to mail letters up in the mountains, in case you hadn't thought about it."

"Thought about it! That's all I did for *years* was think about you. And the more I thought, and no letters came . . . well, then, I didn't have any choice but to think you were dead."

"When you didn't answer, I thought *you* were dead," he countered with a little chuckle.

"No, Sam," she replied even more seriously, just to let him know that she found absolutely no humor in the irony of this. "I mean I thought you were *really* dead. Killed by Indians. Buried alive in a mine shaft. Eaten by grizzlies. *Really* dead."

"I never got any letters, either, but I never really believed you were dead."

"Then why'd you stop writing?" She tried to keep the plaintive sadness from her voice. She couldn't let him see how much he'd really hurt her. "You might've been roaming around up in the mountains and hard to track down, but I've always been real easy to find. I've always been right here, waiting for you."

Apparently the only excuse he could offer was to shrug his broad shoulders.

Oh, don't do that! she wailed inwardly. It was sheer torture to watch every movement he made and not embrace him, press him against her body, and enjoy the feel of him that she'd missed for so long. But she forced herself to hold perfectly still. Why should she show him how much she'd missed him when he hadn't given a tinker's damn about her?

She could feel the tears welling in her eyes. She was about to let her emotions get the best of her, and she was determined she couldn't do that. She'd shed enough tears for him.

"I've been a fool, and you're an idiot." She tried to keep even the slightest hint of weakening out of her voice.

"But I'm an alive idiot, sweetheart." He grinned mischievously at her and moved to step up onto the porch again. "And I'd sure like to show you just how alive I really am."

She couldn't allow herself to return his playful grin. Once she surrendered to him on that point, she'd end up in his arms. Then she'd never settle this argument.

"You know, sweetheart," he said as he took the second step, "I figure we've got a whole lot of catching up to do, and I've got a pretty good idea where I want to start."

"Oh, no, Sam. *You've* got a lot of catching up to do," she countered. She shook her head almost as hard as she was shaking her hands out in front of her, trying to keep him away. "Things have changed a lot around here."

He stopped, but his eyes still gleamed in the light of the afternoon sun as he watched her with evident appreciation— and anticipation.

"No, sweetheart, you haven't changed a bit. You're still just as pretty as—"

"Don't try sweet-talking me, Sam. It won't work anymore. I know darn good and well I'm not as young or as thin as I used to be. I've changed. Everything's changed around here—a lot more than you'd believe."

"Yeah, I can see. The house used to be white." He nodded toward the blue house. "Why'd you paint it?"

"In seven years a house needs repainting," she shot back. "Time doesn't stand still, and the rain doesn't stop falling or the wind blowing just because you go away."

Her life had gone on, too, without Sam. But she'd have to deal with that later, *if* they managed to get around to the subject.

Then he nodded back at the mangy horse he'd left tied to the hitching post on the other side of the whitewashed picket fence surrounding their farmhouse. "And that used to be a plain rail fence."

She gave a little snort. "Where did you get that awful horse? He looks like he's going to drop dead any minute."

He chuckled again. "Yeah, he does look a little worse for the trip."

"I don't believe he looked much better than that when you first started." After leaving her with all their troubles, it sort of figured that, when Sam returned, he'd bring more trouble back with him. "I swear, Sam, if he dies here, and I have to get rid of the carcass—"

"He's not going to die. I'll take care of him."

She gave him a scornful glance up and down. "You couldn't even take care of yourself. You don't look like you fared any better than the horse."

Even though he was only thirty-two, his auburn hair had faded and grayed a little at the temples. There were lines in his tanned face at the corners of his eyes. He needed to shave the dark auburn stubble that roughened his strong jaw.

His dusty boots were scarred at the toes, worn at the heels, and cracked where they bent across the instep. His jeans were patched and baggy. He'd lost some weight.

Served him right, she decided. He was the one who had stayed away so long and missed all her good home cooking that would have kept him healthy.

The shirt that covered his muscled arms and broad, hairy chest was worn and patched.

She could still remember what it felt like to fall asleep with her head on his chest, listening to his steady heartbeat reverberating through his body and moving her very own heart. She enjoyed feeling the soft, curling hairs tickling her nose. She could remember even more vividly, and painfully, what it felt like to try to sleep without him.

A ragged carpetbag hung over the worn saddle on the horse. The top crumpled over as if there really wasn't much inside. It looked as if life had been pretty hard on Sam. Well,

it had been pretty hard on all of them, Bertha thought
bitterly.

"You didn't find any silver mine out there in Nevada,"
she accused.

All the pain and frustration of years of working the farm
alone, of waking and sleeping alone, began to pour out.

"Or if you did, you wasted it all on whiskey and wild
women, and now that you've got no money and nowhere
else to go, you think you can come back here and expect me
to welcome you with open arms."

She slapped her hand against the porch railing, then held
her hand out for him to see the calluses that lined her palm.

"I've worked my fingers to the bone to keep us from ever
being beholden to anyone ever again. What did you do,
Sam? Did you ever send me a lick of money to help keep up
this place? As if you ever had any," she added in a grumble.

"I was up in the mountains, down in the mines."

"Out on the town—"

"No, sweetheart."

"Squandering what little money you made."

"No. I never."

"Only because you didn't have any. Do you know how
hard I had to work this farm—alone—to pay the bills?"

"Of course I remember how hard it is, or I wouldn't have
gone away to try to find—"

"Do you even care?"

"Of course I—"

"Oh, horse puckies!" She slammed both fists down on the
porch rail. "You didn't care enough to write, or to send a
dollar or two toward the bills. Do you even know—"

She stopped immediately on a quick intake of breath, then
gave an angry sniff. He didn't know, the stupid oaf. How
could he? Served him right. He'd know now if he'd
bothered to keep writing to her, and told her where he was
each time he started drifting around again.

She pressed her lips together to stop herself from blurting

out the news. The way she felt now, he didn't deserve that, either.

"But . . . well, I'm home now."

"After all this time, you have the nerve to call this place your home?" she demanded. "Do you think you can just waltz back into my life, say the magic words, and all the doors will be open to you again? Who the devil do you think you are? Ali Baba without his forty thieves? Well, you've robbed me, all right, of seven years of my life. I won't let you take any more."

"I won't take anything, Bertha," he said. "I only wanted to come home and—"

"You think you can just pick up where you left off and everything will be the same, don't you?" She railed on, never giving him a chance to respond. "Well, you're wrong. Dead wrong. I don't know what you've been doing with your life, but I've made something out of this place for myself—by myself! You don't deserve to share it. Get out of here, Sam Hamilton!"

She clamped her lips shut and turned her back on him, so she wouldn't make the mistake of adding, "Before I change my mind."

Instead she told him, "I wish you'd never come back."

As soon as she'd said it, she knew she'd made an even bigger mistake. But this one she couldn't take back.

She waited, studying how the blue paint had settled into the grain of the wood in the clapboards on the side of the house. She listened for Sam to make some reply.

Any reply.

But he just stood there. She didn't need to see him to know that. She could feel his presence. She could feel his dark eyes watching her—just waiting for her to give in, she thought angrily.

Why couldn't he explain why he'd stayed away so long? she wondered. *Was* there an explanation? Why couldn't he say *something*?

All she could hear was the heel of his boot as he kicked at the brick sidewalk. Why wasn't he leaving?

She wasn't going to give in this time, as she had with every other argument she could remember. She was always the one who had given in. Just because he could smile at her with those eyes, and wrap those arms around her body, and kiss her . . .

She'd changed in the past seven years. Now she wasn't about to give in to him and his sweet-talking. She had too much to lose.

"Go away, Sam," she repeated without looking backward. "There are a couple of decent hotels in town now, and a few more that aren't so decent. Miss Sadie's House is still in business, if that's where your tastes lie, which wouldn't surprise me." She pressed her lips together tightly before continuing. "You can stay in one of them—for a while, before you move on."

She didn't hear a sound. She peeked over her shoulder to see what he was doing. He still hadn't moved, and he didn't make any reply.

"I told you, go away!"

She drew in a deep breath and clapped her hand over her mouth so the breath wouldn't escape in the shuddering sob that threatened to arise. She pressed her fingers to her lips and closed her eyes tightly against the gathering tears.

"Bertha?" She heard Arthur call to her from inside the house.

She couldn't risk answering him right away, and having him hear her voice crack with the tears she was trying desperately to hold back. She didn't want Arthur to see how much Sam's return upset her. She especially didn't want Sam to know that after all this time, he still had that much power over her emotions.

"Bertha, is something wrong out there?"

She heard Arthur's voice and footsteps growing louder as he approached the screen door. She sniffed back the tears and was at last able to lift her head.

Arthur pushed open the screen door. It screeched and slammed shut with a wood-and-wire crack. He came to stand beside her.

She still couldn't turn to him. Even though she'd managed to hold back the tears, she knew her eyes were probably rimmed with red, and that would be a dead giveaway.

The best she could do was manage to answer in a singsong voice, "No, Arthur. Everything is just fine."

Arthur eyed Sam suspiciously. His voice grew low and threatening. "If this saddle tramp is causing you any trouble—"

"No, no," Bertha replied.

"I'll get the sheriff—"

"No!"

"Mommy?" Miranda pressed her button nose against the dusty screen. She stuck her head out the front door. The tip of her nose was smudged from the screen. She quickly ducked behind Bertha.

"Mommy?" Sam repeated.

Bertha's heart jolted as she turned to him. She watched as Sam's scrutiny alternated between herself and her daughter. They shared the same fair hair and blue eyes, the same tiny stature. What other family resemblances might Sam recognize? she wondered.

"Go back inside, Miranda," Bertha told her.

But Miranda continued to hide behind Bertha for safety, clutching at her skirt with one hand. With the other she pointed her finger at Sam. Her nose curled up in disgust. "Who's *he*?"

Before Bertha could answer, Arthur assured Miranda with a pat on the top of her head. "That dirty old man won't hurt you, dear. He's just some pathetic drifter, begging for a handout. We'll give him something to eat and send him on his way."

Sam wasn't watching Miranda anymore. He was glaring at the man standing beside Bertha. "Who in tarnation are *you*?" he demanded. "I don't remember ever seeing you in town."

"Somehow I don't find that surprising," Arthur replied. "It appears to me as if you had a little trouble remembering there was a town."

"Oh, I remember, all right. You just better hope I don't remember too much about you."

"Arthur Quinn's the name," the man responded as if he wasn't afraid of who knew what about him. He tucked his thumbs under his suspenders and leaned back proudly. "I don't know what business this is of yours, mister, so I suggest you best be moving along."

Sam's lip curled up in a sneer. "I'll tell you what business it is of mine. I want to know exactly what you're doing here with my wife."

"*Your* wife?" Arthur countered.

"Yeah, *my* wife," Sam insisted. "What are you doing with my wife?"

"Helping her on the farm," Arthur answered smoothly. He gave a little snicker of disgust. "Somebody had to. I don't see why it should concern you anymore anyway. You've been gone so long, she thought you were dead. Why don't you take that as a suggestion?"

"Why don't *you* take *your* suggestion and—"

"*You're* the vermin who abandoned her, leaving her in a—"

"That's all right, Arthur," Bertha cut in quickly. She held her arms out, as if to separate the two squabbling men. The last thing she needed was a fistfight on her front porch. The blood probably wouldn't match the blue paint. "Let's just drop the subject."

Sam nodded toward the little girl still huddled behind Bertha's skirt.

"How old is she, Bertha? Looks like around five or six." Sam glared at her. The ice in his gaze made her own blood run cold. "You claim you were always here waiting for me.

Seems to me like you didn't wait too long to believe I was six feet under."

"It's not what you think, Sam."

"After all this time, how do you know what I think?"

"It's not—"

"You don't owe this man any excuses, Bertha," Arthur told her.

"That's all right. I see the way it is. Sorry to have troubled you folks. Good-bye, Bertha."

She watched him turn on his heel and walk toward his horse. He stopped and bent down to retrieve his battered hat, jammed it on his head, and continued on his way.

Each step he took tugged a little more at her heart until she thought he'd tear it right out of her. She felt as if her heart snapped in two within her breast as Sam mounted and rode out of her life for the second time.

"Well, as I live and breathe!" Rachel Pickett exclaimed as she caught a glimpse of the man through the big, flapping, wet sheets her older son was helping her to hang on the line.

"Who is it, Mom?" Del asked.

One hand resting on her rounded stomach, she turned to the two small children who were playing beside the wicker laundry basket at her feet.

"Willy, Alice. Quick! Go get Daddy," she told them. "Run, run!"

The boy sprang to his feet immediately and took off. His pudgy younger sister needed a little more help from the laundry basket before she was balanced enough to move.

Del started laughing, his voice cracking up and down the scale. "Remember how you used to send me running every time Chester the He-Cow got loose?"

Rachel gave a deep, theatrical sigh. "Poor old Chester. Gone for hide and bones years ago."

"Yeah, but he left a passel of little Chesters and Chester-ettes mooing around here."

"Del! If I've told you once, I've told you a thousand times—"

"A gentleman doesn't speak of such things in front of a lady," he finished for her.

She shook her head in mock forlorn. "I was raising such a nice little boy."

"Until you started shooting at Tom Pickett," Del added with a chuckle.

"I know it's your father's bad influence on you. I should've shot him when I had the chance." Then she laughed. The last thing she'd ever want to do was lose Tom Pickett.

"Don't worry, Mom. I'll behave in front of the company."

At last her visitor had drawn close enough to hear her.

"Sam Hamilton!" Rachel exclaimed.

"How do, Mrs. Pickett?" Sam touched the brim of his hat.

Seeing her in a family way, he was sorry his arrival had startled her. Maybe he should've let her, too, know he was coming. Tarnation, maybe he should've taken out an advertisement in the Grasonville *Herald* and notified the whole dang town. He'd been hoping he could stop by and see old friends without encountering any problems.

"I never thought . . ." Some of her wide-eyed wonder had left her, but she still had a bewildered smile. "Well, honestly, Mr. Hamilton, I never thought I'd see you again."

Sam gave a bitter little chuckle. "You're not the first person I've heard say that today."

"But they . . . she . . . I mean, we heard you were . . . that you had . . . passed away," she mumbled.

"No, just her wishing, I guess."

"Oh, no! It's just that—"

"That's all right, Mrs. Pickett. I've already had a little talk with Bertha. I know exactly where I stand."

"Oh, but, well . . ."

Sam knew he wasn't a man given to fancy notions. He wasn't imagining the uncertainty in Mrs. Pickett's voice.

Partly to change the subject, and partly out of his own curiosity, he turned to the lanky boy standing beside her.

"This can't be Wendell?"

"No, sir. It's Del," he responded with a wide grin.

Rachel gestured between them. "Del, you were so young. You probably don't remember—"

"Sure I do. How could I forget? I really looked up to you when I was little." He extended his hand. "Welcome back, Mr. Hamilton."

Sam returned the boy's firm shake. It was strange to see almost eye-to-eye with the towheaded little boy he remembered as only about knee-high to a grasshopper. He grinned at the bit of dark fuzz starting to show at the corners of Del's upper lip.

Yeah, little sissy Wendell sure had grown into a fine youth. But the way Del had said he remembered him made Sam wonder if it was for good things or for bad. If Bertha believed he'd abandoned her, even if she'd told all the townspeople he was dead, what had they chosen to suppose on their own?

Del had said he'd looked up to him when he was little. Sam could remember playing with the lonely little boy so eager for a father. Not having any children of his own, Sam had been just as happy playing with Del. But what did Del think of him now?

"Let me water your horse for you," the youth offered. Taking the reins, he moved off toward the barn.

"Sam! You ol' hound-dog," Tom Pickett called as he sauntered across the field. The fair-haired boy and curly-haired little girl frolicked around his feet.

"Tom, you must've known I was coming and started out a week ago for this very spot, or you never would've gotten here on time. I've never seen a slower-moving man."

Tom just grinned. "You're moving pretty good yourself for a man in your condition. I heard you were dead."

"Oh, we've already been through all that."

Tom frowned and nodded. "So, you've been to see Mrs. Hamilton already."

"Yep," Sam said, rubbing the back of his neck.

Tom started rubbing the back of his neck, too, and made some kind of grunting sound, as if he understood exactly what Sam meant. Maybe they could talk a little later, Sam thought, when Rachel wasn't around.

"These all yours?" Sam asked, gesturing to the smaller children.

"Nope. Sally—she's seven—is feeding the chickens around back."

"These are Willy and Alice," Rachel said, laying a hand on each one's head in turn.

"Well, you might be slow on your feet, but you've sure been keeping the stork flying," Sam told him, trying to keep his voice low so as not to offend Mrs. Pickett.

Tom's grin widened. "A man's got to have some hobbies."

"Now stop!" Rachel declared, blushing to the roots of her blond hair. She clapped her hands over Alice's ears. "Not in front of the little ones."

"Handsome family. You're a lucky man, Tom. I wish Bertha and I'd been able to—"

"You dang fool. Haven't you seen—?"

"Mr. Hamilton, I have to show you the house." Rachel interjected as she seized him by the arm and fairly dragged him away. "Not our business, Tom," Sam heard her mumble. Then she turned to him and said brightly, "I don't believe you've had a chance to see all the changes we've made."

He wanted to stop and ask Tom what he was talking about. But Mrs. Pickett was chattering so rapidly that he couldn't fit a word in edgewise. Well, he was home now. There'd be time.

If he hadn't remembered they lived on the farm right next to him, Sam would hardly have recognized the old Williams

Pla...
sho... n

"...
"It's ...
town ...

"Y... ...
aroun... ...
block... and two ...
porch.

"Yo... ...
for coo...ing and ...
and two bedrooms ...
through ...

"We ... ...
the stai... ...
back.

Linda Shertzer

16

"Come see how they made the parlor
actually use it now. They even ext
wraps around the whole house,
outside on rainy days. We're ho
so Sally can start taking les
"Randa! Randa!" Alic
excitedly, then made
There was a kn
Sam would
a darned sh
"Rach

"I can... ... ... with a chuckle.

He als... ...mbered now Rachel, when she was still the Widow Williams, had kept this room neat as a new pin, and bare as an old maid's pillow.

The room was still so clean that the floorboards practically shone with all the polishing. But there were pies, cookies, and loaves of bread set out cooling, and dusty herbs drying from the ceiling.

Sam had missed all these things. He longed to be a family with Bertha again. Well, he thought with a bitter smile, some things you just can't have. And some things you can if you just try hard enough. He sure intended to try.

A basket of wriggling puppies guarded by the mother dog was huddled close to the stove. Sam could remember a time when Mrs. Pickett wouldn't allow a "filthy animal" in the house.

Remembering what Bertha had said about him, and knowing what close friends she and Mrs. Pickett had been, he was surprised *he* was allowed in the house.

"Tom and some friends put up the addition about three years ago," Rachel said. She led him farther into the house.

bigger—and we
nded the porch so it
o the kids can still play
ping to get a piano next year,
sons."

e shouted and jumped up and down
a dash for the doorway.

ock on the screen door. "Hello! Rachel?"
recognize her friendly call anywhere. It was
ame she still didn't feel so friendly toward him.
el? Are you there?"

ll be right out, Bertha."

Yeah, you go on out, Mrs. Pickett, Sam thought as he
stood in the parlor. That would be a whole lot better than
Bertha coming in and seeing him again right now.

"You don't mind if Miranda comes over again today to
play, do you?"

"Of course not."

He heard the distinctive slam of the screen door.

"Thanks. I've got so much to do and . . . well, you just
wouldn't believe the horrible day I've had already."

"Yes, I think I would," Rachel answered slowly.

Sam leaned over to Tom and whispered, "Hey, while you
were doing all that building, you didn't happen to add a
back door to this place, did you?"

"Yep, but you got to go through the kitchen to get to it."

Sam exhaled noisily.

"Sorry. I didn't think you'd be over here trying to hide out
from your wife."

"Think Mrs. Pickett would mind my climbing out the
window?"

Tom shrugged. "You could try. But if you put a tear in
them sissy lace curtains she ordered all the way from
Chicago, she'll have your guts for garters. And don't think
she can't do it, too."

Sam nodded, remembering how the whole town was

abuzz the time Rachel took potshots at Tom for building his fence where she thought it had no right to be.

"You're so lucky, Rachel," Bertha said. "So many beautiful children."

"Miranda's beautiful, too."

Bertha giggled. "I know she is. But you've got so many of them. Miranda gets lonesome with no one else to play with."

"I remember how lonesome Del was before I married Tom, and we . . . well, we sort of got carried away with too much of a good thing."

"I didn't know there was any such thing as too much of a good thing," Bertha responded with an embarrassed giggle. "Oh, please, don't remind me!"

"Oh, mercy! If our mothers could hear us now, they'd turn in their graves!"

Sam heard the two of them making little snickering sounds, like two kids laughing in church over something they weren't even supposed to know about.

Miranda and Alice, and an older girl Sam assumed was Sally back from the chicken yard, made a little parade carrying armfuls of dolls and doll clothes from the kitchen into the parlor. Miranda looked so small compared to the others.

"Where's Del?" Miranda asked as the girls passed each other in the doorway.

Sally shrugged.

"Is he working with the cows? Or feeding the horses? Or the chickens?" Miranda persisted.

"Who cares?"

"Cares?" Alice echoed.

"He's just a dumb old boy."

"Dumb."

Miranda sat down and started sorting through the doll clothes with so much intensity that Sam just knew her thoughts were really elsewhere.

"He's . . . he's kind of cute for a dumb old boy."

"Ha! You can say that 'cause he's not your brother."

"Brudder."

"You don't have to put up with him." Sally said with a grimace.

"When I grow up, I'm going to marry him—"

Sally let out a shrill whoop of derision that Alice echoed.

"And we're going to live in a big, red, brick house—like that one in town—"

"Mr. Richardson's?"

Miranda nodded. "That's it."

"That big old ugly thing?"

"Icky!" Alice stuck her tongue out.

"*I* think it's beautiful."

"It's haunted, don't you know," Sally informed her in a gloomy whisper. Her eyes grew wide. "By the restless spirit of his dead wife."

Miranda firmly shook her head. "Nope. No such thing as ghosts."

Sam had to chuckle under his breath. Miranda might be shy around strangers, but she was a real whippersnapper when it came to stating her opinions to her playmates.

No doubt Sally and Alice were sisters—they looked enough like Rachel and Tom both. No question Miranda was Bertha's. Who was her daddy? Sam frowned as he tried to do some ciphering in his head. Oh, heck! Men weren't any good at judging children's ages from their size.

One thing he could tell for sure, though. Miranda didn't talk as if she were only five or six. She had to be older. And if she was older, there couldn't be any doubt about who her daddy was.

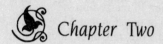 Chapter Two

"Miranda?" Sam said softly, emerging from the corner where he'd been standing with Tom. He could feel his heart swelling with pride. Son of a gun! He could almost feel his eyes misting over at the sight of his very own child. "Is that what your mommy named you?"

Miranda dropped her doll and the doll's little dress. Her mouth dropped open, and her blue eyes grew wide with fright.

"Mommy! Mommy!" she screamed and bolted back to the kitchen.

"What's the matter?"

"Alice, did you bite Miranda again?" Rachel scolded.

"No, Mommy," Miranda said breathlessly. "That man is *here*."

"What man?" Bertha asked.

"The man you chased away."

"Chased . . . away . . ."

Sam could hear realization dawning in Bertha's tone of voice. He knew he couldn't hide any longer. He stepped out into the kitchen.

Bertha had already taken a defensive stance. Hands on hips, she glared at him. "What are you doing here?"

"Visiting old friends."

Clutching her mother's skirts, Miranda peeked out from behind.

"Do you have to follow us here, too?" Bertha demanded.

"I think I was here first." He tried to grin at her, the way he always had before when she was angry and he needed to calm her down. He was hoping it would work even better in front of the neighbors. "Are you following me, Bertha, sweetheart?"

"When Hades freezes over! And don't call me sweetheart!"

It was going to take an awful lot of grinning to calm her down today.

"Stay out of my life, Sam Hamilton."

"I can't."

"Why not?" she snapped. "You've had enough practice."

"I don't want to. I should've known when I first saw her," Sam said, closely watching the shy eyes peeping out of him from behind Bertha's skirt.

"What . . . what are you talking about?"

"But she's so tiny, it sort of confused me at first. Anyway, you know men aren't any good at guessing kids' ages."

"Just leave me and my daughter alone," Bertha warned. Her voice was half command, half plea.

She tried to back away from him, but the clinging child made her stumble. She clutched at Miranda to keep her safe.

"Why didn't you tell me Miranda is *my* daughter?"

"She's *not* your daughter!" Bertha cried angrily.

"Of course she is," he insisted. "I can see it all now. I don't know why I didn't realize immediately."

"Maybe because you were too busy arguing with Mr. Quinn or trying to get your hands on me."

"Why didn't you tell me as soon as you saw me?"

She stared at him in disbelief. "You big idiot! Do you have to ask?"

"I guess not," he replied sheepishly. "You were pretty mad."

"You're darned right. I still am."

"But why didn't you tell me long ago?"

"Because . . . because we'd waited so long," she blurted

out, "and I'd gone to so many doctors, and I was still never able to . . ."

Sam could see the faint blush coloring Bertha's fair cheeks, talking about such personal things in front of the neighbors.

"I even went to see that strange Mrs. MacKenzie across town with all her weird herbs and teas. I couldn't hardly understand a word she said, but I figured all a body had to do was to drink the tea she gave me. So I did, right before you left. It didn't taste too bad, and . . . well, when . . . when I first suspected I was . . . in that condition, you were already gone. And I couldn't believe it anyway. I didn't want to write anything until I was sure. By the time I was sure, I had no idea where you were or how to let you know. And you didn't care enough to ask!"

"Oh, Bertha, I *did* care. Let's not go through that again." He scuffed the heel of his boot against the floor. "If I'd have known, I'd have come right home and taken care of you. If only you'd told me—"

"I would have—"

"You should have—"

"Don't you *dare* try to make me feel guilty for managing to raise my daughter without you!" she snapped.

Bertha could feel Miranda shaking with fear. The poor little thing had probably never seen her mother this loud and angry. Bertha didn't want to frighten her daughter any further with more shouts and accusations at this strange man who had already scared her twice.

She tried to turn to reach behind her to comfort Miranda and still manage to keep an eye on Sam. She wanted to keep him away from both of them. He didn't deserve Miranda.

She looked him directly in the eye and, in a deceptively soft voice, demanded, "Where were you when she was born? When she took her first steps and fell down—you weren't there to pick her up again. Her first word was 'Mama,' not 'Dada.' Why shouldn't it be? She doesn't know who her daddy is."

"Bertha, don't you think you're being a little harsh?" Rachel interrupted.

"Life is harsh, Rachel," Bertha replied. "You of all people ought to know that as well as I do."

"But it doesn't have to stay that way," Rachel insisted.

"Maybe not for you."

"In all fairness, Mrs. Hamilton . . ." Tom began.

"There's been nothing fair about this all along, Mr. Pickett," Bertha told him.

"He does have a right to be with his daughter," Rachel continued. "And Miranda has a right to know who her father is."

"I'm her father, for Pete's sake, Bertha," Sam repeated Rachel's plea.

"You had nothing to do with raising her. She's no more your daughter than the farm is yours anymore."

"I suppose she thinks that Quinn fellow is her daddy." Sam's lips curled just mentioning the man's name.

"No," Bertha answered very quietly. "She thinks her real daddy's dead."

"I'll bet you didn't waste any time telling her that."

"I didn't stand over her cradle reciting it like nursery rhymes, if that's what you mean. I waited until she started wondering and asking why all her friends had daddies and she didn't. Even then, I waited until I couldn't wait any longer."

"But telling her I was dead?"

"What was I supposed to tell her?" she demanded. "That her daddy had abandoned her?"

Sam pressed his jaws together tightly and bowed his head. What else could he say? He looked up to quietly study Miranda. It must have been hard on the little girl, not having a daddy to play with or give her piggyback rides, or to cuddle up on his lap when she was sleepy and tell her stories, when everybody else did. He remembered how kids could taunt the playmate who was different from the rest of them, even in the smallest way.

He'd missed the first really important six years of his daughter's life. Couldn't he at least try to make up for it now, somehow?

Suddenly he looked into Bertha's eyes and started, "I think it's high time she learned her real daddy's still alive."

Arms outstretched, he bent toward Miranda. "You'd like to find out your daddy's still alive, wouldn't you?"

"No!" Miranda clung to Bertha's skirt, shaking her head hard.

"Wouldn't you want to know he loves you very much?"

"No!" She clung to Bertha so tightly she almost pulled her over.

Righting herself, Bertha tried to comfort the child. But Miranda couldn't be coaxed out to where she could hold her more comfortably.

"My daddy's in Heaven. You're not my daddy." Her nose curled up in a sneer. "Go away, you dirty man!"

Sam stood erect. His arms dropped to his side. Bertha could see the hurt and bewilderment in his eyes as he watched their frightened daughter. She could feel a little twinge of sympathy for him at Miranda's rejection—even though it was his own fault.

"Well, what did you expect?" Bertha demanded in a little softer tone. "That she'd welcome you with open arms? Just like you thought *I* would?"

Sam shook his head. "I . . . I just didn't think she'd be afraid of me."

"Why not?" Bertha flung her hand out toward him in a gesture of disgust. "You look like you were dragged through the dirt all the way from Nevada."

"I look that bad?" Sam asked. His eyebrows rose in surprise. "Bad enough to frighten children?"

"Bad enough to scare the hens out of laying."

Sam reached up and stroked his chin. "Well, I guess I haven't had much chance to look in a mirror lately."

"You could've at least cleaned yourself up first before you came calling," Bertha scolded.

"I didn't 'come calling.' I came *home*," he corrected.

"This *isn't* your home," Bertha grumbled.

"I didn't think I had to get all gussied up to come home. I was in such a hurry to see you, I plum overlooked a bath."

"Yeah, seven years is quite a hurry," she shot back. "Well, you've got plenty of time now. I told you before, I'm sure any of the hotels in town could supply you with a bath, at the very least."

"I kind of thought I'd go home. . . ."

Bertha turned around, scooped Miranda up in her arms, and headed for the door. "We've been through this before, and I won't air any more dirty linen in front of the neighbors. She's not your daughter, it's not your home, and . . . and I'm not your wife."

Sam watched Bertha push through the doorway. The screen door slammed shut again. He moved to follow her, but a hand on his elbow prevented him.

"Better think twice about going after her," Tom said with a little grimace. "Leastwise not until you've had a really good soaking in hot water and played with the soap for a while."

"Maybe you're right. You don't suppose I could get a quick bath here and follow her?"

"I don't think following her, even after you've had a bath, would be a good idea at all, Mr. Hamilton," Rachel said. "She needs a little time alone—to think about all this."

"You've really surprised her—surprised us all," Tom told him.

"It's not every day a husband comes back from the dead, you know," Rachel continued. "Bertha just needs a little time to get used to the idea. Then I'm sure she'll come around."

"And Miranda?" Sam asked.

He watched Rachel try to hide a frown of uncertainty.

"Children are such peculiar little creatures. And Miranda . . . well, Miranda's very . . . active. But very adaptable, I'm sure. I'm . . . I'm sure she'll get used to you . . . eventually."

Sam didn't feel very reassured.

"We can still offer you that bath," Tom said, "and a place to sleep."

"We'll just move Del and Willy into the parlor—"

"No, no. I won't hear of it," Sam said, shaking his head.

He wanted a long soak in a tub full of steaming hot water. He wanted to fill his empty stomach with his first good meal in a long time. He wanted to stay close to his home, to his wife, and to the child he'd just discovered he had. But when he looked around at all the little Picketts, and Mrs. Pickett in a family way again, he knew he couldn't impose on them any further.

"I haven't been into town for a long time," he said, heading for the door. "I think I'll ride on in and say howdy. Then I'll check into one of the hotels, at least until Bertha and I can settle this thing."

Tom followed him out onto the front porch.

"Can I have a word with you, Sam?"

Sam stopped and turned around to look at his old friend.

"I know your finances weren't any better than anybody else's around here when you left," Tom said. "If you don't mind my saying so, you don't look like things have improved any. If you need a couple of dollars . . ."

"Tarnation, Tom! No," Sam said. "Keep your money. You got your little ones and the missus to look out for. But I sure do appreciate the offer."

Widow Crenshaw let out a gasp. With one hand she clutched at her heart, and with the other clutched Miss Catherine Barber's sleeve.

"Janet! Are you dying?" Miss Barber demanded. "Oh, not right out here in public . . . in the middle of the sidewalk. It's just so . . . so common!"

"Oh, hush! I'm fine," Widow Crenshaw scolded. She released Miss Barber's sleeve—and her heart. "I'd never do anything so crass. But *that* sight's enough to make Bertha Hamilton faint dead away."

With her lace-gloved pinkie, she pointed delicately toward the end of Main Street.

Miss Barber squinted and leaned forward, trying to see better. Then she shrugged. "Just another drifter coming through town."

"Oh, Catherine, you couldn't see a gnat on your nose! It's Sam Hamilton."

Miss Barber's hand flew to her mouth. "Why, bless my soul! Are you sure?" She leaned forward, squinting harder.

"Who else ever had that audacious color hair? Bertha can just thank her lucky stars the child didn't come out freckled, especially for a girl."

"But . . . but I thought Mr. Hamilton was dead."

"So did everyone else. Especially since that's what Bertha led everybody to believe," Widow Crenshaw said. Her thin lips pursed into a tight knot. "Telling everyone her husband was dead, then feeling free to start keeping company with Arthur Quinn, of all people."

"Well, you must admit, after years of poverty, she set her sights high enough."

"Only other higher sight in town would've been Mr. Richardson."

Miss Barber gave a delicate snort. "As if that miserly, reclusive old curmudgeon would peep out of his bank or his grand house long enough to court a lady!"

"Oh, Catherine, you're only miffed because he never took a shine to you."

Miss Barber gave another snort—a lot less delicate, and changed the subject. "Where do you suppose Mr. Hamilton's been all this time?"

Widow Crenshaw tilted her head as if that would help her examine Sam better. "It appears to me as if he's been rolling in the dirt. That horse doesn't look much better."

"I wonder if Bertha already knows he's back."

Widow Crenshaw leaned just bit closer to her friend and

whispered, "If she doesn't, I wonder if we should tell her?"

"Someone certainly should." Miss Barber nodded emphatically.

"The news might as well come from concerned, caring folks like us," Widow Crenshaw said, preening the gray-streaked brown hair that peeked out from beneath her poke bonnet.

"Yes, it should." Miss Barber nodded again.

Widow Crenshaw pursed her lips. Her eyes narrowed with speculation as she scrutinized Mr. Hamilton. "I also wonder if he knows what she's been up to lately."

"I highly doubt that."

"Then I think it behooves us to enlighten him as well."

"I couldn't agree with you more, Janet."

Widow Crenshaw and Miss Barber waited until Sam had entered the General Store before crossing the street.

Cinnamon, coffee, kerosene. The General Store still smelled the same, Sam thought, taking a deep, appreciative breath as he entered. It still looked pretty much the same, too.

The bell that hung on the front door jingled as he pushed it open.

He shifted the weight of his carpetbag in his hand. He didn't mind leaving it when he stopped at his home, or even at the Picketts'. He could have left it in the Grasonville he knew seven years ago, where everybody knew everybody else—and trusted each other.

But Grasonville was a lot bigger now. The railroad even stopped here, just like Henry Richardson had predicted it would, at a bright red depot with a big Regulator clock and a telegraph and everything.

As he'd ridden into town, Sam had noticed there were a lot of people he didn't recognize living here now. With the railroad, even more strangers were just passing through. He wasn't about to leave his carpetbag unattended in town.

And even if it was the honest old Grasonville he'd left

years ago, he'd changed. He wasn't as trusting anymore. Hard times could make a man awfully suspicious.

The bell jingled again as the door slammed shut. The old man seated near the big, black potbellied stove in the middle of the store raised his head. When he spotted Sam, his watery blue eyes brightened.

"Well, I'll be switched!" Pop Canfield called in a gravelly voice. "Sam! Sam Hamilton, you flea-bitten, egg-suckin' ol' hound dog."

"Pops, you remember me?"

"'Course I do! Who wouldn't?"

Pops looked as old and dried as the crackers in the barrels on either side of the stove.

"Where's your buddy?" Sam asked, gesturing to the empty seat on the other side of the checkerboard.

"Oh, I . . . I suppose he's losing at checkers to Saint Peter now just as bad as he always used to lose to me." Pops gave his thin shoulders a little shrug.

"Tarnation! When did this happen?"

"Oh, 'bout a year after that smack he took to the back of his head. Seems it did more damage than Doc realized."

Sam could hear him trying to sound matter-of-fact, but there was a mist in the old man's pale blue eyes that told Sam that Reuben Taylor was greatly missed.

"Dang shame there ain't some way to see inside a body's head."

"Dang shame," Sam responded.

"I never thought I'd outlive him."

Sam felt a little shiver of cold sadness. It was one thing to return to find a lot of new people in town. It was completely different to discover that some of the old residents had passed away. Well, what did he expect after seven years? he asked himself. It still wasn't easy.

"I know it's a little late, but I'm mighty sorry, Pops. Mighty sorry."

Pops just nodded.

"A checkerboard isn't much good for one. Have you found a new partner?"

Pops shook his head. "Gordon Nichols swears he's going to close down the haberdashery, but I'll believe it when I see it. Mrs. Nichols wouldn't hear of it. She'd rather be the wife of a businessman than have ol' Gordy home all day."

Sam nodded. "That sounds like her." Some things didn't change.

He tapped the curved back of the wooden chair. "I don't suppose Reuben would mind me taking a load off my feet, would he?"

"Course not." Pops straightened in his seat and leaned forward, as if a warm body in the chair opposite him had something to do with his own vitality. "Especially not for someone who's come back from the dead."

Sam settled himself in the chair and set his carpetbag at his feet. "So she really did tell them all I was dead."

"What else?"

The old man was watching him carefully. For somebody who only sat at a checkerboard all day, Pops sure could fathom other people's deepest feelings.

Now it was Sam's turn to shrug. He could hardly tell Pops—and all the other people who had gathered around them—that face-to-face Bertha had accused him of abandoning her and their child.

"She wore mourning for a year, all proper like," a lady told him. She looked like the Widow Crenshaw, only with a lot more wrinkles.

"She even had the little one done up in a bonnet with black edging," the lady standing beside her said.

The only person in town Sam remembered with a squint like that was Miss Catherine Barber. Those two old busybodies had always hung around together anyway.

"You can't hardly blame her for thinking you'd gone on to your Heavenly Reward," Pops continued.

Sam didn't tell Pops that Bertha would probably have sent him in the other direction.

Pops chuckled as he glanced at Sam's ragged clothes. "You *look* like you been dead and buried, and then dug up again."

The crowd around them joined in the laughter.

"Funny you should say that," Sam replied, chuckling, too. "Most people tell me I look like I was dragged here from Nevada."

"So, you really did go all the way to Nevada?" a man asked, and started a barrage of questions that came too fast for Sam to answer each and every one.

"What'd you do out there?"

"What'd you find out here?"

"Did you see any buffalo?"

"Did ya kill any injuns?"

"What made you decide to come back?"

This last question stopped all the others. Sam sat more erect in the chair and looked around the crowd of faces, trying to find the bold questioner.

He didn't have too much trouble. The people on either side of the little man had all stepped back and were staring at him like arrows pointing in the right direction.

Keeping his eyes on the man, Sam stood. He never figured he was much taller than the average fellow, but he knew he towered over this puny little banty rooster. Still, if there was going to be another confrontation, he felt better having a higher vantage point.

"I don't believe I know you, sir," Sam said, glaring down at him.

To Sam's surprise, the little spud stood his ground.

"Sure you do, Mr. Hamilton," the man replied. "I had my office set up in Grasonville long before you left."

Then he had the grit to extend his hand. Sam automatically took it. The man's hand felt like a peeled potato, all cool and slimy.

"Lester Martin, attorney-at-law."

So that explained it.

"I still don't recall ever making your acquaintance."

"Not unless you've tried to sue somebody," Pops remarked.

Sam turned to him. From the way the old man pursed his lips and shot daggers at Mr. Martin, Sam could deduce what his opinion was.

"Not lately," Sam replied.

"You've obviously been to your farm already," Mr. Martin said.

"How do you know?"

"You entered town from the west, so you'd have to pass your farm on the way in. Seems only logical you'd try to stop in. You also weren't surprised to hear about the child."

"That's right," Sam grudgingly conceded.

"I'd also venture to say you received a less than cordial welcome."

Sam grunted. He should've figured the little weasel would bring up something like that in front of everybody.

Mr. Martin eyed him with a smirk. "Otherwise, why would you be here now?"

Sam grunted again. Pops, he would confide in. But he had no intention of telling this spying little weasel anything. On the other hand, Mr. Martin did seem to have a knack for uncovering information he thought might be useful.

Sam turned to glance around the crowd. Half of them looked as if they were just dying to find out why he was at the General Store instead of enjoying a happy reunion with his loving family. The other half looked as if they were waiting for him to tell Mr. Martin to go to blazes.

"Yes, Mr. Hamilton." A familiar voice cut through the anxious silence. "What *are* you doing here?"

The crowd parted, making an aisle between Sam and the door. He felt a little like Moses at the parting of the Red Sea, except it was Arthur Quinn who stood across from him in the doorway, like Pharaoh leading his army, ready to attack. As Mr. Quinn slowly approached, Sam could only stand there and hope God was on his side.

Now, Quinn wasn't any taller than he was, Sam figured,

but he had a good bit more bulk since, unlike Sam, he'd probably been eating regularly. It wasn't going to be easy to intimidate this fellow.

"We seem to keep turning up in the same places, Mr. Quinn," Sam said. "I might ask you the same question."

"What am I doing here?" Quinn repeated. He glanced about him, as if trying to take in all the sights, and gave a hearty laugh. "Why, I own this place, Mr. Hamilton."

Quinn made an expansive gesture with his entire arm that encompassed the general store and nearly everything in it.

"You . . . ?"

Quinn was on his home ground. This might be harder than Sam had originally thought.

"That's right." Quinn proudly tucked his thumbs under his suspenders again.

Sam sure would like to see those suspenders snap, and pop up and hit Quinn right in the nose.

Lots of new people had come to town to build houses and stores. Sam figured somebody would take over the store when Pete Finnerty got shot trying to kill Rachel and Tom. He never figured the same person would come to try to take his place, too.

Oh, Bertha, Sam silently groaned. *After all we went through with Finnerty when he owned the store, now you take up with the new owner! How could you?*

"I thought you'd decided it would be best to keep moving along," Quinn said, glaring at Sam.

Sam returned his glare. "It appears you heard wrong."

Quinn's thumbhold on his suspenders turned into a clenched fist. "I suppose you'll be spending the night in one of the hotels."

"Maybe."

"And moving on tomorrow."

"Maybe. Maybe not. Either way, I don't see any reason to keep you informed of my plans."

Quinn didn't say anything.

"I will tell you one thing, though."

Sam stepped closer to Quinn until they were almost nose to nose. He could see little beads of sweat popping out on Quinn's forehead. Sam tried not to smile. He might not be on home ground, but, after everything else he'd been through, he felt sure he could still glare down any ordinary storekeeper.

His voice was deep and dark as thunderclouds. "Stay away from my wife."

Quinn just smirked at him. "It doesn't look to me as if she wants to be your wife anymore."

"Oh, yes, she does. I've come back to make sure of that."

Some of the people murmured their agreement.

"I'd say that was up to the lady to decide," Quinn replied.

Others in the crowd—probably those who owed him a lot of money—murmured in favor of the storekeeper.

Sam gave the man one last, threatening glare.

"I've made up *my* mind. Don't get in my way, Quinn."

Sam reached down and picked up his carpetbag. He tapped on the top of the checkerboard.

"Good seeing you again, Pops," he said. "I'll be around."

Without saying another word, he shouldered his way past Quinn, then passed through the watching crowd.

As the crowd closed in behind him, several times he felt hearty pats on his back and shoulders from people who were glad to see him return. Other times, he could almost feel the eyes sending daggers to plunge into his back, from people who still couldn't figure out why he'd bothered to return at all, or who wished he hadn't.

"Oh, botheration!" Widow Crenshaw muttered as she dragged Miss Barber after her out of the store. "He's already heard about Bertha and Mr. Quinn."

"And about the little girl."

"Anything we tell him now won't be news," she continued to fuss as she stomped down the boards of the sidewalk. Without news to spread, she apparently had no reason to keep talking. She trudged along in silence.

Miss Barber trudged along behind. "It's just so unfair."

Widow Crenshaw shot her a curious glare. "Unfair?"

"How can Bertha have a good husband like Mr. Hamilton—"

"A what?" Widow Crenshaw demanded.

"Well . . . well, he *was* a good husband before he took off and left," she defended her opinion. "And . . . and he did come back, even if it was a little late."

Widow Crenshaw shrugged. "If that's your idea of a good husband . . . Of course, in your case, a good husband would be anything with pants and a pulse."

"Let's not be crude, Janet," Miss Barber said with a pout. "But now Bertha has Mr. Quinn courting her, too. And some of us have never had *anybody*."

Widow Crenshaw snorted.

"I wonder if it's something you're born with," Miss Barber lamented. "You know, like blue eyes and blond hair and the ability to attract men. Or if it's something you learn from the ladies in your family, like tatting or making pies or the ability to attract men."

Widow Crenshaw stopped dead in he tracks. Miss Barber collided with her rear.

"Don't do that!" Miss Barber protested. "You know I can't see—"

"Oh, hush! I'm thinking."

Miss Barber obeyed implicitly.

"How could Bertha Hamilton subject that young child to such brazen immorality?"

"Immorality?" Miss Barber echoed. "I don't recall as Bertha's done anything truly immoral."

"Well, as you said, she does have this ability to attract men."

"So?"

"It's just not proper to be teaching a young girl that sort of behavior. Is it?"

"I . . . I guess not," Miss Barber mumbled. "Although I sure wish somebody had taught me."

"Of course. Of course," Widow Crenshaw murmured as she tapped her chin with her index finger. "Little Miranda Hamilton is the ace up our sleeve."

"Oh, Janet, I just love when you talk riverboat talk!"

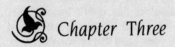 Chapter Three

For the rest of the day Bertha had tried to stay busy so she wouldn't have to think about Sam. It hadn't worked very well. As she served up chicken and dumplings for her and Miranda that evening, she couldn't help remembering how Sam had always said this was his favorite meal.

What was he eating for dinner tonight? she wondered. Was he eating at all? He didn't look as if he could afford much.

Maybe she should have at least given him a meal, her conscience prodded her. She'd have done as much for anyone else in need.

She glanced over to where Sam always used to sit at the head of the table. Of course, then there had been just the two of them, and she had sat beside him.

After he left, and Miranda was old enough to sit up at the table, she hadn't had the heart to take over his place. So she moved to the opposite end and sat Miranda beside her.

Of course, if she did feed him, she would make Sam sit out under the big cottonwood in the front yard like the other drifters she'd given a handout to. Or maybe, if it was raining, she'd have him eat in the bunkhouse with the two hired hands.

Even if she would allow him to enter the house now, she couldn't bear to see him sitting in his old place, as if nothing had changed. He hadn't done a darn thing around here for seven years. He had no right to sit at the head of her table anymore. She wasn't going to let her conscience prod her into doing anything so silly and sentimental.

Thunderation, it didn't matter one bit anyway, she thought as she and Miranda cleaned up after supper. She'd made a home for herself and her daughter that didn't include Sam anymore. He'd made a brief foray back into her life, but she'd make sure it was one and only one—and that he was out of her life again just as quickly.

She'd carry on as she had before, she told herself as she helped Miranda get ready for bed. It would be as if Sam Hamilton had never even existed.

But she knew, as she sat in her rocking chair before the fireplace, mending underclothes by lamplight, that all her brave intentions wouldn't work at all. There would always be a little hollow spot in her heart that ached for Sam.

Every place in this house held a memory of Sam. That's why she'd put up a different fence and painted the house a different color. Even so, she could still see Sam leaning against each and every wall, sitting in every chair, or propping his big, sinewy feet up on the porch rail.

Every time she laughed, she remembered his twinkling brown eyes and mischievous grin. Each time she lay down on her solitary bed, she remembered the feel of his strong arms around her and his firm, warm body pressing close to hers.

She knew in her heart that, even if he went away again, no matter how much she cleaned and scrubbed and re-painted, she'd never get her memories of Sam out of this house, or out of her head, or her heart.

She rocked as she stitched, listening to the crackle of the fire, and the creak of her rocker on the hardwood floor. The wind outside had picked up a little. She could hear the branches of the lilac bushes tapping against the window.

She'd grown used to listening to the silences of her house once Miranda was tucked safely in bed. The small noises were a comforting reminder of all she held dear.

She stopped rocking and listened more intently. It sure

sounded as if the gate of the picket fence had opened and closed.

Darn, had Arthur forgotten to latch it when he left? she wondered. That was very unlike him.

The gate would keep banging back and forth until the nails in the hinges were loose. If she left it alone, she'd probably have to repair it or rebuild it completely tomorrow. She sighed with exasperation as she debated whether she should brave this wind, and go out and latch it securely again.

At last the thought of hammering all those nails won out over a little chill and some loose hairpins. She placed her mending on the table beside her and rose. After throwing the woolen shawl she always kept hanging by the door over her shoulders, she opened the front door to look out.

It was difficult to see in the darkness through the dusty screen in the door. She frowned and looked harder.

Odd. The gate was securely latched.

What if the noise hadn't been the gate after all? she wondered. Maybe it was just another shingle that had blown off the roof, she tried to assure herself. Oh, darn! That was such a bother to fix, too, but there was nothing she could do about it until morning. She wasn't about to try to climb up on the roof in this wind. With a sigh of resignation, she moved to close the door.

Footsteps.

She froze, her hand still resting on the doorknob. She could have sworn she heard footsteps rapidly scraping along the brick walk, approaching the house. She tried to move, to close the door. But her heart was beating so rapidly, she could hardly see straight, much less make her rigid fingers push the door shut.

She heard the footsteps again. This time it sounded as if the prowler was right on the front porch.

They'd never had much trouble in Grasonville before— except maybe for that time Pete Finnerty tried to blow up some people and shoot Tom and Rachel. But the railroad had brought a lot of strangers to town—strangers who might not be exactly trustworthy. Strangers who might take advantage of a woman and a small child living alone on an isolated farm.

Would she have enough time to run to the bunkhouse for help? Would the hired hands even hear her cries in this wind?

There were times like this when Bertha really missed not having Sam around the house. Darn that man, he was never there when she really needed him!

Suddenly she realized the source of all her problems, and her fear disappeared as if blown away by the wind. She frowned, and her fingers tightened in anger on the door-knob. She pulled the door wide open and pressed her forehead against the screen door, trying to see better through it into the darkness.

"Sam! Sam Hamilton! Is that you, you lowly side-winder?" she yelled.

Bertha waited for Sam to show up, grinning, on the other side of the screen, begging to be let in. And she—fool that she was—would probably let him.

The wind whistled, but nothing else happened.

The Sam she remembered was a straightforward kind of man. He wasn't the kind who would go creeping around the house, spying on his wife, scaring her half to death. On the other hand, after so many years, it was almost as if she didn't know Sam at all anymore.

"How dare you come spying on me, you good-for-nothing polecat!" she yelled.

She thought she heard the footsteps moving away into the night.

"You'd better haul your rotten carcass out of here if you know what's good for you!" she threatened. "I didn't want to have the sheriff come and chase you off when Miranda was awake, but if you keep this up, I'll sic him on you faster than you can spit."

Bertha heard only the wind howling through the trees.

* * *

From his seat in the dining room Sam saw them coming at him as soon as they walked in the doorway of the hotel. Widow Crenshaw and Miss Barber stopped just long enough to glance over all the other breakfasting guests.

As soon as Widow Crenshaw spotted him—because Miss Barber couldn't see any farther than the end of her nose—she made a beeline for him, dragging her friend along behind.

If he wasn't so darned hungry, he'd have left his plate and tried to duck out the back door. If he hadn't thought it would slow down his escape, he'd have grabbed his plate and taken it with him.

Before the late Mr. Armistead Crenshaw had passed away, he'd accumulated a sizable fortune selling beef to the Union Army and left it all to his wife.

Jackson Barber, Miss Barber's father, had bequeathed her enough from his rather shady dealing with the Bureau of Indian Affairs to live on comfortably for the rest of her life, so she didn't have to set up some kind of shop to support herself.

Unfortunately, in spite of her wealth, Miss Barber's hopes of marriage had never come true. As he watched her bumping into chairs and people to reach him, Sam wondered why she didn't take some of that money and buy herself a pair of spectacles. A fellow might take more kindly to marrying a lady who could pick him out in a crowd.

Sam watched with dread as they navigated their way through the maze of tables. Having to work for a living would have given each of them something worthwhile to do with their lives, instead of allowing them the leisure to go poking their noses into everybody else's business, where they didn't belong.

"Why, hello, Mr. Hamilton," Widow Crenshaw said in a voice that dripped more syrup than his pancakes. "Oh, do go on eating," she urged. "A big, strong man like you needs his nourishment."

Without even asking if the other chairs at the table were taken, Widow Crenshaw seated herself. Miss Barber sat to his other side. Sam had a sinking feeling in the pit of his stomach that there was no escape for him now.

"It's such a shame you haven't been eating right."

"How do you know how I've been eating?" he asked, and stuck a forkful of pancake into his mouth.

"Why, you're just a shell of your former robust self," Widow Crenshaw said. "But don't worry. Now that you're home, you'll fill out."

Bertha certainly wasn't going to be doing the cooking for him, Sam figured as he sipped his coffee. He wouldn't fill out on hotel food, either. He didn't want to even suspect that these two ladies might have plans to feed him.

"I do hope you're enjoying your stay in town," Miss Barber said.

Sam shrugged. "It could be worse."

Widow Crenshaw heaved a deep sigh and shook her head. "Such a brave man!"

"Yes, indeed," Miss Barber echoed the thought and the sigh.

"You have my sincere admiration for your Christian charity and forbearance."

"I do?"

"I don't know how you can be so optimistic after coming home to find your wife . . . well, um . . . well, *involved* with that Mr. Quinn."

He should have figured that's what all this attention was leading up to. He ducked his head and started chopping off more chunks of pancake with his fork. He speared a chunk, but didn't raise it to his mouth.

"I know everything about that that I want to know," he told them. Then he ate the pancake.

Widow Crenshaw glanced around the hotel dining room and shook her head again. "And her not even allowing you to stay in your very own home."

"Well, what do you expect?" Miss Barber demanded.

"That she would invite him in and let him *know* what's been going on there?"

"What *has* been going on there?" Sam asked cautiously.

"Well, oh, my goodness." Miss Barber fanned herself with the palm of her hand. "It just isn't proper for a maiden lady to say."

Sam decided the shriveled up old maid probably wouldn't know what it was anyway, even if it jumped up and bit her on the nose.

"Oh, I declare!" Widow Crenshaw exclaimed. "That a man should have to stay in a hotel in his own hometown. Shameful. Just shameful, if you ask me."

"Come to think of it, I don't recall ever asking either one of you," Sam said sharply. "Frankly, I don't see what business it is of yours anyway."

He thought his bluntness would send them scurrying back to whatever little rock the two of them had crawled out from under. He shouldn't have underestimated them.

"Well, it's *not* any of my business, Mr. Hamilton," Widow Crenshaw admitted.

"Certainly *that* matter is between you and Mrs. Hamilton," Miss Barber added.

"It's the *child* who concerns us," Widow Crenshaw said.

"How's that?" Sam put his fork down completely. Now they had his undivided attention.

They knew it, too. He could tell by the way they eagerly leaned toward him.

"We think it's an awful shame to allow that dear little lamb to be subjected to a wanton display of her poor, misguided mother's more prurient proclivities."

"What exactly do you mean by that?" Sam demanded. Apparently Widow Crenshaw had invested some of her money in a big dictionary.

"One certainly wonders how she's managed to make the payments on the farm all these years," Widow Crenshaw mused aloud.

"My wife worked hard—"

Widow Crenshaw and Miss Barber snickered behind their hands.

"Then, of course," Widow Crenshaw continued, "lately she's been entertaining Mr. Quinn alone—"

"At night—" Miss Barber added.

"With the child right in the house! The very idea!"

"I'm horrified!" Miss Barber interjected.

"I'm aghast!" Widow Crenshaw was not about to be outdone in her outrage.

"If Miranda's there, then they're not alone," Sam said.

Widow Crenshaw and Miss Barber glanced at each other as if Sam had just let loose a flood of unintelligible gibberish. On the other hand, he had disagreed with him, and that was just about the same thing.

"That's just all the more reason why the child shouldn't be in that house with *that* woman!" Widow Crenshaw stated.

"But Miranda's been with my wife since she was born," Sam said. "Why are you suddenly so concerned now?"

"Oh, Mrs. Hamilton didn't start this until you were dead," Miss Barber tried to explain.

"It's only been a few months since she put off mourning— and started keeping company with Mr. Quinn," Widow Crenshaw clarified. "It wouldn't even matter so much if Miranda were just an infant. But she's going on seven—quite an impressionable age for a young lady, I must tell you."

How would you know? Sam silently questioned. *You only had one son, and that didn't work out so well.*

"Well, what do you have in mind?" he asked.

"What do you mean?" Widow Crenshaw's wrinkled eyelids opened in a wide impression of innocence.

"Since you seem to see the problem so clearly, you must have some sort of a solution," he said. He couldn't wait to hear what these two old busybodies would come up with now.

"You must realize, no matter how deep our concern, this

entire situation was quite out of our hands before you came back, Mr. Hamilton."

Sam nodded, waiting.

Widow Crenshaw placed her hand over her bosom. "Why, it pained me deeply to see that sweet, innocent child growing up under those circumstances and not being able to do a thing about it."

"And now?"

"Why, now that you're here—" She placed her hand over his and applied just the slightest bit of reassuring pressure. "And you've arrived in the very nick of time, I can tell you—we can set this situation to rights. For the good of the child, you understand."

Sam continued to nod.

"She *is* your daughter, after all."

"Yes," he answered cautiously.

"You have every right to be with her, but there's not much chance of that if you're staying at the local hotel."

"True."

"No judge in the land would allow Mrs. Hamilton custody of Miranda," Widow Crenshaw said at last. "You must take the child out of that den of iniquity into your own loving home."

"What? Take her away from Bertha?" Sam was glad he'd swallowed his food. Otherwise, he'd have choked.

Widow Crenshaw nodded emphatically. "It's for her own good."

"For the good of both of them," Miss Barber affirmed.

"Yes, maybe once Mrs. Hamilton sees the error of her ways, she'll repent and reform." Glumly Widow Crenshaw grimaced and added, "Maybe."

"I can't do that!" Sam exclaimed.

Widow Crenshaw eyed him with admonishment. "Not even for the good of your daughter?"

"But I can't—"

"Legally, yes, you can," Miss Barber said.

Legally, perhaps yes. But how could Sam take from

Bertha what she cherished most? He'd come back to make
a peaceful life for himself and his family—not to stir up
trouble between them.

"We had a little discussion with Mr. Martin yesterday
evening," Widow Crenshaw confessed. "He said he'd be
very willing to help you with any legal matters."

"I'm sure he would—for a sizable fee, the little weasel.
But I *won't* do it," Sam insisted. "I won't do that to Bertha
or Miranda."

"That's very commendable of you, Mr. Hamilton," Widow
Crenshaw said. "On the other hand, I had thought you'd be a
little more concerned for your daughter."

"I am, but—"

"Then you *must* take her."

Sam wasn't about to admit to these two old crows that
Miranda was scared to death of him. She'd certainly never
want to come live with him. He wasn't about to admit,
either, that, unlike Bertha, he didn't have the slightest idea
how to raise a child on his own.

"Buy a little house. Then, I'm sure you could always find
some nice widow—"

"Or a nice maiden lady," Miss Barber interjected quickly.

Sam winced at Widow Crenshaw's misplaced kick landed
on his shin instead of Miss Barber's.

"Some competent lady would certainly be willing to work
as your housekeeper and help raise Miranda."

"For a reasonable fee?" Sam said wryly.

"More reasonable than Mr. Martin," Miss Barber told him
bluntly.

Sheriff Amos Duncan was right where Bertha had expected to find him—sitting on the bench outside the
sheriff's office. He looked up from his newspaper and
scratched his head. Then he scratched his sagging paunch
right on the big stain left by a blob from the filling of one
of his wife's apple turnovers.

"So, what can I do for you, little lady?" he asked. He pounded on his chest as if to ease a bubble, then belched.

Bertha felt glad to be getting even this much response out of him. She never could figure out how he kept getting elected sheriff time and again when everyone agreed he was the laziest man on the face of the earth. Maybe it was because nobody else ever ran against him.

She wished he'd been in his office instead. Everybody had stared at her as she'd driven through town in her buckboard. Enough people knew her business already. She didn't need to advertise her problems on the town sidewalk.

"Sheriff, I need to lodge a complaint against Sam Hamilton."

The sheriff scratched his head again. "Already? He ain't even been in town twenty-four hours."

"That still doesn't mean he isn't annoying."

He scraped at the stain on his shirt with one fingernail. Then he stuck his finger into his mouth and sucked on it.

Bertha drew in a deep breath. How disgusting could one man get? How could Mrs. Duncan stand him?

"Shoot, Mrs. Hamilton, if I was to go around arresting every annoying person in town, I'd never have time to get any reading done." He shook the newspaper for emphasis. "And I might just start with you."

He shook the newspaper again, just for good measure. Then he raised it to shield his face from Bertha.

"Sheriff!" she insisted. She looked around guiltily as she noticed several people had started to stare as they passed by. More quietly, she continued, "Sam Hamilton was prowling around my house last night."

"Look, little lady." He lowered his newspaper and grimaced at her. "If you and the mister had some sort of spat—"

"Spat?" she exclaimed. "He left me seven years ago. That's not a spat! Now he comes back, prowling around my house like a thief in the night."

"Ah, now we're getting somewhere." He folded the

newspaper and placed it over what little lap he had left. "Did he steal anything?"

"No."

"Did he wreck anything?"

"No. Well, just a couple of tramped-down bushes that'll grow back."

"Did he kill anything?"

Bertha frowned with surprise. "Of course not!"

"Then I can't do nothing about it." The sheriff raised his newspaper with a noisy shake.

"But—"

This time he didn't even bother to lower the newspaper. "If he ain't broke any laws, I can't arrest him," he stated firmly. "No matter how annoying he is."

Bertha had all she could do to control herself and not snatch the darn newspaper right out of his grubby hands. But there was definitely a crowd gathered around now, eager to hear the latest gossip about the Hamiltons. She wasn't about to give them more fuel for their fires. She tried to ignore the rumble of murmurs and the shuffling of the crowd that had started behind her.

More calmly, she tried to insist, "But he was trespassing, Sheriff."

"Is somebody giving you a problem, Bertha?"

Sam's voice behind her startled her. She whirled around to face him.

He'd had a bath and shaved. His hair was burnished by the morning sun. His skin was tanned and clean-shaven again, the way she always remembered it.

She didn't think he'd be standing so close. There was only enough space between them for her to lift her hand, stretch out her arm, and place her palm on his smooth cheek. She'd feel his warmth and his strength. She'd be tempted to run her finger along the edge of his strong jaw. Then she'd forget all about all the trouble he was causing her, and welcome him back home.

Her heart ached as she stepped back.

"You're darned right somebody's giving me a problem, Sam Hamilton. *You* are."

"What do you need the sheriff for?"

"That's what I was trying to tell her," Sheriff Duncan interjected from behind his paper.

"I don't see how you can get a man arrested for coming home late," Sam told her with a grin.

"Even if it is seven years late!" the sheriff declared. He laughed at his own bad joke, and his stomach bounced up and down in front of him. The crowd joined in his laughter.

Bertha tried to ignore him. "What were you doing sneaking around my house last night, Sam?" she demanded.

"Me? I wasn't anywhere near the house last night."

"Yes, you were, you lying polecat. I heard you banging on the gate and stomping on the porch and moving around in the bushes."

"I wasn't anywhere near the house last night," Sam repeated.

"Naw, you must've just heard the wind, little lady," the sheriff interjected. "It was blowing up something fierce last night."

"The wind doesn't open and close a latched gate," she insisted. "And it doesn't come up on your front porch."

The grin fled from Sam's face, and his eyes grew serious.

Out of the corner of her eye, she saw Sam lift his hand. He placed it on her elbow and gave a little squeeze. Was he trying to be reassuring? It wasn't working. The only thing he was accomplishing was making her even more upset.

His hand was warm and comforting, yet at the same time it raised exciting memories in her. Her heart started to beat faster. Although she'd been nervous to begin with just coming here, it was becoming harder to swallow.

Sparkling feelings that had lain dormant for so long flashed to life. The feelings were growing so strong that she was beginning to have second thoughts about sending Sam away.

She could barely look him in the eye. She tried to glance

around at the crowd, but she had a mortal fear that these people knew exactly what she was feeling.

These *weren't* the kinds of feelings a person wanted to have in the middle of a large crowd of people.

"Someone actually came up on the front porch last night?" Sam asked.

She glared at him. "You know darned good and well you did."

"No, I didn't, Bertha. I swear it." His grip on her elbow tightened just slightly. "After I had dinner in the hotel, I was in my room all night."

She grimaced skeptically. "I suppose you've got witnesses who can prove it."

"Well, sure, the waiter saw me eating," he offered. "But, no. After that I was alone—and I went right to sleep."

"That's a poor alibi."

"Would you rather have me tell you I was with one of Miss Sadie's girls?" he demanded.

Bertha felt her cheeks flame. "You're going to have to think up a better excuse than that if you're going to try to come spying on me, trespassing—"

"Excuse me, Mrs. Hamilton," the voice interrupted. "He wasn't exactly trespassing."

Bertha turned to see Mr. Martin elbowing his way through the crowd that had gathered around them. She thought she noted a look of perverse pleasure as some people firmly refused to budge for the little man and he had to squeeze through the spaces between them.

He wore the hat he always wore, although Bertha had sat behind him in church one Christmas service when he'd actually shown up. She knew there was a bald spot on his head that he was trying hard to cover. But being that short sort of put it right under everybody's noses anyway.

The lawyer's beady little eyes were glowing with smug satisfaction.

"Mr. Martin! What business is it of yours anyway?" Bertha demanded.

"I never told you I wanted your services, Martin," Sam fairly growled.

"Nevertheless, Mrs. Hamilton, Mr. Hamilton was not trespassing," Mr. Martin continued, undaunted.

"What do you mean?" Bertha and Sam both demanded.

"I was perusing the land records yesterday evening, and I happened to notice, Mrs. Hamilton, that when you decided your husband was actually dead, you went through a year of mourning, and even had a memorial service for him in church—real nice one it was, too."

He paused. Was he waiting for her to thank him? Bertha wondered. Or was he just pausing to give a more dramatic effect to his announcement?

At last he continued, "But it seems you never bothered to have Mr. Hamilton's name removed from the deed to the property."

"So—?"

"So Mr. Hamilton actually does still own his land and has every right to live in that house," Mr. Martin finished. He was grinning so broadly that Bertha could almost believe he considered this a personal triumph.

"Oh, no. Oh, no," Bertha repeated, shaking her head.

Sheriff Duncan was chuckling again. "So, when are you moving in, Sam?"

The crowd started murmuring again.

Sam gave the sheriff a look of disgust. The man didn't even deserve an answer. He shot Mr. Martin a look of contempt.

"I expect you're thinking of charging me for this information," he said.

"Well, I did—"

"I never agreed to any of this, Martin," Sam told him.

He didn't want Bertha to believe he and the little weasel had gotten together and concocted this whole rotten scheme just so he could move in on her—even though she probably would anyway.

"I've got a whole store full of witnesses to that. So don't

you dare think you'll get one Yankee dollar out of me for these so-called 'services' of yours."

Mr. Martin pursed his lips and stood there, silently watching. Like a miniature vulture, perched and waiting, he obviously wasn't done yet.

At last Sam looked at Bertha, who was still muttering, "Oh, no, you're not coming to live with me and Miranda." Her blue eyes drooped with dismay.

He wouldn't hurt Bertha for all the world. Just because the lawyer had said he had a legal right to live there didn't mean he *had* to.

He wouldn't hurt Miranda for all the world, either. He knew his own daughter was scared at the very sight of him. What would she do if he actually moved in and she had to see him all the time?

But there was the story Bertha had just been telling the sheriff. Standing at the edge of the crowd, he'd overheard most of it. He couldn't believe she'd made up the yarn just to get him in trouble. It hadn't been him sneaking around the house last night. But somebody obviously had been. He didn't want to try to speculate on who.

He didn't like to think of his wife and daughter in any possible danger. They'd be safer if he was around to guard them, to watch out for them. After his long absence, didn't he owe it to them? But he'd never be able to convince Bertha of that.

So he supposed the only thing he could do was pretend he believed Mr. Martin's words because he wanted to claim the house he'd worked for. In reality, he didn't give a hang about the land or the house. What really mattered to him was that he was able to stay close to the woman he loved, and his daughter, to protect them both.

"I guess I'll just go get my things out of the hotel, and I'll be moving in," Sam said.

"What?" Bertha exclaimed. "You can't!"

"Yes, I can."

"You won't!"

"Yes, I will."

"I'll fight you on this, Sam," she threatened. "I'll get my own lawyer, no matter what it costs, and I'll take this to whatever court I have to."

"Frankly, I don't think you'll have much luck, Mrs. Hamilton," Mr. Martin said with a smug grin.

"I'll do what I have to do, Mr. Martin," she replied.

"It seems the courts don't look too kindly on women alone," Mr. Martin continued. "Especially on women fighting against their own husbands."

"But—" Bertha sputtered.

"Especially on women who've been keeping company with another man in their husband's absence."

Sam watched Bertha's pretty face grow red with anger and frustration. Let her fuss at Martin, Sam figured. At least she was mad at somebody besides him for a change. He knew he wouldn't actually take this into court. He knew darn good and well he wouldn't give Martin the satisfaction—or the attorney's fee. More important, he'd never hurt Bertha like that.

Bertha turned away from the lawyer and peered at Sam intently. In a low whisper she grumbled, "Oh, Sam. Don't you dare do this to me in front of all these people. Please."

She nodded her head backward at the group of people surrounding them.

"Do what?" he asked quietly.

"Embarrass me like this."

"But you were embarrassing me by accusing me of prowling around."

"Look, you can come around later."

"No. I think I really want everyone in town to know I'm living in my own house, on my own farm, with my little daughter and my loving wife."

Bertha's shoulders slumped in defeat. "You're really trying my patience, Sam."

"Come along, sweetheart," Sam said.

He put his arm around her shoulders and began to lead

her away from the crowd. She angrily shook off his embrace.

"I'll follow you back to our house."

"You're just lucky I left Miranda playing at the Picketts'," she whispered to him as they walked along. "That way she won't witness when I murder her father on the way home."

Maybe he'd been away so long, he'd forget the way to the farm and get lost, and she wouldn't have to put up with him living in her house.

Don't be silly, she told herself as she pulled on the reins, guiding the horse down the road. There's only one road, straight out of town, that goes right past the farm. Besides, he'd already been back there once.

Well, maybe the flea-bitten nag he was riding would drop dead, fall on him, and kill him, and she wouldn't have to put up with him living in her house.

Yeah, but then you'd be stuck with the expense of burying both of them, she told herself.

Well, maybe he'd eaten some rotten food in the hotel and would drop dead of ptomaine poisoning any minute now, and she wouldn't have to put up with him living in her house.

As all these arguments with herself ran through her mind on the way to her farm, Bertha realized she was a drowning woman, just clutching at straws. Sam and the horse were both perfectly healthy, and they were following her wagon at a steady clip. That miserable carpetbag was still hanging from his saddle, flopping against the side of his horse as if it would beat it to death.

At least she should be grateful they were following her. The road was wide enough that Sam could have pulled up alongside her and insisted on chatting as they went along. Of course, it would only be to gloat over his victory, the miserable polecat, she thought glumly.

As she turned into her yard, she noticed Miranda waiting for her on the front porch with Rachel. It was bad enough she was going to have to try to set some rules for Sam to abide by while he was staying in her house. It was going to be even more difficult trying to explain to Miranda what was happening.

"Mommy!" Miranda cried with excitement and bounded off the front step to run to greet the wagon.

"Rachel," Bertha called, pulling the horse to a halt. "You really shouldn't have walked her all the way over here."

Going to get Miranda would have brought Bertha a little more time to think up an explanation for this mess that a six-year-old would understand.

"Oh, I don't mind," Rachel answered. "Willy and Alice are napping, and Sally's home doing her chores. And the walk was good for me, you know." She patted her stomach.

Suddenly Miranda spotted Sam reining up behind the wagon. She scrambled up onto the seat and clung to her mother.

"What's *he* doing here again?" she demanded. Her nose was wrinkled, and she was frowning angrily.

"Well, Miranda, sweetheart . . ." Bertha began.

She looked over to Sam, who was silently watching. She was just as glad he kept his mouth shut. It didn't matter if he said a word or not. Miranda would never listen to him.

Bertha noticed Rachel was watching them, too, with intense interest. She wished her friend could help her out with a good explanation.

"Miranda, it seems that . . . well, I . . . I've told you this man is really your daddy—"

"No, he's not!"

Bertha didn't see any sense in arguing with the child over that point right now when she had a much more pressing problem. She put her arm over the little girl's shoulders and tried to hug her. She figured Miranda was going to need all the comforting she could get.

"That means he's really my husband, too," she continued her explanation. "And usually husbands and wives live together. So, Sam . . . your daddy . . . well, he's coming to live with us—"

"No!"

Miranda pulled sharply out of Bertha's arms.

"No, you can't have that man live here with us!" she protested. "He's dirty and smelly."

"He had a bath," Bertha tried to console her.

"He'll eat all our food and mess up our house. You *can't* have him stay here. I won't live here if you do!"

She jumped down from the wagon seat and darted across the yard, heading for the Picketts' farm.

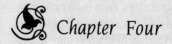 Chapter Four

"Miranda!" Sam cried, and took off after her at a run.

Miranda must have heard him, because her little legs started to pump even harder up the little worn path just to get her away.

"Don't chase her, you big dummy!" Bertha scolded, standing her ground. "She's already afraid of you."

Sam skidded to a halt, ripping up little clumps of grass with the heels of his boots. Angrily he whirled around.

"I'll get my horse."

Bertha laughed. "Sheriff Duncan could outrun that nag. Just let her go."

"What do you mean, let her go? She's only six years old. She can't just go running off like that."

He turned again to watch the top of Miranda's blond head disappear behind the hill. Bertha could see his lean muscles, tensed to take off again any second.

"There are snakes and wild animals and—"

"We're in the middle of a farm in Kansas, for Pete's sake, not the wild mountains of Nevada. I don't think she's going to be running into any bears."

Bertha shook her head.

"Oh, it figures you wouldn't understand anything about raising children in general, and your own daughter in particular."

Suddenly Sam was no longer the sheepish, apologetic prodigal he'd been when he first arrived. It was all the fault of that darned lawyer and his legal documents! It was almost as if, now that Sam knew he had a right to stay here in spite of all her protests, he'd regained all his old self-confidence—and a whole lot more he didn't need, either, Bertha thought glumly.

Now he was the strong man she remembered, confronting his wife in an argument. Well, in the time they'd been together before he left, they'd done their fair share of disagreeing. She supposed they could continue right where they left off—except this time there wouldn't be the fun of kissing and making up afterward.

Frowning darkly, he pointed his index finger directly at her throat. "Don't start that 'you weren't around' stuff with me again, Bertha," he warned.

Her heart pounded in her chest. Her eyes widened and, even though he was too far away to actually touch her, she could feel a power emanating from him. She leaned her head back anyway.

Just because he'd made her flinch didn't mean she had to let him think he had her completely cowed. She stared him coldly in the eye.

"Don't you start jumping to conclusions, either. Just because you've got a guilty conscience about having that sleazy lawyer help you to finagle your way into living in my house—"

"*Your* house?"

"Don't go around accusing me of picking on you without any cause," she finished.

"I didn't—"

"And let me tell you, as far as my complaining about you not being here, well, now I'm stuck with having you around more than I ever care to. But I wasn't even going to bring that up. All I meant was, you didn't know that Miranda usually does this when she's angry."

"She runs away?" he demanded incredulously.

"No. She runs over to the Picketts."

"Why?"

"Why not? It's only just over the rise. There are lots of children there for her to play with. When she comes home a little later, or when I go to get her, she's usually forgotten all about what made her angry in the first place." She screwed her mouth up in a bitter grimace. "Although, in this case, I don't think that's likely."

Neither of them said anything for a moment.

Rachel broke the awkward silence. "Well, looks like I'll be heading home." She stepped carefully off the front porch.

"If you can wait until I unhitch the horse and turn him out, I'll walk with you," Bertha offered. "I've got a feeling I'm going to have to bring Miranda home this time."

Rachel walked a little closer toward her friend. "Probably dragging her kicking and screaming all the way," she whispered as she nodded in Sam's direction.

Bertha gave her a weak smile. "The trouble is, who's going to drag *me* back home?"

Rachel just shrugged.

Bertha grabbed the horse's bridle and started to lead him toward the barn.

Sam took the other side of the bridle. "I'll take care of the horses," he volunteered.

She turned and stared at him, eyebrows raised in surprise. "You?"

"Why not?"

"Are you going to start telling me they're your horses?" she accused. "To my recollection, there was nothing in that deed about the farm animals."

He glared at her. "Look, Bertha. I'm just trying to make things a little easier for you to go get Miranda faster. Will you at least accept that without making a fuss?"

Her gaze dropped to the ground. She pressed her lips together, trying to think up some sort of answer. She couldn't let him think he'd gotten the last word. But nothing smart or snappy came to mind. It really would be a big help to her if he did take care of the horses, she grudgingly acknowledged to herself.

At last she just said, "Thank you, Sam. Come on, Rachel."

The two women began to stroll over the little rise that separated their farms.

"I take it this arrangement is *not* your idea," Rachel said.

"Did you think it was?"

"Well, if worst comes to worst, we can always bed Miranda down with my girls."

"Is there any room for me?"

Bertha gave a little half-laugh. What if Rachel said yes? Could she really leave her home? This time, could *she* leave Sam?

"Thanks anyway. But, no. I'm standing my ground on this one," Bertha said determinedly. Then she sighed. "Unfortunately for poor little Miranda, I really think it's better if she starts getting used to him. Who knows how long he's going to stay around this time?"

"He was around for seven years the first time," Rachel reminded her.

Bertha didn't find that the least bit comforting.

Sam unsaddled his own horse, unhitched the other, brushed them both down, and turned them out in the pasture in no time at all. He paused just long enough to carefully store his carpetbag behind the sofa in a corner of the parlor. He fairly ran the whole way to the Picketts.

He knocked on their screen door. He had all he could do to remain polite and patient while he waited what seemed like forever.

"Come on in, Mr. Hamilton," Rachel called cheerfully in response.

Bertha and Rachel were both sitting at the kitchen table, drinking coffee as if nothing out of the ordinary had happened. He almost choked with anger and surprise.

"Where is she?" he demanded, looking from Bertha to Rachel and back again.

Both women confronted him with a finger placed to their lips for silence.

"Shhh," Rachel whispered. "Alice and Willy are still napping."

"I told you, she'll show up in about ten minutes," Bertha said with forced patience, as if she were tired of repeatedly trying to explain something very simple to a very dense child.

"But where is she *now*?"

She blew on her coffee to cool it, then took a sip before she answered. Sam felt down in his very bones she was just doing this to annoy him.

"It seems as if Miranda didn't come here to play after all," she said. "She must have gone to her hiding place."

"Hiding place?" Sam repeated. "It's bad enough the child runs away. Now you tell me she hides, too."

"She must be *very* angry," Rachel observed.

"She only does this when she's very angry," Bertha explained, as if he were too stupid to have heard or understood Rachel.

Sam paced rapidly back and forth across the kitchen floor. Every once in a while he had to dodge one of the puppies that had managed to stumble out of the basket, or one of the many toys strung across the room. He slapped his arms at this sides in frustration.

"I don't believe you're just sitting there. What are you waiting for? Why don't you go get her?"

Cup halfway to her lips, Bertha paused and stared at him. "Because I don't know where her hiding place is."

"Go look for it!" he demanded. Then he smirked at her sarcastically. "Of course, that's only a suggestion, since I don't know much about raising kids."

"We have looked."

"Try again."

"I *have* tried." She slammed the cup down on the table. "Do you think I'm some kind of terrible mother who doesn't care where her daughter is?"

"It sure looks that way to me."

"All right!" Bertha stood up so quickly, the chair almost toppled over backward. She marched over to him, grabbed him by the arm, and started hauling him toward the door. "We'll go out and search the barn, the stables, the corn crib, the chicken coop—"

She stepped in the doorway, suddenly aware of what she was doing. For the first time since he'd returned, she was actually touching him.

He was as warm and strong as she remembered. The feel of his taut muscles under her fingers reminded her of how she used to hold him when they made love.

Since he'd had a bath, he smelled like he used to, too—coffee and leather, hair tonic and wool. She remembered everything. All the little things that had made their marriage so wonderful flooded back now, overwhelming her.

How they'd lingered over their coffee after dinner, discussing all their plans for the future—plans that somehow never seemed to come true.

How he smelled before he cleaned up when he came in after riding around the farm all day—the pungent scent of a hardworking man.

How, on Saturday night, he'd take a long bath in the big tub in front of the fireplace and she'd help scrub his back. He'd comb his hair in the cloudy little mirror over the bureau. Then, with a playful gleam in his eyes, he'd climb into bed with her on clean muslin sheets under warm woolen blankets, and the night would stretch into dawn.

Then they'd both try very hard to keep each other awake in church the next morning—and not succeed very well at all.

Now she'd be spending her days and nights with him again. But everything had changed. Hadn't it? And there was definitely no going back. Was there?

She released his arm and backed away.

"Is there any other place you can think of that I—in my

stupidity and inexperience—might have overlooked?" she snapped.

Her voice cracked with the emotions she tried to push down. She hoped he'd think it was anger that made it hard for her to speak, and not—no, she didn't want to give a name to the emotion. That would make it dangerously close to "longing"—or even "love." She wasn't ready to acknowledge that she still might feel that for Sam. She might never be ready.

"Have you looked in the trees?" Sam suggested.

"She's not a squirrel."

"Along the riverbank?"

"She's not a muskrat, either, you big dummy."

"Don't think I'm so stupid. *You* were going to look in the chicken coop."

Behind her, Bertha heard Rachel snickering. As she continued to look Sam in the eye, she could feel her own lips starting to twitch. When you looked at it that way, it was a pretty ridiculous argument.

Sam's eyes started to dance merrily. Now she had all she could do not to break out laughing. She knew if she let just one giggle escape she'd fall victim to his impish charm all over again. She had to remain firm. She couldn't let one silly grin make her give in so easily this time.

Footsteps on the porch made Bertha jump. They were too loud and heavy to be Miranda's. She saw Sam give a start, too.

"Look, if you're going to come over here all the time, you've got to go play with Sally and Alice, okay?" Del's loud complaint carried all the way inside. "You've got to stop following me around like a puppy. I've got work to do."

"I can watch you work," Miranda said.

"No, you can't. It's dangerous."

"It is not."

"Farm equipment can be *dangerous*," Del insisted.

"You'll protect me."

"Yeah? Who's going to protect me from you, you little pest?"

She giggled. "You don't need protecting from me, silly. I'm going to marry you," she told him confidently.

"Yeah? Well, you're going to have to find me first, you sawed-off runt."

"Ha! That's the easy part. I already found your secret hiding place."

"I know, and you took it over, you pint-sized thief."

"We were *both* supposed to hide there—together. *You* were the one who ran off."

"I'm *not* sharing my place with any pesky little kid."

"Yeah? Well, you'll change your mind once I get bosoms."

"I will not! And you're not supposed to talk about those kinds of things," he scolded.

"Oh, Del, I can talk to *you* about anything."

"No, you can't. And anyway, I found another place all my own. You'll *never* find this one."

"Oh, yes, I will."

"Geez, were you born this way or do you take annoyance lessons in school?" Del muttered. The screen door screeched as he pulled it open.

Bertha hurried to the door. Sam wasn't far behind. As she stopped and backed up to allow Del and Miranda to enter, Sam bumped into her. He held her at the waist to keep her from losing her balance. His touch was gentle, but if he had confined her with iron bands, she couldn't have been able to breathe any more easily.

"I'm fine. I'm fine," she insisted, pulling quickly away. She bent to pick up Miranda, who never took her admiring gaze off Del.

"Honest, Mrs. Hamilton, she's *got* to stop following me around," Del complained.

"Where was she, Del?" Sam asked.

"Um . . . well . . ." Del scuffed his heel against the floor. It was pretty clear, in spite of all his complaints and protests, Miranda had Del wrapped around her little finger.

"Del?"

"Don't pester the boy, Sam," Bertha interrupted. "It doesn't matter."

"Of course it matters. Suppose she runs away again?"

"She will. But at least Del is the one person who knows how to find her," Bertha explained. "If she finds a new hiding place, maybe no one will know where she is."

Sam reached up and rubbed the back of his neck. He supposed this was Bertha's sort of logic. The worst part was, it was beginning to make sense to him.

But Bertha wasn't worrying about Sam or Del or hiding places anymore. She turned her complete attention to Miranda.

"I've been so worried about you," she told her, lowering her to the floor again.

"I was right here, Mommy."

"She's *always* here, Mrs. Hamilton," Del grumbled.

Before Bertha could thank him for retrieving her daughter, the youth turned and beat a hasty retreat back to his chores.

If she were a thirteen-year-old boy, she wouldn't blame him. She even felt sorry for him. Even though she was Miranda's loving mother, she knew that once the girl made up her mind she wanted something, she wouldn't stop until she got it, and woe to anyone who tried. Clearly Miranda had set her sights on Del.

Now that Del was gone, Miranda turned to Bertha.

"You know I always come here, Mommy."

"I know, but . . . but you know how mommies like to worry. It gives them something to do. And you went so fast this time."

At last Miranda's gaze shifted to Sam. Her expression changed, too, from blatant, unconditional adoration to peevish anger.

"I had to get away from *him*!"

"I'm afraid you won't be able to do that, Miranda,"

Bertha said. She had to make this sound as convincing as possible, even to herself. "I told you, Mr. Hamilton—your daddy—is going to be living with us now."

Miranda scuffed the toes of her shoes against the bare wood.

"Well, then, I guess you can look for me over here a lot."

"You can play here as long as Mrs. Pickett doesn't mind." Bertha threw Rachel a silent plea for help.

"Of course, Miranda," Rachel chimed in. "Once your chores at home are done, you can come almost every day—just like before—and play with Sally and Alice. And once the new baby comes, I'm going to be needing lots of help from you girls."

"But Mr. Hamilton is going to be living with us now." Bertha glanced over at Sam. Then she spoke low, so only her daughter could hear her. "There's nothing we can do about it. We're both just going to have to make the best of this horrible situation."

"You don't want him, either," Miranda stated, obviously with no concept of what a whisper was. "Then why is he staying?"

"It . . . it has something to do with property deeds and the law."

"So?"

"Maybe someday when you're older you'll understand," Bertha finished with a sigh.

She was older, and she wished she understood. Oh, she understood how an oversight on a land deed could get her in this predicament. Not removing his name. That's where her maudlin sentimentality got her!

What she couldn't understand was how Sam could forget her for all those years and then insist on wanting to live with her now. If it was just the farm he wanted, he could have had her evicted. Why did he have to insist on being here *with* her? Hadn't thoughts of him tormented her all these years? Why did he still want to torment her so?

If she had trouble understanding Sam, she had even more

trouble understanding her own feelings. How could she have missed the husband she loved so badly, and yet now hate him for wanting to intrude on the life she'd managed to make without him?

And what was she going to do about their daughter?

"Come on, Miranda," she said. "It's time we were heading home."

Bertha held out her hand. Reluctantly the little girl reached up and took it.

"Thanks for watching her, Rachel." Turning to Miranda, she prodded, "What do you say to Mrs. Pickett?"

"Thank you, Mrs. Pickett," Miranda responded dutifully.

Rachel had made her way toward the door. She placed her hand on the top of Miranda's head. "Anytime you want to run away, you'll make sure you come here to me, won't you?"

"Yes, ma'am."

Rachel lowered her voice to a whisper. "Just don't run away too often. It really worries your mother, and you wouldn't want to do that, would you?"

"No, ma'am."

Rachel leaned a bit closer to the child's ear. "And try not to let Mr. Hamilton being in your house bother you too much. Now that he's had a shave and a bath, he doesn't look so much like a big red bear, does he?"

Miranda giggled, but continued to eye Sam cautiously.

As the three of them walked home, Miranda was still so wary that she insisted on keeping Bertha protectively between them.

"Why did you run away from me, Miranda?" Sam asked.

"'Cause you're not my daddy and you don't belong in my house. Mommy and I don't need you—and we don't want you."

"Maybe your mommy ought to tell me that herself," he said.

"I thought I already had," Bertha responded without even looking at him.

Sam watched Bertha as they walked along. The years hadn't changed the way the sun shone on the waves of her fair hair. She might insist she had made it clear she didn't want him, but she was walking beside him, not hurrying on ahead or lagging behind. Could it be that, in spite of her protests, she was at least learning to tolerate his presence? Could she learn again to really enjoy having him around? He could always hope.

"But your mommy hasn't run away, Miranda," he said.

"She's too slow."

"Where did you go?"

"Right where you found me." She kicked at a full-blown dandelion top, scattering fuzzy seeds to the wind.

"No. When I first saw you, you were on Mrs. Pickett's front porch, and you weren't there when I passed by the first time, so you must have been someplace else then. Where were you?"

"My hiding place."

"Where's that?"

Miranda twisted her face into a grimace. "Do you think I'm going to tell *you*?"

He gave a little chuckle. "I guess not."

"Miranda, mind your manners," Bertha scolded. She turned and tried to assure him. "I really did raise her with better manners than that."

He nodded. "It's a shame she only uses them for Mrs. Pickett."

"I use them for people who should get them," Miranda told him.

"Well, then, will you *please* tell your mother where your hiding place is so she doesn't worry so much anymore?"

Miranda grunted. "It wouldn't be much of a hiding place if everybody knew where it was."

"No, I guess not," Sam agreed. "But Del knows where it is."

Miranda nodded. "But he won't tell," she answered confidently. "He's going to marry me."

"I see."

Sam moved around behind Bertha to continue walking by Miranda's side. The little girl immediately crossed over in front of Bertha and took her other hand. He'd try again later, he decided.

The walked along for a bit. Then Miranda turned to Bertha.

"If he's going to live with us, do I have to call him Daddy?" she grumbled.

Before Bertha could say anything, Sam answered softly, "I wish you would, Miranda. Will you call me Daddy?"

"No."

"Miranda, your manners," Bertha tried again.

"No, *sir*. I don't think so."

He moved around to walk beside Miranda again.

"Then could you call me Pa?"

"No, *sir*." She quickly scooted over to Bertha's other side, almost tripping her.

"Will you two stop doing that!" Bertha demanded. "You're making me dizzy."

So much for trying to get closer to his daughter—at least for now.

"What will you call me, Miranda?" he asked.

"Nothing."

"Why?"

"'Cause I won't be needing to call you at all, so I don't have to call you anything."

They walked in silence the rest of the way. Bertha was grateful that at least everybody stayed in his place.

Even as they climbed the porch steps and entered the house, Bertha said nothing. What was there to say? He was here, and there was nothing she could do about it.

Miranda bolted for her room and slammed the door shut. Bertha had the sudden impulse to do the same, but then who would do the cooking?

Sam stood in the doorway, as if he were waiting for something.

What could he possibly want? she wondered to herself. He'd already gotten everything he'd aimed for.

"What? No welcome home?" he asked, grinning broadly.

She just glared at him steadily for a minute or two. Then she grabbed the frying pan and a large knife and set them on the table.

"I have to start dinner." She shoved two pieces of wood into the firebox of the big, black cast-iron stove. "You can take what little you brought with you and put it in the parlor."

"I already did," he said.

Bertha peeled a large onion, laid it on the wooden chopping board, and gave it a good whack with the knife, cleaving it in two. What a shame it wasn't Sam's head.

"I guess maybe I shouldn't have done that," he said, disappearing into the parlor.

You shouldn't even have come back, Bertha told him silently. With murderous thoughts in her head, she gave the onion another whack with the knife, slicing it in quarters. You can force me to keep you here, Sam Hamilton, she silently warned him, but you have to sleep sometime. She gave the onion one more chop. She was starting to feel a little better.

Sam reappeared in the kitchen, holding up the ragged carpetbag. "See?"

She gave it a brief glance. "Yeah, I see." She turned back to her chopping. "If you've seen one carpetbag, you've seen them all. This one isn't all that special to begin with."

Undaunted by her reply, he continued, "I only put it in the parlor because I was trying to be polite."

"Polite?"

"Yeah. I thought it would be mighty rude to put this in the bedroom when you weren't home."

He strolled boldly into her bedroom.

She dropped the knife in her surprise. "What? Wait! What do you think you're doing?"

As she ran after him, she wished she had the nerve to go

back and get the knife. Even if she didn't intend to use it, it might appear to give her a little more authority when she tried to kick him out.

She skidded to a halt in the doorway. There was no way on earth she was going to enter that room when he was in it. She watched with horror as he placed the bag on the bed.

"What do you think you're doing?" she demanded.

"I live here. This was my bedroom before. It might as well be mine now, too."

"Oh, no."

"Oh, yes."

"Then just where am I supposed to sleep?"

He nodded down to the bed in front of him, to the very side where she used to lay, cuddled up beside him, before she'd gotten the whole darned big lonely bed to herself. Now she'd grown used to sleeping alone—sort of.

"This is your bedroom, too. It always was. No sense in changing now."

"Now you've gone too far!" she cried, striking her palm against the door in frustration. "You've got the house, the farm, the horses . . . but *I'm* not part of the land deed."

"No. You're part of our marriage license."

She stood there, silently breathing in and out very hard for a few moments.

"So I'm stuck here with nowhere else to go. All right, so I'll cook for you, and clean, and do your laundry. But you don't have *me!*" she cried, jabbing her finger at her breast. "You'll never have me again."

Soft and low, Sam said, "What a shame, Bertha. What a gosh-darn shame."

She'd have been ready for any kind of argument, but she didn't know what to reply to his gentle remark. At last she decided to just ignore it—for the time being.

She whirled around, marched back to the stove, retrieved her knife, and proceeded to chop the onion into teeny, tiny pieces.

This time it didn't make her feel any better.

*   *   *

Sam speared the last piece of smoked sausage with his fork and held it up. Did the darn fool think he was admiring some fancy work of art? Bertha wondered.

From his place at the head of the table, he looked down at her. She'd cringed when he took his customary spot. Then she'd deliberately set her and Miranda's plates at the far end of the long table.

He might think nothing had changed, but she was about to show him in no uncertain terms that, even at mealtimes, he was still not a part of her family.

"Ah, my favorite dinner," he said, grinning at her with satisfaction. Then he popped the sausage into his mouth.

"I thought chicken and dumplings was your favorite," Bertha mumbled. She hadn't said much throughout the meal, in spite of Sam's incessant chatter about the beauty of the Nevada countryside and the peculiar characters he'd met in the mining towns. But this last bit of blatant hogwash was too much for her to bear.

"Oh, yeah, it is," he responded quickly. "So's this."

"I've got a feeling if I'd served hog's ass and hominy grits tonight, you'd have said it was your favorite," she grumbled. "Don't try sweet-talking me again, Sam."

He shrugged. "Can I help it if you're a mighty good cook? You know, that's another thing about you I really missed—"

She rose and snatched the plate out from under him. "Well, dinner's over now. I'm mighty good at doing the dishes, too. You want to admire that?"

She cleared the table without saying another word. Miranda had gobbled down her meal, then retreated to her room again.

Come back here, you little coward, Bertha mentally scolded her. *Don't leave me here alone with this man.*

She just hoped her daughter wouldn't keep her up all night with a bellyache from bolting her food. She was going to need all the rest she could get just to have the energy and wits to confront Sam every day until he decided to leave again.

While she filled the washbasin with hot sudsy water, Sam settled into the rocking chair in front of the fire and proceeded to hum in time to the creaking of the rockers. Even though she kept her back to him, the sound of his off-key little tunes were a constant reminder to her that he was here. She didn't want to break any of the dishes she'd so carefully brought all the way from Ohio, but she was awfully tempted to throw a few at him just to shut him up.

She dried her hands on her apron. She glanced over at Sam. His eyes were closed, and his head rested against the back of the rocker. He wasn't rocking and he'd stopped that annoying humming. Maybe he was asleep.

Tiptoeing so she wouldn't wake him, Bertha hurried into her bedroom. All throughout the meal, she'd been trying to think of some way to avoid being with Sam in the bedroom. She'd finally come up with what she thought was a fairly workable solution. She'd succeed, too, if only she could be very, very quiet.

She wasn't about to do this while he was awake and risk getting stuck in the small room, so close to a bed and Sam, with his brown eyes full of fire and silver tongue full of ready compliments. Thank goodness his "favorite meal" had lulled him to sleep.

She pulled open the cupboard and scooped up an armload of her skirts and bodices. She scooted into Miranda's room as quickly as she could without making a sound and dumped them all in a corner. She'd hang them later, after the move was complete and Sam couldn't stop her.

"Mommy, what are you doing?"

"Shhh."

"We're not packing to leave, are we?"

"Of course not," Bertha whispered.

"Don't let him scare you away, Mommy. *I'm* not afraid of him anymore."

Oh, no, of course you're not, Bertha thought with an

inward laugh. It only took you two tries at hiding from him to decide that.

"I'm not afraid of him, either," Bertha told her daughter. "I'm moving in here with you."

"Here? Now?" Her pale eyebrows drooped.

"Don't look so delighted. It's only until he leaves."

Miranda heaved her little shoulders up and down in a sigh of resignation, and turned back to her doll. "I hope he leaves real soon. You snore."

"Thank you very much. I hope he leaves soon, too. You used to wet the bed," she teased.

"I was just a baby then!"

Bertha laughed quietly. "I know. You're a big girl now."

"You're darned tootin'," Miranda finished with an emphatic nod.

Bertha only needed to make one more trip for her underclothes and nightgowns. If worst came to worst, she might be able to get away with wearing the same work dress for a few days in a row, but she couldn't do without a fresh supply of underthings.

She'd always modestly considered herself a rather observant woman. She noticed when pictures weren't hung straight on walls, when Miranda's braids were uneven, pieces of untrimmed thread or lint on a dress, who was in church on Sunday morning and who was not—although she never gossiped about it afterward. She could have sworn that when she entered the bedroom, Sam was still dozing in the rocker.

How then, in less time than it took for her to open the drawer and gather up her underthings, could he be standing so close behind her?

"Sam! You scared the life out of me," she scolded.

Standing between the foot of the bed and the wardrobe, he just grinned at her.

In order to get to the door, Bertha would have to climb over the bed, or else pass by so close that she couldn't help touching him again.

She made sure she held her underthings all doubled up in front of her, like a barrier. She'd have to press them all again, but that didn't matter now. Maybe he'd be sitting in the rocker when she ironed, and she could bash him over the head with the heavy iron. Just to be humane, she'd let it cool first. No sense leaving a burn mark with the bump.

"Did you study sneaking up on people with the Indians while you were out there?"

"No. Anyway, they don't sneak. They're just mighty quiet."

"Oh." She blinked at his correction. Then she frowned again. "Why are you following me? What in tarnation do you want now anyway?"

"I just wondered what you were doing in here."

"I'm . . ." She glanced down at her armful of white, lace-edged drawers. "I'm moving my things into Miranda's room."

"Why? There's enough room for both of us—"

"Oh, no, there's not. I don't even think there's room enough in this house—in the whole darned town—for both of us, but I'm not about to call you out for a showdown. So I'm moving into Miranda's room instead."

"Oh. I'm sorry to hear that."

"You shouldn't be surprised. You know darn good and well I refuse to sleep with you—in here or anywhere else. So don't make a fuss about it," she warned. "Just let me through."

She started to step forward. Sam moved to block her way. She didn't know why she should have been so silly in thinking that he'd let her pass that easily.

"Let me by, Sam," she said. She tried to make her voice sound threatening—almost an "or else." Or else what? she wondered. Or else I'll toss my underthings in your face and climb over the bed?

"I want to talk to you."

"Fine. Let me put these things in Miranda's room. Then we'll sit by the fire and have a nice, long chat. I'll heat up the coffee," she offered with a forced brightness she didn't feel. "I think there are still a few cinnamon rolls—"

"No. Right here is fine."

"Fine for you. Not for me."

"It used to be fine for you in here, Bertha." His voice had turned very gentle. Yet it held a deep undertone of power and longing—and of desire that would not be denied much longer.

"It used to be *wonderful* for me in here, Sam," she reluctantly admitted. "But all that *used to be*."

She shook her head as she studied the small, flat metal buttons on the shirt that stretched across his broad chest. It was difficult to meet his burning gaze.

"It's different now, and I don't think it can be the same between us ever again."

"You won't even give it a try?"

She never should have hesitated. She should have just told him no—outright and in no uncertain terms. But that second of hesitation gave Sam the opening he needed.

Slowly he took one step toward her.

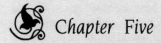 Chapter Five

"No, Sam. No," Bertha protested.

She wanted to run away from him, but she couldn't move her feet. He took another step toward her. Now they were standing so close that his chest pressed against her arms folded over the clothing in front of her. He placed both of his hands on her arms.

She couldn't allow herself to relax. Once he started to hold her close the way he used to, once she could feel his heart beating within his broad chest, feel his warm breath on her cheeks, feel his lips on hers—all the old feelings that she kept so carefully imprisoned would riotously escape, and she would be a helpless hostage to her own emotions.

She braced herself, waiting to feel him pull her toward him. She'd have to resist—for Miranda's sake, and for her own good. Down deep inside, she feared that, however good her intentions, she couldn't.

But he didn't step closer. He didn't even move his hands up and down her arm. He just continued to hold her.

"I still love you, Bertha," he whispered.

She didn't say a thing.

"I traveled all this way just to come back to you."

She still didn't say a word.

"The only thing on my mind the whole way was how much I wanted to hold you in my arms and love you again."

She drew in a deep breath, as if she might be ready to say

something, but then she just pressed her lips tightly together and remained silent.

"I should've figured after all this time you might be a tad perturbed at me."

"A tad?" she repeated.

"All right, a lot," he corrected with a mischievous chuckle. "But it did make you talk to me."

She didn't return his grin. "I don't think it's funny, Sam."

"I don't think it's funny, either." He stopped grinning and looked down at her intently. "Sometimes I missed you so much it hurt."

"I hurt, too, Sam. I still do."

"But I hadn't finished what we'd sent me out there to do, Bertha," he continued as if she hadn't spoken. "I hadn't made the money we needed to keep the farm."

"And all the time I spent waiting for you, I discovered something. I found out I didn't need you after all," she told him with a proud lift of her chin. "I did it myself. I made it on my own—for Miranda and me. Not for you—at least, not anymore."

"I always worked—for what I thought was the two of us. I'd have worked even harder if I'd known there were three of us."

"You would have known—"

He placed one finger over her lips to still her argument. She was glad. She'd had enough of it, too.

But the touch of his callused fingertip against her lips made her shiver, not from cold but from warmth. She could feel with more intensity the heat of his body, and the rising heat of her own longing. If he didn't remove his finger soon, she was afraid she'd burst into flames.

"I worked hard all day, so that I was exhausted and fell into bed every night." His hand moved across her cheek and over her shoulder in a gentle caress, down to hold her arm again.

His voice had taken on a soft, low tone. He wasn't trying

to argue with her now. He was telling her something very special.

"Then I didn't have to lay awake, thinking about how soft you'd feel next to me, how warm your body would be next to mine, how much I missed you."

Bertha swallowed hard and clutched the bundle of clothes more tightly. How could he, half a continent away, have done the exact same thing she had done?

"Even then, sometimes I'd wake up in the middle of the night and not be able to get back to sleep again just for thinking about you."

How could he know?

"I never stopped thinking about you," he continued. "Why else would I come back?"

She shook herself from the dream of the picture he was painting for her with his smooth words.

"You needed a place to sleep and someone to cook for you," she answered him bluntly.

"I could have found that anywhere."

"Well, a wife is . . ." she began hesitantly. She could feel the warmth flooding her cheeks. She also doubted the wisdom of bringing up this point in the bedroom. But some problems between them still needed resolving. "A wife is . . . good for . . . a few other things, too."

"I could have gotten that anywhere, too, and you know it. But I didn't, Bertha. It was damned tough sometimes," he added with a slight chuckle, "but I never did."

One hand released her arm and moved slowly up to cup her chin. His touch was soft and gentle as he raised her face to his.

"Oh, sure, I met a few guys who set up new families without giving a hang about the wives and children they left behind. But I only, ever, always, wanted to come back to you."

Now that she was looking up into his deep brown eyes, watching the bright twinkle against the darkness like stars in the night sky, she found it impossible to turn away.

"I've always gotten something very special from you and you alone. Something more than just cooking food, washing clothes, and . . . other things besides just being together in bed."

She could feel the pressure of his gentle grasp on her arm drawing her closer to him. She knew she should pull away, but couldn't manage to make herself move.

"You're the only one I want to share my home, my heart, my life with."

"Share?" she repeated. She pulled back a little and glared up at him. "It seems to me, with a little help from Mr. Martin, you've managed to get the whole darned thing."

He moved his hands away, just enough so he wasn't touching her anymore, but not enough that she could escape.

"Just say the word, Bertha, and I'll leave."

"Just like that, huh?"

He nodded. "Just like that."

She grimaced skeptically. "It wasn't that easy this morning."

Sam tilted his head a little to the side and grinned. "Can I help it if I only want to be near you?"

"That sounds good now, Sam," she said. She couldn't let the silver-tongued devil think he had convinced her to take him back, but she was helpless to resist. "But—"

"No *buts*."

Now he held her arms again. She could feel one hand slowly smoothing up her arm and over her shoulder. With the warm palm of his hand, he followed the rise of her collarbone across the soft indentation at the base of her throat. His hand rose until just the edge of his thumb supported her chin.

He held her tenderly, but with a strength that denied her escape. She couldn't have moved, even if she'd wanted to. Slowly he lowered his face to hers.

The insistent knocking at the door startled her.

"Hello! Hello, Bertha!"

"Oh, my goodness! It's Arthur," she exclaimed.

"Quinn? That bastard!" He released her quickly.

"Are you there, Bertha? He hasn't killed you yet, has he?"

With a squeal she tossed the armful of underclothes up into Sam's face.

From under the clothes she heard him muttering, "What in thunderation is Quinn doing here?"

Bertha started to scramble across the top of the bed. She should have known better than to try to run on a feather-stuffed ticking laid over rope supports.

Her feet sank into the soft cushioning. The holes where the ropes gave way made the ticking fold around her ankles, trapping her. As she pulled her ankles out, one shoe stuck in the mattress.

She just kept going. As she tried to make her last jump off the bed, she became hopelessly entangled in her skirt and tumbled to the floor.

She rolled over and landed upright on her bottom, legs sprawled out in front of her, with her skirt bunched up to her knees and her head spinning round and round.

She looked across the room toward the front door. Arthur stood with his nose pressed to the screen and his hands cupped around his eyes, peering in.

At least it was harmless Arthur, and not Mr. Martin, come to gloat over the successful results of his manipulation.

Worse yet, it could have been Widow Crenshaw and Miss Barber, those two old busybodies. For the past seven years they'd found something snide to say about her every time her back was turned. She didn't need them spreading any more rumors now. At least she knew she could trust Arthur not to gossip about her.

His timely interruption had broken the spell Sam always managed to cast over her whenever she was near him. Even now, after all these years, he had a power over her that she realized she was still helpless to resist. Sitting there with her head still spinning, and not just from her tumble, she knew she had to do something to keep him away from her permanently.

"Looks like I've come at a bad time," Arthur remarked.

"No, no." Her fingers fumbled with the folds of fabric, trying to pull her skirt down over her ankles. But she was sitting on the back of the skirt and couldn't pull it any farther down than her knees. Would Arthur notice she only wore one shoe? Or would he be too busy examining her legs?

"I suppose you two are having fun," Arthur said. There didn't seem to be much humor in his voice.

"No, no," Bertha protested, scrambling to her feet. She smoothed down her skirt as she headed for the door. Would Arthur notice she only made one thump on the floor, like Long John Silver? "It's not what you think."

"As a matter of fact, Quinn, I don't give a damn what you think," Sam called threateningly from across the room.

Bertha looked back over her shoulder. Sam was leaning against the doorjamb of the bedroom, his arms crossed over his chest. Thunderation! If the son of a gun didn't have a pair of her drawers slung over his shoulder. Her face blazed with heat, and she felt sick to her stomach. Arthur would have to be blind not to see them!

Her head had stopped spinning from Sam's soft words and gentle touch, but she still wanted to cling to the doorknob for whatever support it could give her.

"In fact, I'll thank you not to think about me and my wife at all," Sam warned.

"I can't say what I think of you in polite company, Mr. Hamilton," Arthur replied as he stepped boldly into the room. "But I can tell you I avoid thinking of you whenever I can."

"I appreciate that."

"However, I do take great interest in what happens to Bertha." Arthur turned deliberately from Sam to her. "As a matter of fact, that's why I'm here."

"Why are you here, Arthur?" she asked.

Considering the size of the crowd that had gathered around them this morning, and considering how sooner or later everyone liked to play at town crier, Arthur must have eventually heard something from someone about Sam's moving back in. She couldn't imagine why he would take it into his head to visit her now.

"Yes, Arthur," Sam mocked Bertha's tone of voice. He pulled her drawers from his shoulder, but continued to hold them chest-high, and to shift them very noticeably from one hand to the other. "Why *are* you here?"

Before Arthur could say anything, Bertha took him by the arm and began leading him into the parlor.

"Why don't you have a seat in here while I heat up the coffee?" she told him. "I think there are a few cinnamon rolls left. Then we can all have a nice, neighborly chat."

"Bertha and I were just about to do the same thing, weren't we, dear? Sort of." Sam still kept tossing her drawers around.

Why don't you just wear them on your head? Or wave them in front of Arthur's nose? she silently demanded. If she could get hold of them, she'd gladly strangle Sam with them, with Arthur standing there as a witness. Maybe she ought to call Miranda out of her bedroom. She'd probably get a good deal of satisfaction out of watching, too.

"Of course, you're not exactly a neighbor, Quinn," Sam continued, "seeing as how you must live in town."

"Right now I live over the store. When I marry, of course, I'll buy a house."

"Well, that's a nice ambition, Quinn—a house of your own. Not somebody else's. You just keep thinking about that."

Bertha situated Arthur in the most comfortable chair, then headed for the kitchen. "I'll be right back," she called musically over her shoulder.

On the way out she passed Sam, who was standing there blocking the doorway.

"Give me those darned things," she demanded in a hoarse whisper. Snatching the drawers from his hands, she rolled them into a tiny bundle and shoved them into the cupboard. "What in tarnation do you think you're doing?"

"What the heck does this Quinn fellow think he's doing, coming over here tonight?" Sam apparently had little regard for whispering.

"I don't know."

She took the cinnamon rolls from the cupboard and placed them on a plate. She intended to go in and talk to him to find out. But Sam was always interrupting with insults, and Arthur didn't seem to be able to control his own hostility any better. She might be able to talk some sense with either one individually, but never together. How could she tell her husband she wanted to be alone with the man who'd been courting her?

"You two don't seem to be able to find a kind word for each other. Why don't you just stay away from each other?"

"Nope, can't do that." Sam's eyes narrowed. "Quinn seems pretty familiar with this place, and I'd sure like to know why."

"He . . . he's been here before, a time or two."

"A time or two—or three? What are you doing entertaining him? For Pete's sake, you're a married woman!"

She slammed the coffeepot down on the warm stove. "I haven't done anything to be ashamed of." She tried to keep her voice to a whisper, but her anger was making her speak more loudly than she'd intended.

"Having him come here while I was gone wasn't exactly—"

"Excuse me. While I believed you were dead." In a more normal tone of voice, she continued, "Anyway, let's not discuss it now. I have a guest."

"*We* have a guest," he corrected.

She knew there'd be no keeping these two apart. And there wouldn't be any peace, either. With a sigh she started toward the parlor, then turned back.

"If you *have* to be here, at least make yourself useful and bring the coffeepot."

"Sure, sweetheart. Does Quinn take sugar or rat poison? One lump or two?"

Showing a cheerfulness she didn't really feel, she carried the cups and plate of rolls into the parlor. She could hear Sam's boots clomping on the floor as he followed her. At least he made two noises. But she could just picture coffee sloshed all over her clean floor. If she didn't mop it up tonight, the place would be crawling with ants by the morning.

She took her seat in the chair opposite Arthur. She took care to try to keep her feet tucked under her skirt, so Arthur couldn't see her stockinged toes.

"I'd heard rumors Sam was actually living here again, Bertha," Arthur said. "I came to see how you were. I couldn't believe—"

"I don't know why you'd find it so hard to believe a man would be living with his own wife," Sam grumbled as he set the coffeepot on the table beside Bertha.

He sat down on the sofa and threw one long leg over the arm. He picked up a roll from the plate and bit into it with all the finesse of a ravening wolf.

"Hey, Quinn. Don't say I'm not a good host." He picked up another roll. "Here, try one."

He tossed it at Arthur's head with admirable accuracy. Arthur managed to catch it, but it crumbled in two through the sieve of his fingers, sending a shower of crumbs into his hair.

Bertha stared at Sam in horror. What in the world had happened to his manners? Had he forgotten them all while he was away? Was he trying to embarrass her in front of Arthur? Or was he deliberately showing himself up as a lumbering, uncouth clod for some other reason?

Arthur seemed unaffected. He set what was left of the roll on the table.

"Bertha, I couldn't believe you'd willingly allowed Mr. Hamilton back into the house."

She shot Sam an angry look. "I haven't. Apparently Mr.

Martin discovered that I'd neglected to have Sam's name removed from the deed, making him the owner still."

"Lester Martin?" Arthur exclaimed with a scowl on his face. He gave a derisive laugh. "He's the best lawyer money can buy. Figures he'd try to make a big to-do out of a little oversight. But don't worry. My mother's uncle is a retired judge. I'll wire him first thing tomorrow, to see what we can do to stop—"

"We?" Sam growled.

"No, Arthur. Please. Not right now," Bertha pleaded. She couldn't afford a lawyer, much less a judge.

Arthur harrumphed. "Very well, Bertha. Whatever you think is best—for now. Anyway, I also recalled this is our usual night for—"

"Usual night?" Sam interrupted. "Do you mean to tell me he *usually* comes here, Bertha?"

She could feel her throat tightening and her face growing hotter. If these two were going to argue, she hoped they wouldn't come to blows. Great-Aunt Sophie's lamp was perched on the table between them, and she'd always hoped to be able to pass it on to Miranda someday when she married.

"I've been coming here almost every Thursday evening since Bertha came out of mourning for you," Arthur answered without hesitation.

"Oh, my goodness!" Bertha's hand flew to her mouth. "I'm sorry, Arthur. In all the confusion, I forgot."

"And, pray tell, what do you two *usually* do?" Before Arthur could reply, Sam added, "Later on, we'll discuss the *unusual* stuff."

"There *was* no unusual stuff," Arthur answered with deadly seriousness. "At first I helped with all the little repairs needed around the house."

"I'm listening."

"You left the place in really poor condition, Hamilton," Arthur accused. "Any man with a decent conscience would've been ashamed to leave his pregnant wife living like that. There were so many things that Bertha couldn't do alone, and the hired hands just couldn't manage to get to."

"Of course, *you* could," Sam answered, his voice dripping with skepticism.

"Of course," Arthur replied confidently. "Then we discovered something we both enjoyed."

Sam's eyes grew dark. He glared at Arthur. "Such as?"

"Dominoes."

Sam began to grin. "Dominoes?"

"Yes, most people don't appreciate how challenging—"

"Dominoes?" Sam turned to Bertha. "We don't even have any dominoes."

"Arthur gave me—us," she quickly corrected, "a set of them."

"Oh, he did?"

"We carry them in the store. And it's an appropriate gift for a gentleman to give a lady."

"If you're so danged appropriate, what are you doing calling on a married woman?" Sam demanded. Then he turned to Bertha. "You like to play dominoes?"

She nodded.

"You never told me you played dominoes."

"You never asked."

"Well, that never stopped you before from telling me a whole lot of others things."

"My father taught me when I was a little girl." She shrugged. "I didn't think you liked to play, so I never—"

"Of course, we usually found other things to do besides play children's games." Sam gave Bertha a wink and a broad leer that Arthur couldn't have missed.

Arthur cleared his throat, drawing attention back to himself. "We've made a weekly game of dominoes for several months now. I saw no reason to stop our entertainment just because you'd returned. We were just beginning to let Miranda join in. She really seems to enjoy the game, too."

"The three of you. Real cozy and family-like, huh?" Sam asked.

Arthur paused a moment before replying. He smiled smugly at Sam. "I guess you might say that. At least the child doesn't try to hide when she sees me."

"Oh, Arthur." Sam eyed the man coolly, as if he wasn't any more threatening than a pismire, and gave a mocking laugh. "How could anybody be afraid of *you*?"

Bertha knew Arthur couldn't possibly see what Sam was doing because he held the hand with the roll in it on the other side, down by his hip. But she could watch the whole thing as Sam's hand turned into a fist around the roll and crumpled it until nothing was left but doughy crumbs. She'd have to sweep up tonight or the place would be crawling with field mice by the morning.

Apparently, no matter what he said or how coolly he said it, Sam viewed Arthur as a very real threat.

Bertha just hoped she wasn't also cleaning up shards of Great-aunt Sophie's lamp, broken teeth, and pools of blood.

"Well, Quinn," Sam said, still appearing very calm. "I do appreciate your looking after things on the farm while I was away, and I can understand your wanting to help out a pretty lady. Of course, in all honesty, I can't really say I appreciate all the attention when the pretty lady is my wife."

"A woman gets lonely, Hamilton."

"But I'm back now, and she won't be lonesome anymore."

"For a while anyway, I suppose."

"Nope. Not anymore," Sam stated insistently. "But I can't see as any of this is any concern of yours. Frankly, I don't think it was any concern of yours to begin with. So I'll be thanking you to leave now."

"Sam! Mr. Quinn is my guest."

"Well, he's not mine."

"Don't tell me anything again about this being *your* house," she warned. "Even a housekeeper's allowed to have callers—in peace."

How could she have put herself in the category of an employee? She wanted to bite off her own tongue.

But she could see Sam's face turning red from her last remark. He wasn't the kind to embarrass. Only anger could cause this reaction in him. She couldn't see why he should be angry. It wasn't as if she'd done anything wrong. As a matter of fact, if anyone around here had the right to be angry, she did.

"That's all right, Bertha," Arthur said, rising. "I don't think we're going to have much of a game tonight. I guess I'll just head home. I've got to open the store bright and early tomorrow morning. At least I'm gainfully employed and not a burden to others."

Bertha rose quickly and followed Arthur to the door. She hoped it would take Sam a little longer to untangle his long legs from the sofa cushions and wipe the crumbs from between his fingers. She needed just a little time alone with Arthur, time that she didn't think she'd ever get again—at least not while Sam still stayed around.

"Arthur," she began.

His hand still resting on the doorknob, he turned slowly, almost as if he knew what she was about to say and didn't want to hear it. He was right. She knew he wasn't going to like this. She also knew enough about him to know he wasn't going to accept this that easily.

"You know I've enjoyed your company, Arthur. But . . . I think, in light of everything . . ."

She didn't know how to continue. She really had enjoyed having Arthur around, to talk to as an adult, all those long lonely evenings. And she had *really* appreciated his help with all the bothersome little things that arose on a farm.

Arthur Quinn wasn't a bad-looking man. He was a good businessman, a sober churchgoing man, good with children, and a good neighbor. If Sam had really been dead, she supposed she could have made a contented life with Arthur. She felt certain he'd have raised Miranda as his own. She'd have at least been a dutiful wife to him, and they probably would have played a lot of dominoes.

But things were different now.

She wasn't really sure how she was going to say what she had to say.

"Seeing as how Sam's come back, and is living here . . . I've had enough hurtful gossip about me already. . . . And you really don't need people spreading tales about you, either."

Her mind flitted from one lame excuse to another. Arthur listened silently to her feeble attempts to explain herself.

"You're a good man, Arthur. Someday you'll find a wonderful girl. But you deserve better than to wait around for a married woman's husband to abandon her again. I've got to think of Miranda and the reputation that'll precede her everywhere she goes in this town for years to come. . . ."

"Not of yourself and not of us," he stated flatly. "Just about Miranda. And Sam."

"Yes." It was the only honest answer she could give him. "I think it's best if you don't come here again, Arthur."

"I'll stay away for a while, Bertha," he answered. "Just until he leaves you again."

"I'm back to stay, Quinn," Sam's voice behind her echoed through the kitchen. "And you're gone for good."

Arthur didn't even say good evening as he closed the door behind him.

Bertha turned and leaned her back against the door. She looked across the room toward her own bedroom. Then her gaze moved to Miranda's room. That's where she'd be spending her nights from now on. Right now she wished she had the strength left to cross the room and tumble into bed.

"You told him you didn't want to see him anymore."

She turned to look at Sam. He was standing there with the most incredibly self-satisfied grin on his face.

Now she knew she didn't have the strength to make it across the room, much less past Sam.

"How dare you eavesdrop on my private conversations."

She was even too emotionally exhausted to become angry, or show it properly.

Sam said nothing to defend himself or his less than polite actions. He just continued to grin and repeated, "You told him you didn't want to see him anymore."

"I did not. I . . . I only told him not to come here again for a little while."

Sam shrugged. "Same thing."

"It is not."

"The way I look at it—"

She pushed herself away from the door, planted her feet apart, and placed her fists on her hips.

"*You* are looking at it all cockeyed, just like you always do. I won't have you pecking at each other like two roosters in one henhouse. I've already got too much to do to spend my time cleaning up after you've had your little battles."

"We didn't—"

"Yes, you did. I'll thank you to get the broom and clean up that mess you made of the rolls in the parlor while I get the scrub brush and clean the coffee you probably spilled on the kitchen floor."

"I didn't spill any, see." He pointed to the clean and dry kitchen floor.

Did he expect her to thank him?

Then he grinned at her. "But I'll be more than happy to help you clean the sofa. As I recall . . ."

Bertha didn't respond. She just grabbed her broom and dustpan from beside the stove and marched into the parlor. She tried to pretend she was too busy furiously sweeping up the crumbs to notice that Sam had followed her.

He must have been watching her awful carefully. As soon as she had all the crumbs neatly collected in the dustpan, he began to turn down the wick on Great-aunt Sophie's lamp.

"What do you think you're doing? I'm working in here."

"Put down the broom, Bertha."

"It's late. I'm tired. Go to bed, Sam."

"That's exactly what I was thinking."

"Fine. I'll see you in the morning."

"I was sort of thinking I'd see you in the morning, too, across the pillow from me."

She sighed and watched him silently for a moment. Then she pushed past him into the kitchen.

"Blow the flame out when you're finished in there," she told him.

She dumped the crumbs in the dustbin beside the stove and replaced everything. Brushing the remaining bits of crumbs from her palms, she headed toward Miranda's room. When she reached the door, she stopped, hand on the doorknob.

Sam was standing at the doorway to what once was their room. His dark eyes were studying her intently.

"I'm only saying this once more," she told him. "So you'd better be sure it sinks into that hard head of yours this time. I'll do your cooking, cleaning, and laundry. But as far as I'm concerned, you're living here just as if I'd taken in a boarder."

The corners of his lips curled up in a grin. "Would you treat me better if I helped with the dishes and learned to play dominoes?"

"No."

With a hand that trembled in spite of her efforts to remain calm, she twisted the doorknob and gave a push. Safely in the dark of Miranda's room, Bertha leaned her back against the door and stifled a sob.

Why did he have to make this situation so difficult? She wondered. Why did he have to make it so easy for her to hate him?

Sam lay in his bed alone. He stared up at the ceiling, watching the moonlight shading light and dark between the clouds. What he was really thinking about was Bertha, just on the other side of the wall.

She should be in here with him. She should have been

beside him all along. He never would have left her if he'd known things would take this kind of turn.

He listened to the breeze whispering through the trees. Some sounds never changed, no matter where you were. A dog barked in the distance. He was used to the yelp of the coyote and the howl of the wolf. He could hear one of the cows in the barn lowing. He had to admit it was a more comforting sound that the growl of a grizzly bear moving past your camp.

He hadn't forced himself in here to protect Bertha and Miranda from dogs and cows.

Listen as he might, he never heard anyone in the bushes, or any footsteps coming up on the porch. People just didn't do that sort of thing in Grasonville.

It had to have been Bertha's imagination—that was all. Either that, or she really was making up tales just to get him in trouble.

"Mighty peculiar, if you ask me," Widow Crenshaw said as she and Miss Barber sat rocking in the front parlor of the Crenshaw house.

They hadn't bothered to light the lamps. The glare on the windowpanes interfered with seeing everything that was going on outside.

"What's that?" Miss Barber asked.

The two rocking chairs faced the big front window that looked out over Main Street, but Miss Barber couldn't see past the dust specks on the windowpanes. Once the weather got really warm, they'd move the rocking chairs out on the front porch and watch everyone go by. Then Miss Barber wouldn't be able to see past the big red geraniums Widow Crenshaw always planted along the front of the porch.

"Mr. Quinn seems to be returning to his home a tad early this evening," Widow Crenshaw mentioned.

Miss Barber turned and squinted at the clock resting on the mantle. "What time is it?"

"Barely seven. On a Thursday night he usually doesn't

come riding back into town until nine. Now, what do you suppose could've happened to make him return so early?"

"I'd say he'd received a less than cordial welcome at the Hamilton farm," Miss Barber replied, rocking even harder.

"Catherine, you may be shortsighted, but you never really miss all that much."

"Why, thank you, Janet."

"The question is, who kicked him out? Bertha? Or Mr. Hamilton? Or did he leave of his own free will?"

"Bertha," Miss Barber asserted with an emphatic nod. "She wouldn't want to risk gossip, having her husband and the man who'd been courting her with her at the same time."

Widow Crenshaw snickered. "She ought to know it doesn't matter what she does. No one in this town is safe from gossip while we're still breathing—and they all know it."

"Mr. Hamilton?" Miss Barber amended with a little less certainty. "He's taken over the house and taken back his wife."

Widow Crenshaw laughed gain. "It's only been two days. You know Bertha better than that. She doesn't give in that easily."

Miss Barber twisted her lips. She had one last chance.

"Mr. Quinn wouldn't leave on his own," she stated. "In the five years he's been in this town, we've never seen him walk away from anything he had a real interest in."

Widow Crenshaw stopped laughing. She leaned a little closer to Miss Barber. "And in the five years he's been in this town, I've never seen him take such an interest in anything more than he has in Bertha Hamilton."

Miss Barber frowned and pursed her lips. She rocked all the harder, muttering, "Two men at the same time."

"Will you stop dwelling on that, Catherine! Now, think about this. What court in the land would allow such a brazen, morally corrupt woman to raise a small, impressionable child?"

"I really don't know, Janet." From the tone of her voice,

it seemed as if she didn't really care, either. She was probably still dwelling on Bertha—and Sam and Arthur.

"None, I tell you."

"You're probably right."

"Of course I'm right. I'm always right."

"You know, it's odd. Bertha Hamilton's not a breathtaking beauty."

"No."

"She's not exactly witty or talented."

"No, not really." Widow Crenshaw shifted in her seat. "What the heck are you getting at, Catherine?"

Miss Barber sighed heavily and rocked all the harder. "I just wish I knew how she does it."

Widow Crenshaw let out a low hum. "If we want to find out, then I think it's high time you and I paid Mrs. Hamilton a neighborly visit."

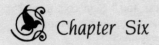 *Chapter Six*

"Would you like some more pancakes, Miranda?" Bertha asked the next morning. She stood at the stove, dripping spoon and bowl of batter in hand, ready to pour.

"No, thank you, Mommy."

"I'll take another stack, please," Sam said, pointing to his empty plate.

He wasn't hungry, Bertha thought to herself. How could he be? He'd had three stacks already. He was just trying to do the same thing he'd done last night at supper—all that silly flattery about her good cooking just to win her over. It hadn't worked then. It wasn't going to work now—or ever. When would he learn?

The batter sizzled as it hit the hot griddle.

He was nothing more than a stranger, taking up space in her house, she kept trying to tell herself, and him. No matter what he said—if he said he loved the food—well, it was just her job to cook it for him. If he said he hated it—well, too bad. He could eat it or go somewhere else to live.

"They sure are delicious pancakes, aren't they, Miranda?" Sam asked.

The little girl eyed him from her safe spot at the other end of the table. "Yes, sir."

"Are you sure you don't want some more?"

"No, thank you, sir."

"Don't you think you're carrying this 'sir' business a little too far?"

"No, *sir*. I'm being polite, like Mommy taught me."

"Oh. Well, yeah, being polite is important."

Just listening to the two of them, Bertha had to grin. Very few people were a match for Miranda.

"But a little girl needs to eat, too," Sam continued, "if she's going to grow up to be as pretty as her mommy."

"I'm short. I don't need to eat much."

"You need to eat if you don't want to stay three feet four the rest of your life."

"I ate enough yesterday to get me to three feet five. Tomorrow I'll eat enough to get me to three feet five and a half. There's not much sense in rushing. Then I'll grow out of my clothes too fast and won't have anything that fits."

Let's see you come up with an answer to that one, Mr. Samuel I-Want-to-Be-Your-Daddy-So-Much Hamilton, she silently challenged.

Sam, undaunted, continued. "My grandma always used to tell my sisters that eating burnt pancakes gives you curly hair."

No fair changing the subject, you big coward! Bertha thought.

"My mommy's a good cook. She doesn't burn the pancakes."

"Of course not. But just in case . . ."

"I wouldn't eat them anyway. I don't want curly hair," Miranda answered.

"Why not?"

"I've seen Dorothy Halstead in town. It's too darn hard to brush the knots out of, and if she doesn't tie it down, it fluffs up around her head like fur on a scared cat."

Bertha thought Sam chuckled way too loud for the actual humor of Miranda's comment.

"Your mother's hair is very pretty."

Bertha silently wondered if Sam was talking for Miranda's benefit or for hers.

"Mommy's hair's not curly. What does that have to do with anything, anyway?"

"It's still pretty, isn't it?"

"Yes, sir."

"Don't you want hair like hers?"

"I already got it. See." She pulled on a hank of her hair and held it out from her head. "And I didn't have to eat any awful burnt pancakes to get it, either. I just had to be born."

Bertha plopped the plate of still steaming pancakes down in front of Sam.

"You're going to have to do better than that if you're trying to make Miranda like you," she told him quietly, so that Miranda at the other end of the table couldn't hear. The ornery little whippersnapper didn't need any encouraging. "Want more coffee?"

"Thanks. At least she's not running away screaming from me anymore," he replied as he poured corn syrup on his stack.

"Maybe Rachel's pointing out to her that you don't look like a big red bear anymore worked."

Sam chuckled. "You can always count on Mrs. Pickett to say just the right thing."

Bertha brought the coffeepot from the stove and refilled his cup.

"I was thinking of checking on what the hired hands are doing with the corn in the north field this morning."

Bertha shrugged. Anything was fine as long as it kept him out of her hair.

"Miranda, would you like to watch me work?"

Thunderation, that man didn't know when to quit!

"No, sir."

"Why not?"

"Watching people work is boring."

"Seems to me like you really wanted to watch Del work."

"That was Del. I don't want to watch *you*," she replied with a sneer.

Before Bertha could scold Miranda again for not minding her manners, Sam asked, "Am I that boring?"

Apparently he wasn't as bothered as she was by Miranda's lack of tact.

"No, sir."

"Then why not?"

"Farm equipment is dangerous," she repeated Del's warning.

"I'll protect you," Sam offered.

"I want Del to protect me, not *you*."

Sam laughed. "How about if we invite Del over here and—"

"No!" Miranda sprang to her feet. "No. Why don't grown-ups ever listen? I don't want to do anything with you."

"But, Miranda—"

She stamped her foot on the floor. Sam could see tears edging her lower lids, threatening to drip down her cheeks. She gave a big sniff, as if trying to pull them back in again.

"Just stop asking me, will you?"

"Why?"

"Because . . . because I don't care if some stupid piece of paper says you have to live here with us," she blurted out. "I don't care how hard you try, you're not my real daddy."

"But, I *am*—"

"No!" She alternately stamped both feet hard and waved both fists in the air. "My real daddy's dead. I wish he was alive—and *you* were dead instead!"

Miranda bolted for the door.

"Miranda! Not again!" Sam called after her.

"Now see what you've done," Bertha scolded him.

Miranda pushed the screen door so hard it hit something with a thump.

Odd, Bertha thought, it didn't sound like the side of the house.

"Well, bless my soul!"

From where she stood in the kitchen, Bertha couldn't see who was at the door, but she'd recognize that whining voice anywhere. Miss Catherine Barber. Now she figured the screen door hadn't hit her. Miss Barber had probably walked smack into it. Bertha knew Widow Crenshaw would be with her, too, standing on the porch, waiting to come waddling into her house and nosing into her life.

What in the world were those two doing here this early in the morning anyway? She hoped the screen door had whacked them both really hard. Even if they'd shown up later, why on earth did they have to come at exactly the same time Miranda decided to run away again?

To make matters worse, they'd probably seen Sam shoot up from his chair and rush to the door after the fleeing little girl. It must have looked like some kind of horrendous scene from some badly written and even more badly performed melodrama, instead of just Miranda's usual hasty trip to the Picketts.

Bertha quickly removed her apron and reached up to make sure her hairpins were in place. Her life and her kitchen were a shambles right now, and those two old buzzards wouldn't miss a hair out of place on a fly on the wall. They wouldn't hesitate to tell everyone in town about how badly Bertha Hamilton kept house, either.

As Widow Crenshaw entered, she straightened the large hat that the blow from the screen door had set askew. Bertha couldn't resist a chuckle.

"What on earth is wrong with that child?" Widow Crenshaw demanded.

"She doesn't like people who ask too many questions," Bertha replied.

"Clearly the child is very upset," Miss Barber said.

Nothing beyond the end of her nose was clear to Miss Barber, Bertha thought.

"What have you done to upset her?" Widow Crenshaw demanded.

Bertha stared at her with insulted surprise. "*I* haven't done a thing." She threw Sam an accusing glance.

"That's the whole problem," he muttered.

"Now is *not* the time, Sam," Bertha warned in a deceptively pleasant voice.

It was bad enough the two old women knew she and Sam were at each other's throats. No sense in letting them believe she was having trouble with her daughter, too. Why couldn't they see it was Sam causing the trouble? Probably because it was the truth, and the truth is always so much harder to believe.

"My dear Mrs. Hamilton," Widow Crenshaw said as she settled herself, uninvited, into Bertha's rocking chair. She folded her white-gloved hands primly over her bag.

Miss Barber sat in the ladderback chair beside the hearth. Bertha noticed her throwing a wistful glance at the more comfortable rocking chair before she assumed the same prim pose as Widow Crenshaw.

"There seems to be something of a problem here," Widow Crenshaw continued. "If you'd like to talk to me about it—"

What? And have it blabbed all over town within twenty-four hours? She couldn't actually say that, Bertha decided, very disappointed. She'd have to be a little more tactful, but not too much.

"Mrs. Crenshaw, I've never considered you a confidante before," she told her. "I don't see any reason to start now."

If Widow Crenshaw was offended by Bertha's bluntness, she never showed it. She was probably so intent on what she wanted to say the she'd never even noticed.

"But, my dear Mrs. Hamilton, your little girl has just run screaming from the house—"

"She wasn't screaming."

"And you don't seem to be doing a thing about it," Widow Crenshaw continued, as if Bertha had never even spoken.

"There's no need to do anything," Bertha replied.

It rankled her that she was even bothering to give an explanation to these old biddies. However she explained Miranda's unusual behavior, she knew Widow Crenshaw and Miss Barber would manage to twist and turn the truth until it sounded about as much like what Bertha had actually said as cow bells were like church chimes.

"She'll be back soon," Bertha said confidently. Silently she prayed that this wouldn't be one of the times Miranda decided to spend all day playing with Sally and Alice, or following Del around.

"How can you be so sure?" Widow Crenshaw demanded. "Your husband doesn't seem as unconcerned with his daughter's welfare as you."

"My husband hasn't seen her do this many times over the past couple of years," Bertha started to explain.

"Many times?" Widow Crenshaw echoed.

"Couple of years?" Miss Barber repeated at the same time.

Oh, now you've done it, Bertha scolded herself. All this nonsense of Miranda's had just been between the Picketts and her. Now everyone in town would know Miranda was in the habit of running off whenever she didn't get her way. And this time it was all Sam's fault!

Bertha threw her hands up in the air and exclaimed, "Oh, botheration! What business is it of yours, anyway?"

Widow Crenshaw stared at her as if that were the silliest question in the history of mankind. Of course, she believed that everything that happened within a fifty-mile radius of town was her direct business.

"I'm rather concerned about any mother who could misplace her child and not worry about her," Widow Crenshaw replied sharply.

Bertha stared at the woman in amazement. "I haven't misplaced her. I know exactly where she is. She's at the Picketts'."

"She wasn't there yesterday," Sam interjected.

"Yes, she was!"

She glared at him. Any other time the two of them would just have their usual disagreement. But how *dare* he contradict her in front of Widow Crenshaw and Miss

Barber—of all people! When they left, she was sure going to give him a piece of her mind to feast on. In fact, she'd like to shove it right down his throat, and hoped he'd choke on it.

"How do you know she's at the Picketts'?" Sam asked. "Yesterday, she was in her 'hiding place.' That could be almost anywhere. You don't even know where it is, and you didn't make much of an effort to find out, either."

Bertha blinked with surprise and hurt. She'd never imagined Sam would attack her mothering instincts, especially in front of strangers.

"Well . . . well, she came back within minutes. It *has* to be on the Picketts' farm."

Sam didn't say anything. Why did she feel that this indicated his disbelief? Why did she feel the need to continue to defend herself?

"It was Del's hiding place before she took it over, so it must be on their farm."

"A thirteen-year-old boy can do a lot of traveling."

"But Miranda's only six years old and small for her age, so the hiding place has to be on the Picketts' farm."

Widow Crenshaw and Miss Barber just sat there, watching and listening to everything. All the while they nodded their heads knowingly.

But, just like everyone who sought to stick their nose in other people's business, Bertha thought, they didn't really know anything at all.

She raised her chin and stared at them confidently. "She'll be back. Just you wait."

Why did she tell them that? The last thing she needed right now was to have those two old buzzards perched in her kitchen, watching and waiting.

Widow Crenshaw eyed her skeptically. Miss Barber just blinked out of focus.

"You'll see," Bertha asserted.

Widow Crenshaw and Miss Barber settled back into their

chairs as if they were prepared to wait until the Second Coming.

"Excuse me, I have work to do." Bertha returned to the kitchen table, retied her apron around her waist, and began to clear the rest of the dishes.

No matter how hard she pumped, the water only trickled into the dishpan. At this rate it would never fill up. There must be a hole in the bottom of the dishpan that she'd have to get Fred the Blacksmith to fix. It seemed as if, no matter how long she kept pumping, the pan took all morning to fill up.

No matter how hard she scrubbed, the food and grease continued to cling to the plates and pans as if somebody had glued them there.

Even the two passenger pigeons perched in the little maple trees outside seemed to be cooing a little more slowly, as the morning shadows crept across the lawn. It was as if the March of Time itself was conspiring to draw out this wait to its ultimate, nerve-shattering eternity.

"My dear Mrs. Hamilton, I don't know how you can just stand there," Widow Crenshaw complained.

"I'm not just standing here," Bertha replied over her shoulder. "I'm washing the breakfast dishes."

"Well, I don't know how you can be so calm about it."

"There's really not much to get excited about, just washing dishes," Bertha replied with a shrug.

She figured that's all Widow Crenshaw would see from behind. She'd miss Bertha's grimace and the murderous look in her eyes specifically for her. Bertha's hope that maybe she'd wing Miss Barber, too, as a not-so-innocent bystander.

Widow Crenshaw pursed her lips and folded her hands neatly in her lap. "I mean," she stressed, "I don't know how you can just go about your daily work with your daughter missing."

"She's *not* missing."

As if Bertha's words meant no more to her than the

splashing of the dishwater, Widow Crenshaw continued, this time apparently for the benefit of Miss Barber.

"If I did not know precisely where my child was, why . . . why . . ." Her hand fluttered at her bosom. "Why, Catherine, I'd be a . . . a helpless pile of nerves, prostrate on the floor."

"Oh, yes, indeed. Me, too."

Bertha wondered how that sentiment didn't seem to apply to the fact that, as soon as Mr. Crenshaw passed away, their only son, Eustace, had taken off for California and never been heard from again.

"I'd have every able-bodied man and dog in town out searching for her."

"Oh, yes, indeed. Me, too."

"Don't forget to look in the chicken coop," Sam advised.

How could he say such things with a perfectly straight face? Bertha could almost forgive him for his earlier, damaging comments. A little laugh escaped. Then she coughed and splashed the water around, trying to hide the unexpected outburst.

Widow Crenshaw turned to Sam. "As a matter of fact, I'm surprised you, as a concerned father, are not out there searching for her, Mr. Hamilton. You seemed eager enough to bolt for the door in the beginning."

Bertha's fingers tightened around the forks she was washing. Sam had opened his mouth already this morning, and enough stupid things had come out to last her a lifetime. What incriminating things would he say about her now?

"I'm not very good at tracking," Sam replied.

"Well, send someone—"

"She'll be back," he answered.

Bertha's grasp on the utensils eased.

"But—"

"She'll be back," he stated very firmly.

Bertha wasn't surprised by the sound of confidence in his voice. Sam had always been a confident man. But she was

plum bedazzled that he would be agreeing with her—
especially now.

She stood there, studying him, waiting for him to say or
do something that would give her a clue to the reason
behind his change of heart. He didn't say anything, and she
really wasn't surprised.

She could practically see Widow Crenshaw and Miss
Barber straining their ears for a word to eventually pass
along. How could he speak plainly to her in front of them?

She could practically see Widow Crenshaw and Miss
Barber popping their beady little eyes out of their sockets,
searching for some gesture that would reveal the situation
between her and Sam.

They could watch all they wanted, she thought, and
mentally tossed her head with a proud arrogance. They'd
never detect the little lift of one of Sam's eyebrows and the
twinkle in his eyes as he looked back at her from across the
room. That had been *their* little secret signal from their
courting days. She could never forget, but she was surprised
Sam had remembered.

It wasn't false flatteries about curly hair and good
cooking. It wasn't broad winks and leers used in a crude
attempt to get her back into his bed. It was something
genuine—no matter how faint or remote at the moment.
Once, it had held them together against the rest of the world.
It was drawing them together again. Was this secret sign
between them his way of apologizing? Could she risk
allowing Sam closer once more?

"Mommy? Is *he* still here?" Miranda called through the
screen door.

Bertha had all she could do to tear her gaze away from
Sam's. But somehow she managed. On the other hand, it
was just too tempting—so she didn't even bother to
resist—turning to Widow Crenshaw and Miss Barber.

She gave them the ultimate in self-satisfied grins. "I *told*
you she'd be back."

Widow Crenshaw rose and straightened her hat. Miss

Barber rose and, although her hat hadn't suffered any damage, she straightened hers, too.

"You're a very lucky woman, Mrs. Hamilton," Widow Crenshaw said.

"I don't think you realize how lucky you are," Miss Barber said.

Bertha thought she detected just a hint of wistfulness in her voice. This time she couldn't decide if Miss Barber were eyeing the rocking chair, Miranda, or Sam. The rocking chair she could have. Miranda, of course, was a charming child anyone would long to raise. But Bertha didn't care to speculate one bit on why Miss Barber would covet Sam.

"If I were you, I'd thank my lucky stars the child had enough sense to come back," Widow Crenshaw said.

"My lucky stars had nothing to do with it, Mrs. Crenshaw," Bertha told her. "I know my child—as any good mother would—and as no mere stranger possibly could. Good day." As if in afterthought, she added, "Do be careful of the screen door."

Sam chuckled softly.

Widow Crenshaw let out a loud snort and headed for the door. Miss Barber, following closely behind, sniffed, too.

Sam knelt with one knee to the floor to be eye-to-eye with Miranda. "I'm so glad you came home."

She scooted around behind Bertha. "I didn't come home for you. I came home for my mommy."

"I know. But I still—"

"Sam, why do you insist on doing this?" Bertha demanded, interposing herself between the two of them. "You can see plain as day she doesn't like you."

He rose with a sigh of disappointment. "But she's my daughter."

"She's been your daughter for the past seven years, and I didn't see you rushing around here in such an all-fired hurry then."

"I just want her to accept me—"

"You can't rush her into doing that."

"But I have so much catching up to do."

"You don't have to do it all in one day. Are you in such a hurry because you know you're not going to be around here very long?"

He rose and looked her in the eye. "I'm here to stay, Bertha," he repeated yet again. "Maybe one of these days I'll be able to make you believe me."

With Miranda still clinging to her skirt, Bertha turned away from him. "Go to work, Sam."

Miranda called over her shoulder, "And I don't want to watch you!"

The loud clattering brought Bertha hurrying out of Miranda's room. Sam had set up the big tin tub in front of the fireplace and was pouring pots of warm water into it.

It wasn't so much that her mouth dropped open with surprise. It was the sudden thudding of her heart against her chest that worried her.

The room was well lit. She could see perfectly well that the tub was still only half full, and that he was still fully dressed beside it. But all she could picture was the Sam of her memories, wet and warm and naked, standing in the tub in the firelight.

She shook her head to chase the wonderful—and very disturbing—picture from her head. She had to swallow hard before she was able to speak calmly.

"What in the world are you doing?"

"Taking a bath."

"A bath?"

"Yeah, you know, one of those things where you take off your clothes and get all wet. Some people even use soap."

"I sort of figured that."

"Sometimes the person taking the bath even has someone scrub his back for him," he added with a little wink in her direction.

"How interesting." Bertha specifically tried to keep any hint of interest out of her voice. She knew very well if Sam thought she was the least bit susceptible, he'd be inviting her not only to scrub his back, but to join him in the tub as well.

"You didn't think I was filling this thing to float toy boats, did you?"

"I don't care if you float out to sea in it," she said.

Of course she knew he was going to take off his clothes and get in it. She just didn't think she'd be able to bear watching him, or even sitting in Miranda's room thinking about it. She started to return to Miranda.

"Just try to be a little more quiet, please," she requested. "I'm trying to get Miranda settled into bed."

"Oh, yeah. Sorry," Sam said as he poured in another bucketful. "She's got to get up early tomorrow, too."

"Too?"

"Sure. We all have to get up early tomorrow for church."

She stopped. "What do you mean, we *all*?" she asked cautiously.

"I was kind of hoping we'd go as a family."

So that was it. He'd never stop, would he?

"Miranda and I always go as a family. If you want to come along—"

"No, Bertha." He set the bucket down with a clunk and crossed his arms stubbornly over his chest. "I won't just 'come along.' Whether you like it or not, we *are* a family again. And we really need to go to church together—as a family."

She frowned and eyed him suspiciously. "You were a fairly regular churchgoing man before, but there wasn't anything fanatic about it. Did you have some kind of miraculous conversion up there in the mountains?"

"No."

"Saved from being eaten by a grizzly and you promised to go to church every Sunday for the rest of your life?"

"No," he answered with a chuckle.

"Or maybe more likely you had a really good hand at poker?"

"Don't be silly, Bertha." He laughed again, but not as heartily this time. Was he, too, growing weary of them constantly taking potshots at each other?

"Then why this insistence . . . ?"

Sam eyed her steadily. "You know very well why I want everyone in town to see the three of us show up in church *together* tomorrow morning, my first Sunday back."

Bertha just sighed. "I know very well why you want *certain people* in town to see you and me together anywhere."

"Can you blame me?"

He was giving her that impish grin again. But there was nothing puckish in the flickering of his dark eyes in the firelight. The flames reflected there revealed pure masculine desire. Her heart beat more fiercely when she recalled all the wonderful things they used to do after their bath.

"No, Sam," she admitted without the slightest hesitation. She didn't even mind him hearing the little catch in her throat. "I can't say as I really blame you."

She watched his grin widen. She could tell by the way he was standing there, he was poised, ready to move toward her at the slightest signal of approval from her. She couldn't give him one. She couldn't let him think a few days of flatteries and innuendoes had made up for the neglect of years.

"On the other hand, I can't really say as I agree with you, either. I don't know who you're trying to fool. Everyone in town knows all our business, probably right down to who's sleeping where."

"Not if they believe what Quinn tells them about what he saw the other day."

So there was more reason than just trying to irritate Arthur for why he was tossing her drawers around the house the other night.

"But it's not true."

"When did that ever stop any of them from believing

something? Especially if he has Widow Crenshaw and Miss Barber backing up his story."

She drew in a deep breath and shuddered at the mention of their names. Sam was right. Right about now, people would be willing to believe anything about her and Sam.

"No, no." She shook her head, as if that would make it all right. "Arthur's a gentleman. He wouldn't tell."

"No, probably not. I don't think he's the kind of fellow who likes to advertise when he's lost."

"He hasn't lost," she blurted out.

When she saw the look on Sam's face, she wished she hadn't said a word. Every other time they'd talked about Arthur Quinn, Sam had been angry or had made insulting remarks about the man.

This time he looked more than hurt. The spark was gone from his eyes, replaced with a deep, searching gaze. He looked like a man whose only hope had been ripped from him, and the only person who could restore that hope for him was the one person who had destroyed it.

"He hasn't won, either," she added quietly.

Apparently that was the signal Sam had been waiting for. He took several steps toward her.

"There . . . there isn't a contest between you two."

She took a few quick little steps backward. She still didn't want him getting any ideas that had no basis in fact.

"I'm not some kind of prize you two can fight over," she insisted.

That didn't stop him. Sam continued to move toward her.

"Of course not. You're my wife. You'll always be my wife. I don't care if Quinn does manage to get his senile old uncle to help you get a divorce and get me kicked out of here. I'll always consider you and only you my wife."

His gaze was sweeping over her face and body as he drew ever nearer. Was he taking inventory to make sure everything he'd left was still in place? Or was he remembering what used to be, and speculating on how it might be again?

"I already won you, years ago," he murmured intensely. "I don't intend to lose you now. I'll never let you go."

"But you did."

His gaze snapped directly to her eyes and wouldn't release her.

"Can't you let go of the past?"

She tried to look away, but couldn't. There was nothing else in this room, nothing else in the entire world, that held her more than Sam.

"For so long, that's all I had of you—just memories."

This time he didn't bother with a tentative touch on her arm. Swiftly he enveloped her completely in his embrace.

"No more memories, sweetheart. We've got a whole future ahead of us, if only you'll let us have it."

Before she could reply, he pulled her closer to him, cradling her against his warm chest. Their bodies molded together like spoons in a drawer. The heat between them melded them together.

He shifted her in his arms so that she looked into his face. His face drew nearer to hers. Slowly he placed his lips upon hers.

She tried to remain still. She tried not to let him know by even the slightest motion how close she was coming to being ready to give in. But the warmth of his lips, and the sweet tenderness of their first kiss in seven years, overtook her completely.

Her arms moved up to embraced him.

"Let me be your future, Bertha," he whispered against her cheek. "You're my future. Without you—and Miranda, whether she thinks so or not—I don't have a life."

"But you see, that's the problem, Sam. Without you, I still do. What do I do with that life now?"

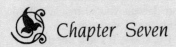 Chapter Seven

"Then make me a part of your life, Bertha," Sam whispered in her ear. "I can be a part of your new life, too."

He placed a gentle kiss on her earlobe, then nuzzled the small hollow at the base of her ear. He trailed his lips over her cheek until he encountered her mouth once more.

"Let me be a part of you again," he murmured against her lips.

His mouth pressed against hers. There was no tentative softness in this kiss as there had been in the first. Now he was insistent in the passion that had lain sleeping within him all these lonely years. Bertha could feel her own dormant yearnings begin to awaken in response.

"I've waited so long," he told her. "Let me be a part of you tonight, my love."

While his lips continued to cover her own mouth, cheeks, and neck with the heat of his kisses, his hands moved slowly up and down her arms and shoulders in a gentle but feverish caress. Every inch of her flesh that he touched burned to feel him again. A warm glow of aching desire spread throughout her body.

Gradually his hands slid into the hollow at the small of her back. He pressed her body against his until she could feel through her skirt the strength of his desire.

She closed her eyes and breathed deeply. He felt good. He smelled good. His kisses tasted good. The only thing that wasn't good about Sam was his absence.

"I can't. I can't," she murmured, but she still clung to him with a fierce passion.

He slowed the pace of his frantic kisses. He simply held her close to him and pressed his cheek against hers.

"Yes, you can, sweetheart. I want you so much. All you have to do is want me as much as I want you."

"I do, but . . . no. No, I'm sorry. It's just not that easy, Sam."

"But it is that hard." He gave a low chuckle and pulled her against him again.

"You're incorrigible!" she whispered in return.

His wit and his scandalous whispered suggestions had been part of what had made her love him to begin with. She couldn't allow herself to fall victim to them again—not at the cost of her daughter.

"That's why you love me. Admit it."

"No, I . . ."

She managed to squeeze her hands between them, palms pressed flat against his chest.

"No, no. I'm sorry. It's not that simple, Sam. I'm sorry."

She continued to push against him, and tried to take a step back at the same time. His fervent kisses had sapped the strength from her legs. She felt as weak as a newborn lamb, barely able to stand.

There was no strength in her arms, either. She could barely keep him at a distance. Was it because his passion had drained her, too, or because she truly didn't want to be apart from him any longer?

No, it was her own frustration. She was only human. She'd missed him with an aching longing. That hadn't ended, even though he had gone away. And even a woman could only bear so much.

She could hear him swallow between heavy, stifled breaths. The pounding of her own heart made it difficult for her to breathe, too.

"Are you still so reluctant when you can see how much I want you . . . need you?"

"Yes!"

He had stopped kissing her, but his arms still held her. She was glad. She wasn't such a fool anymore that she'd be happy to see him go. She just wasn't so sure she was ready for him to really stay all that quickly.

She knew her body was more than ready for everything else, having her husband back included.

But she wasn't so sure that her heart and mind were ready yet. There were still old hurts to resolve, and new problems constantly arising. Loving with just the body was the easy part. Things got so much more complicated when a person's heart and mind were involved.

"Well, no. Not reluctant, exactly."

"Then what would you call it—exactly?"

"Just . . . cautious."

"Still? Oh, Bertha, my love. Haven't I convinced you by now that I'm here to stay?"

"After four days?"

She backed up enough so that he had to release her completely. She felt his hands slip unwillingly from her arms and slide slowly across her waist. She ached to feel his touch again. How could she tell which hurt worse? Sam being gone and not having him, or Sam coming back and not being able to trust him again?

"No?"

"No," she answered quickly. Then she shook her head and, more quickly, she continued, "No. Not 'no.' Just 'not yet.' "

Standing several feet away from her now, he grinned at her. Did he think her simple answer had meant more than she'd really intended? He lifted one eyebrow and had the boldness to ask, "Then how about tomorrow after church?"

"Sam, you are, if nothing else, a persistent man."

"I'm a man who's missed his wife. Thunderation, Bertha! I'm a man in pain from missing you so much."

"I have a different kind of pain," she replied. "I need time to get used to you being around again."

"You want to get used to me? Do you want a courtship? Is that it?" he demanded. "Do you want a man who'll sit and play games with you? Or a man who'll take you in his arms and love you the way I want to?"

He stepped forward quickly, before she could move away. Before she could protest, his arms were around her, his lips pressing against hers.

This time she pushed him roughly away.

"I want a man who'll be a trustworthy husband to me and a dependable father to my child—not someone who just comes waltzing in and out whenever he pleases. Just . . . just go take your bath!"

She made a dash for Miranda's bedroom and closed the door behind her. She'd promised her daughter one more bedtime story.

It took a few moments to calm her ragged breathing and swallow the tears that clung tightly to the verge of falling. At last she was able to speak.

As she recited Little Red Riding-Hood one more time and noticed Miranda's eyes were still as perky as ever, she thought if she was lucky, she could stretch it out another time or two before her daughter finally wound down and fell asleep. Maybe, if she was really lucky, Sam would be all clean and dry, dressed and asleep in bed by the time she was done.

But it was awfully hard to sit there without thinking about him, warm and naked, on the other side of the door.

"Why don't I just make a run for the Picketts and get it over with?" Miranda asked, looking up as Bertha tied the ribbon of her Sunday bonnet under her chin.

"They're going to church, too," Bertha replied.

What if, Sam speculated, the real reason she'd been so agreeable about going to church today had nothing to do with religion? Suppose she was only going to see Quinn. And here he was inviting himself along. Yep, the more he thought about it, going along with them was a mighty good idea.

"We're all going to church together," Sam told her.

"I'm going with *her*," Miranda told him, pointing at Bertha.

"Would you mind if I came along?"

"Yes, we would," Miranda stated without a moment's hesitation.

Well, that pretty much dampened any remaining hopes he might have for winning his daughter's affection.

"You got a horse. Why don't you ride him?"

"He just traveled all the way here from Nevada. He's pretty tired."

"I guess you can't go, then."

Apparently she had more sympathy for the horse than she had for him.

"We've got plenty of other horses around here," he told her.

"But aren't you too tired to go to church, too?"

"Nope. I sat all the way."

"I guess I can't get out of it. All right," Miranda replied with a grimace. "But I get the back of the buckboard. I'm not sitting next to *him*." She dashed out the door, heading toward the wagon.

"I suppose you'll be wanting to sit in the back with Miranda," Sam said as they headed for the buckboard at a little slower pace.

"No, I think I can manage to sit beside you without cringing," she replied.

"That's a good sign, Bertha."

"No, it's not. I can sit across from you and eat without vomiting, too."

Sam chuckled. "Now I know where Miranda gets her sharp wit."

"You mean her sharp tongue, don't you?" she corrected with a laugh.

He shrugged. "Same thing."

He helped her up onto the seat of the buckboard, then moved around the horse to his own side. He climbed up and took up the reins. A click of his tongue and a slap of the reins set the horse to trotting.

"You know," he told her as they rode along, "I think I'm getting better, too."

"How do you figure that?"

"I can suffer through each meal, making stupid, boring comments about the crops and the weather."

"And silly compliments about my cooking," she interjected.

"That, too. I can sit and eat everything you give me without making a single comment about it, and watch you at the opposite end of the table without doing what I really wanted to do."

"What's that?" She knew darn good and well what his answer was going to be, and she still asked. Did she have some sort of gluttonous appetite for punishment?

"I really want to take you in my arms, sweep the dishes aside, and make passionate love to you right on the table—provided that first Miranda skedaddles over to the Picketts'. I want you back in our bed again, too."

He noticed her slowly edging her way to the far end of the seat.

"But I know as soon as I mention it, you'll be fleeing over the rise faster than Miranda ever went."

"Sam!" A delicate blush was beginning to color her cheeks. "Don't . . . don't you *dare* talk that way in front of Miranda."

He tilted his head toward the rear of the buckboard. "She's way in the back, Bertha. She can't hear a word we're saying."

"But . . . but I can." She seemed to search in frustration for the right protest. At last she said, "Please, don't talk to me that way, either. You might as well save your breath."

"I'd hold my breath until I turned blue if I thought—"

"Don't," she stated flatly. "It didn't work for Miranda, and it won't work for you."

"She holds her breath, too?"

"She used to when she was little, to get her own way. That was before she learned to run and figured out the Picketts were just over the rise."

He chuckled. "It seems I have an awful lot to catch up on."

She shook her head without smiling. "No. Some things you miss once, you don't get a second chance."

"You're absolutely right," he said.

She turned to look at him in surprise. "You're the man who's been making such a nuisance of yourself pleading for a second chance. Now suddenly you're saying you don't deserve one."

He nodded. "Sometimes you just have to start all over again."

He could see the caution in her blue eyes, made all the lighter by the shadow the brim of her bonnet cast over her face. The surprise was gone. She'd probably figured he'd try any means he could to get her back again—and he would.

She didn't look angry. That was good. Maybe it meant she'd try to accept one of the ways he tried to win her back. Maybe, if he tried hard enough, one of them would even work.

"Brothers and sisters, what a glorious morning!" Reverend Knutson began with a shout. "Hallelujah!"

Miranda jumped in her seat. "Oh, brother!"

"Hush," Bertha scolded.

"Does he have to be so loud?" she complained, hands over her ears, elbows stuck out to the side like bony chicken wings.

"Yes, so he can be heard over people who talk in the pews," Bertha responded quickly. "Now put your hands down. Everyone's staring."

"That's 'cause they want to know what I'm doing, but they can't hear us, so they got to look."

Bertha just glared at her.

"Looking doesn't make any noise. So why does he still have to be so loud?"

Bertha's glare transformed into the supreme "mother's look"—the silent communication that signaled the bounds of a mother's patience, beyond which the wise child knew there was no trespassing. Her mother had used it on her, rarely but with consistent results, but then she had been a model child. Her grandmother had probably used it, too. Miranda would probably use it on her own children someday, if somebody didn't strangle the little nuisance first.

Miranda lowered her hands, but squinted her eyes, as if not seeing as well would somehow block out the sound. She squirmed around to see the entire Pickett clan lined up across one whole pew in the back.

"Why can't I go back and sit with the Picketts?" she pleaded.

"I don't think there's room in the pew."

"Oh, I can squeeze in next to Del real easy."

"I think Del might have a problem with that."

Miranda gave a dejected sigh. "Men! At least you didn't make me sit next to *him*." She shot Sam, seated to Bertha's other side, a menacing look.

He grinned back at her. "Remember, you can't go running off to your hiding place from here."

"Ha! I can find a hiding place anywhere."

"I *will* sit you two side by side—with you in the middle so you can't go running off," Bertha pointedly told Miranda, "if you don't hush immediately." She glanced threateningly back and forth between them. "Both of you."

"Whatever you say, dear," Sam replied and concentrated on the altar.

Miranda clapped her hands firmly over her mouth and sat staring at the minister.

"We have much cause for rejoicing this beautiful morning," Reverend Knutson continued.

Bertha couldn't imagine what.

First she'd suffered through more of Sam's foolish flatteries over breakfast.

Then Miranda threatened to run off to the Picketts' again when Sam had insisted that the three of them sit together as a family.

When they'd entered the church, Sam had seized Bertha's elbow and walked her down the aisle, leaving Miranda to follow behind, grumbling and scuffing her heels against the floor the whole way.

Bertha and Miranda usually sat in the fourth pew from the front of the little Evangelical church, on the side farthest from the pump organ.

If she sat by the organ, she couldn't hear a word while it was playing, not so much from the loud notes from the reeds as from the creaking and wheezing of the body of the old instrument, and from the old body that played the instrument. Every Sunday they prayed for Miss Meecham's relief from the rheumatism, and listened to her complain about it the rest of the week.

Even when the pump organ was silent, Bertha couldn't see around it, so she usually dozed off during the sermon.

But if she sat in the back of the church, she spent more time inspecting the ladies' hats and dresses, and which men were growing balder by the week. Up front, she knew she'd concentrate on the sermon.

Today was the first time she'd really regretted that choice. As Sam led her to the pew, she could feel all the eyes of the congregation silently following her. She wondered how the trustees had managed to lengthen the aisle since last week. It never used to take that long to get to her seat.

When they settled themselves into their pew, Sam squeezed in right beside her. It wasn't exactly crowded this morning, either—not like it was on Christmas and Easter. Then why did he have to sit so close that their elbows touched?

Why did they have to share a hymnal? There should have been plenty to go around, seeing as how last year Mr. Potter had dedicated two dozen in memory of his late wife, who used to always sing in the choir and drown out everyone else.

Bertha could almost believe Sam had sneaked into church late last night or real early this morning and taken all the books out of this particular pew. That would account for the shortage.

And how had he managed to have a nice, wool, Sunday-go-to-meeting suit, a starched white shirt, and a fancy blue necktie stuffed in the bottom of that ratty old carpetbag? she wondered. What kind of use could he have for clothes like that out in Nevada? All of it looked like fine quality fabric, too, she couldn't help notice.

She was tempted to reach out and touch the soft-looking material. After last night, she was really tempted to discover just how the wool would feel, stretched across his muscular back and shoulders. And how would he feel when she touched only his bare skin? she wondered.

Shame on you, Bertha, she scolded herself, thinking such thoughts in church! But she couldn't help herself.

What would happen if she could touch the lapels, and caress the muscles of his chest with the flat of her hand—right here in church?

What would happen if she grabbed that nice necktie and tried to strangle him with it—right here in church?

Either way, people would be sure to talk about her.

"Now, I know all you farming brothers are praying for rain," Reverend Knutson was saying. "But we've got to be thankful for this bright morning, too. Crops need sunshine as well as rain to grow."

Bertha had to agree. Sunshine was very good right now. A steady downpour would stick Sam and her in the house together much too long. Sunshine gave him the chance to work in the fields—*out* of the house.

She made a mental note to be thankful that it was spring,

and the days would be getting longer. Then he could work
out in the field even more—that is, provided he bothered to
stay around that long.

"We also give thanks this morning for the recovery of
little Flora Baker from the croup."

"Amen," the congregation agreed.

"And for the recovery of Marvin Platt from his infected
toenail."

"Amen," the congregation agreed with that, too.

"Mr. and Mrs. Lucas Stanley are pleased to announce the
safe delivery of Isaac, their fifth son. Mother and baby are
doing fine."

"Amen," the congregation repeated, although everyone
there knew perfectly well Mrs. Stanley had really wanted a
girl this time.

"The Baldwins have a special joy in that their new
porcelain tub has finally arrived from St. Louis. The family
wishes me to announce that you're all welcome to stop by
their house to see it today after services. Refreshments will
be served."

"Amen!" the congregation rejoiced.

While Bertha was in complete accord and thanksgiving
for all these blessings, and wished all the recipients well, as
the minister droned on, she found herself drifting off to
daydreams.

"We've particularly got to give thanks for the sudden,
very unexpected return—"

Bertha's head shot up. She stared at the minister. She
could feel her eyes growing wider and her cheeks growing
hotter. *Everyone* knew Sam was back. Why did the minister
have to announce it in church and draw more attention to the
fact? Why did he have to include it in with the blessings?

"—of one who's been gone a long time, and has now
returned to the Grasonville fold. For those of you who've
never met him—or who might not recognize him anymore—
Mr. Samuel Hamilton—Brother Sam, raise your hand!" Reverend Knutson's hand shot out, pointing him out in the pew.

Sam grinned and reluctantly lifted his hand only about shoulder height.

"Brother Samuel left us several years ago to work out West," the minister continued. No one could say the man wasn't tactful. "We're sure his loving wife and devoted daughter are rejoicing in his return."

Bertha waited for the snickers behind cupped hands. She herself almost broke out with a bitter laugh—one that perceptive people would definitely remark upon. For the less perceptive, who didn't remark upon it immediately, there was always Widow Crenshaw and Miss Barber to give their interpretations of the situation. She couldn't risk it. Unfortunately she had forgotten about Miranda.

The child started to giggle. She giggled a little louder.

"Hush!"

That only set her to laughing more. The more she tried to stop, the funnier everything got.

"Miranda, this is not funny," Bertha warned.

"Oh, yes, it is," the child managed to say between gasps of laughter.

Bertha could feel dozens of pairs of eyes boring into her head, just trying to figure it out. If the mere mention of Sam's return set their daughter to laughing, what was Bertha really thinking?

She noticed Arthur, back in the pew where he used to sit before he'd come to join her a few months ago. He wasn't watching Miranda. He was watching her. She quickly averted her eyes. It had been difficult enough trying to explain to him why she didn't want him coming around anymore. How was she going to explain *this* to him?

Did Arthur agree that the very idea of Sam's return to the embrace of his loving family was laughable? Or had her last remark as she sent him away made him believe that she and Sam were truly man and wife again? Of course, Sam practically flinging her drawers in Arthur's face had probably only served to reinforce the supposition.

Bertha noticed Widow Crenshaw and Miss Barber, sitting

right behind Arthur. What kind of stories were they beginning to concoct in their evil little minds from this incident? What sort of lies and temptations were those two little devils, virtually perched on each of his shoulders, whispering into Arthur's ears?

Suddenly it occurred to her that she didn't give a tinker's damn what Arthur believed about her. He might be perfectly likable, but she'd never felt for him what she felt for Sam. Not once in all these months while they had been keeping company had she ever believed she was in love with Arthur. Not once had she felt any desire for him to hold her the way she longed for her husband's embrace.

Sitting there quietly, with Sam and Arthur separated so she didn't have to worry about them whaling the tar out of each other, she was able to look at the two men and decide. It only took a second or two before she smiled to herself at her own foolishness. There really hadn't been any doubt.

Other people had probably had more important, or more startling, or more spiritual revelations sitting in church. But it came as quite a shock for Bertha to finally realize she still loved Sam with all her heart. She could never be in love with anyone else the way she loved him.

No matter what happened—whether he left again, or he stayed to further complicate her life—she knew no one else could ever take his place. What did it matter if he only stayed for a little while? No one stayed forever. Just look at poor little Addie Newcomb, married only two months, then carried off with the stomach fever. Sam was here now. She'd enjoy having him around while she could.

"And so, brothers and sisters"—Reverend Knutson seemed on the verge of ending this part of the service—"in honor of his return, and all our other joys, if there is a particular hymn—"

Miranda's hand shot up. "Oh! Oh! I've got one." She bounced around on her fanny in the seat. Frantically she waved her hand. "Oh, oh! Please, pick me. Please. Please."

"Well, my, my." Reverend Knutson folded his hands in

front of himself and blinked at Miranda from over the top of the pulpit. "It seems that one of the littlest lambs in the fold is so caught up in this spirit of joy that she can't contain her choice of hymn."

He leaned forward a little more and smiled at Miranda.

"And just what might your special hymn be, young lady?"

Miss Meecham poised her fingers over the keys, ready for whatever notes were required.

Miranda lowered her hand and stopped bouncing. She sat up very straight and tall, and used her very best reciting voice, so everyone could hear her, just like Miss Potter had taught her in school.

"This is very special, 'cause it tells exactly how my mommy feels ever since *he* came back." She shot Sam a dark look that only Reverend Knutson could see.

"What could it be, child?" the minister asked. "'Oh, Happy Day'?"

"No, sir."

"'Happy the Home When God Is There'?"

Very innocently, very seriously, she looked up at the minister and announced, "'Rescue the Perishing.'"

A little snicker arose in the back of the church and ruffled through the pews.

"Miranda," Bertha whispered, "I think when we get home, it would be a good idea if you spent the rest of the day in your room, so I don't murder you."

Sam caught Miranda on the way out of the church, while Bertha was busy fending off the friendly, the curious, and the merely rude. This time he didn't try to kneel or bend down to meet her eye to eye. There was nothing about this matter that could be settled between equals. He crossed his arms over his chest and glared down at her from his full height.

"Well, little girl, I guess you think you're pretty clever."

She chuckled. "I sure embarrassed you, didn't I?"

"Nope."

She stopped grinning and studied him. "Sure I did."

"Not me." He shook his head.

"Yeah, right. You just won't admit—"

"You can't embarrass me. Remember, I'm the one who can just pack up and travel on out of here any time I please."

"Then why don't you?"

Sam ignored that comment, for now.

"I don't give a hang what anyone says about me once I'm gone. But I know your mother does. You sure embarrassed her—and yourself—this morning with that little shot at trying to be funny."

"Mommy's not embarrassed."

Miranda, her face completely blank of any expression, continued to stare him directly in the eyes, and watch and wait.

He wished he could see what was going on behind that devious, innocent little face. Was his scolding having any effect on her? None of the flattery or cajoling he'd tried had worked. Sooner or later something would have to. He had to keep talking.

"How do you know? Think about it, Miranda. Your mother's got to live in this town the rest of her life. I know they've gossiped about you all since I left. How do you think she's going to feel with all those people talking about how she drove her husband away twice?"

"She didn't drive you away. I did!"

"Maybe." He wasn't going to let her think there was even the remotest chance she'd succeed. "But I think you're old enough to have figured out by now that gossiping doesn't always tell the truth."

Her gaze shifted all around Sam, but she stopped looking directly at him.

"Well, it didn't embarrass *me*."

"You know how they're always saying how much like your mother you are. They'll talk about you that way, too," he continued.

"No, they won't. They'll all be dead."

"So is Reuben Taylor. Do you still hear people talking about him?"

Miranda grimaced. "Geez, yeah. Every time you go into the General Store, Pops has to start."

"See what I mean?" Sam shrugged the emphasize the absolutely veracity of his claim. "When your mother's a lonely old woman, living all by herself on the farm, people will still be saying, 'What a shame about poor old Mrs. Hamilton. Sam came back once, but the daughter was so mean, she drove him away. That's why Bertha's all alone today.'"

He reached up and began stroking his chin, as if thinking really hard about the future.

"Only six years old and already driving men away. I wonder how that'll sound to any young fellows who might come courting? I wonder what Del would think of a girl who—"

"Okay, okay! You made your point. Geez!"

She twisted her lips around and frowned and kicked at the grass. She pulled up the edge of her dress and twisted the hem around her finger.

"I suppose you expect me to tell you I'm sorry."

"No. But your mother would probably like to hear it."

"Geez!" she muttered loudly as she turned away. "Who the heck do you think you are, my father?"

Sam hoped his talk had done some good. But then he watched as Miranda ran off to play with the other children who were running around the cemetery while their parents chatted. He should've figured better than to expect her to find Bertha and apologize right away.

Well, what did you expect from the kid, Sam? he asked himself. You know she doesn't like you. Did you really expect her to listen to you, too?

Miranda joined a group of girls on the swings, but didn't do much swinging. She just sat there, as if she were thinking.

Maybe she really she was thinking seriously about what he had said to her, he hoped, and what hurt feelings her thoughtless actions might have caused. More likely, the little imp was thinking up more ways to pester him.

Bertha came and stood beside him, watching Miranda, too. She was close, but their shoulders never actually touched. It was so tempting to lean just slightly to the right to make contact. Nothing rude or showy, especially while they were standing in the churchyard with so many people milling around after Sunday morning service. Just enough contact between them to let all the Doubting Thomases know she was his and he was home to stay. Now if he could just convince Bertha.

"Why the grumpy look?" she asked.

"You noticed?" He hadn't even realized he'd kept the frown on his face while scolding Miranda. He did his best to look pleasant for Bertha.

"How could I miss it?" she countered with a laugh. "It's such a contrast to your usual smiling face—or should I say simpering grin—when you try to sweet-talk Miranda."

"Me? Simpering?"

"With the best of them." She nodded emphatically, never taking her eyes off Miranda.

Sam shrugged. "At least you think I can do something right."

She nodded. "A few things."

The pleasant look he was trying for turned into a downright grin. "I'd be real happy to do a whole lot of things so you can really decide which are good—and which are terrific."

She shook her head and gave a little laugh. "You never give up, do you?"

"Not as long as there's breath in me."

"Well, just keep breathing. Meanwhile . . . I didn't expect this, but I have some things to discuss with the Ladies' Charitable Aid Society. An emergency has come up."

"You? And the Ladies' Charitable Aid Society?" Sam chuckled. "As I recall, you said they were nothing but a bunch of old busybodies, more interested in seeing who needed charity than in giving it."

"Yes, well . . ." She cleared her throat. "Well, they do good works after all, even if they do tend to argue amongst themselves about it beforehand, and gossip and brag about it afterward. And they gave me something to do while you were gone."

"Then you can turn in your resignation now. I promise, you'll never need to go looking for something to do again."

She didn't reply to his remark. She only nodded toward the laughing children.

"Miranda will be fine out there. I know you'd just find the meeting unbelievably boring—"

"That's all right."

"It shouldn't take long."

"No, no. You just go have your meeting." He waved her off magnanimously. "There are a lot of people and things in town that I haven't seen in years. I think I'll do a little catching up."

Sam strolled around the churchyard for a while, nodding and smiling to folks he passed, stopping to chat with some of the men he'd known real well.

Bertha would be safe from Quinn without him, Sam thought confidently. Miranda made a darned good chaperon. Pops was there, too. He might not be an eagle-eyed watchdog, but his very presence might keep Quinn from making any more advances on Bertha. Tom and Rachel would keep an eye out for his interests. Heck, Bertha had the entire Ladies' Charitable Aid Society meeting surrounding her like a better bodyguard than any Roman emperor ever had.

Of course, his own pride made him think that just the warning he'd given Quinn would be enough to keep the man away from his wife.

There was also the fact that Bertha had told Quinn not to

come to their house anymore, Sam recalled with a grin. She couldn't be too interested in the fellow if she could make it through a whole week without being with him.

On the other hand, Sam thought with a grimace, she'd made it through seven years without being with him. He guessed that meant she wasn't too interested in him anymore, either.

"Say, young feller," Pops called to him. "How're you doing?"

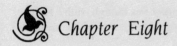 Chapter Eight

Sam hardly recognized the man without his checkerboard in front of him and the potbellied stove behind him.

Pops Canfield was seated on a bench under the big black walnut tree near the street. The few gray hairs he had left were slicked back with hair tonic. He had on his best gray suit with a tiny white pinstripe running through the fabric. He must have tied the big black cravat himself because it was a mite crooked, but still sported the little garnet stickpin he claimed to have gotten as a young man in New Orleans with General Jackson.

"Pops." Sam hurried over. "Look at you, all done up handsome."

"Handsome? Poppycock! I look like they dressed me for the funeral, then somebody propped me up here, and they all went off and forgot to bury me."

Sam chuckled.

Pops tugged at his collar. "Tarnation, I feel stiff as a corpse in this darn thing."

"Well, you look and smell a whole lot better than one."

"Thanks." Pops stopped fooling with his collar and looked up at Sam. "You look pretty hang-dog yourself, if I got to say so. How's things going with you and the Mrs.?"

Sam took a deep breath. He set one foot on the edge of the bench and leaned his elbow on it. "About as good as anybody could expect, I reckon."

"I see she keeps you clean and pressed."

"Yeah."

"I figure she's been feeding you good."

"Oh, yeah." With a weak chuckle Sam patted his stomach.

"Still ain't sleeping too good yet though, huh? Kind of stretched out all cold and lonesome instead of all warm and cuddled up?"

"Pops!" Sam had seen and heard a lot in his thirty-two years. But he never expected to have a man old enough to be his grandfather talking with him about such personal matters.

"I guess that kind of answers my question, don't it?"

Sam ran his fingers through his hair. "That was a heck of a question."

"Well, consarn it, boy. I expected a heck of an answer. What the dickens is wrong with you?"

"Nothing's wrong with me, Pops."

The old man shook his head. "What's this younger generation coming to?"

"If they all act like Bertha, there isn't going to be much of a coming generation."

"Well, I can't tell you what to do, boy, but me personally, I'd be doing something about it right smart."

"I have been."

"Well, keep doing it, and don't give up. She'll come around eventually."

"Yeah, probably not until they got *me* dressed for the funeral. And I wouldn't be surprised if Bertha wasn't the one who did me in."

"I would. She still loves you, boy. Always did."

Sam just looked at Pops. The man was getting mighty old, maybe even as old as the tree he was leaning against. Nobody in town rightly knew exactly how old he was, but rumor had it he was past eighty. Maybe his saying such preposterous things was a hint he was getting senile.

"Ain't you got enough sense to see that?"

"I guess not. But what makes you so sure?"

"'Cause I been watching her these past seven years, and you ain't."

"Now you sound like Bertha."

Pops chuckled. "You know, she might've gone into mourning for you for a whole year, but she never did go through all the folderol to have you declared legally dead."

"She couldn't afford it."

"She had a nice memorial service, but she never had a plaque or a stone set up."

"Too expensive."

"Not even a wooden cross. She never had your name removed from the deed to the farm, either. Don't that count for something?"

"Carelessness? Forgetfulness?"

"Nope. She loves you so much she couldn't bear to face the fact that you were dead. Leaving your name on the deed made it like you were still alive for her."

"But she even forgot she did that," Sam protested.

"She didn't remarry," Pops offered instead.

Sam let out a sound that was half groan, half grumble.

Pops' gnarled hand waved the thought away. "Oh, forget about Arthur Quinn, will you!"

"I'd be glad to. I just wish Bertha would."

"She already has."

"How do you know? You got some kind of crystal ball hidden in that checkerboard of yours?"

Pops snickered. "Nope. I keep 'em under it."

"Geez, Pops! You *are* a dirty old man."

"Just trying to help you keep your mind on what's really important in life."

"And what's that?"

"Quinn ain't important."

"I know that."

"Bertha is. That little girl of yours is."

"I know that, too."

"Sure, you know. But you don't understand. Can't you see with your own two eyes, boy? She still loves you."

"How do you know?"

"She doesn't care about Quinn—never did. He was just somebody who came by when she was lonesome while you were gone."

"Is that what you think?" Sam could hardly tell this nice old gentleman he was full of horse poop.

"That's what I know. I got eyes—and for as old and bleary as they are, they're better than yours. I never did—never will—see her eyes light up for Quinn like they do whenever she sees you."

"That's not the light of love, Pops. That's the fire she wants to have me burned at the stake with."

The old man laughed heartily. Then his misty blue eyes pinned Sam's and he spoke earnestly. "That's a lady's fire, boy. You don't get no truer flame than that."

"Well, if you say so, Pops." Sam placed both feet on the ground and looked toward the church steeple, shining pure and white in the bright spring sunlight. "I just hope you got that on good authority."

The old man leaned his head back against the trunk of the tree and crossed his arms confidently over his chest. "The best, Sam. It's human nature. It's Mother Nature."

Sam could still hear Pops chuckling to himself as he started to walk down Main Street.

Bertha looked around. Miranda was still playing with the Pickett children. Rachel and Tom were sitting cozily next to each other on the bench under the walnut tree, watching them. They didn't appear to notice her at all. Pops was standing over where they'd buried Reuben Taylor.

The meeting of the Ladies' Charitable Aid Society was going to take longer than it rightly should, Bertha fretted to herself as she stepped back into the darkened church. Once Widow Crenshaw got to arguing with Mrs. Nichols about whose idea was whose, and who was going to pay for all these great ideas, you could pretty much count the whole day wasted.

She turned to descend the narrow stairs to the basement. She was surprised to see Arthur standing there in the shadows of the alcove. He was leaning against the clean, whitewashed wall, arms crossed over his chest. Clearly, he'd been waiting here. She didn't like to suspect that he'd been waiting specifically for her, but it was too much of a coincidence otherwise.

"Arthur, what are you doing here?" she asked.

"I don't open the store on Sunday, and there's not much reason to go home to an empty house."

"Don't sound so pathetic," she chided him. "It's not like you."

"All right," he said, pushing himself off from the wall and standing upright before her. "In that case, I'll come right to the point. I've come to rescue the perishing."

She gave a weak little laugh. She didn't like anybody remembering Miranda's silliness enough to make a reference to it.

"What on earth are you talking about?"

He stepped closer to her. "I heard what Miranda said. I saw what went on this morning."

"You and everybody else."

"But everybody else isn't as concerned about you as I am. I've come to save you."

She couldn't help but stare at him, partially in amusement at his foolish dramatics. Was he going to pull a lance and shield out of his coat pocket? But partially she watched him with worry for what this was all leading to.

"I'm not perishing, Arthur. And I don't need rescuing."

He seized her hands and gazed at her in earnest adoration. "Admit it, Bertha. You're miserable now that Sam's home."

"I am not." She tried to disengage her hands, but Arthur wouldn't let go.

"He lied to you."

"He did not." She tried to pull away again.

"He cheated on you."

"No." At last she managed to free herself.

"He doesn't deserve you, Bertha."

"I . . . I don't know about that. But I *am* still his wife."

"See, you have doubts yourself about him not being the right husband for you."

"Be that as it may, he *is* my husband," Bertha insisted.

"But you miss me, don't you?"

She looked him straight in the eye. "In all honesty, Arthur, no, not really."

"Of course you do," he insisted, looking around. They were all alone. He raised his hand to caress her cheek. She pulled back. "You just can't admit it in public."

She looked about them. "Arthur, we're alone in a deserted church stairwell. That's hardly in public."

"It's a public building."

"Arthur, you're not listening."

"Neither are you. I told you, my great-uncle's a judge." His voice took on excitement with his planning. "He knows people. He has influence. He'll make Lester Martin look like horsemeat in court. We'll get you that divorce, and make sure you keep the farm and Miranda."

"I don't want a divorce."

"I know there'll be some problems with people accepting it," he continued, deaf to her protests in his enthusiasm. "But once you've married me, there won't be any stigma attached to you or Miranda."

"I can't marry you."

"Yes, you can. We'll fix it—"

"No, I can't."

He stopped and stared at her. "You mean you won't."

"Very well then," Bertha stated with determination. "If that's what you want to hear, I won't."

His eyes grew wider. "But . . . but, Bertha," he stammered. "I thought you loved me."

"I . . . I never said that. I mean, I think you're a fine man, and you really play a good game of dominoes, but . . ."

His shoulders slumped. "Has nothing I've said or done these past few months made you love me?"

"I like you very much, but—"

"Is there anything I could say or do to make you change your mind?"

"I haven't changed my mind about you, Arthur. At least, not yet."

"Then why not—?"

"I like you, Arthur. I just don't love you."

"You could learn to . . .."

"Now, don't go sounding like a bad melodrama," she scolded. "I've had more than enough of them lately."

"What?"

How could he know—how could she explain—all the peculiar things everyone at her house had been up to?

"I'm a married woman, Arthur. I intend to stay married—for better or for worse. I know times have been better between Sam and me—"

"What are you going to do when it gets worse?"

"That's an awful question, Arthur. I've already been through about as bad as it can be."

Arthur turned and headed for the church door. With his hand on the doorknob, he turned back to her.

There had been such sadness in his eyes that Bertha was almost sorry she'd had to banish his dreams and chase him away. But now that sadness was gone, replaced with a wild determination that she'd never seen in his eyes before. Bertha had always been a little cautious of people with looks she'd never seen before.

"I wish there were some way to convince you to change your mind," he said.

When he opened the door, the bright sunlight blinded her for a moment. Then the door closed and she was left alone in the dark and quiet of the church.

She sighed and leaned against the wall. Right about now, going downstairs and confronting the Ladies Charitable Aid Society was the last thing she wanted to do.

*   *   *

Of course, Sam had noticed the big train station right away the first time he'd come to town. All brick, with a big green roof, and lots of white gingerbread trim all around, and a huge clock set up on top. He would bet Yankee dollars Henry Richardson had a lot to do with the designing and building of that station, not to mention overseeing how it got paid for.

Used to be, the bank was the only brick building in town, besides Henry Richardson's big, useless mansion. There were a lot more brick buildings sprung up around the bank now—offices for other lawyers, a branch of the county land office, an office for the Bureau of Indian Affairs, and a chapter of the Grange. Pale sandstone carvings of big leaves and little faces—probably meant to signify Commerce or Industry, but looking more like lost gargoyles with indigestion—topped the doors and windows.

All Henry Richardson's money hadn't done him a damn bit of good, Sam reflected as he stood there studying the big mansion. The lilacs and rosebushes lined up against the fence had grown tall and looked as if they hadn't been pruned since Sam had left. The white lace curtains covered by heavy red velvet draperies were still drawn tight, but the red had faded to a dusty brown. It looked as if Richardson were trying to erect some sort of shield against the outside world.

The man's wife and only son had died a long time ago. Rachel Williams turned him down and married Tom Pickett instead, and he never seemed to think any of the other ladies in town were ever good enough for him. But that couldn't be the only reason for his becoming a hermit. What could have happened to Henry Richardson to turn him into such a bitter old man before his time?

If Bertha found a way to kick him out of her life, Sam wondered, would he turn out the same way?

Trying to flee such grim thoughts, Sam continued to wander around the town. He was surprised to see Mrs.

MacKenzie's son had opened a bookstore. Son of a gun! And here, all this time, he'd thought Ian only knew about plowing fields and milking cows. MacKenzie and Sons. How many boys did he and his wife have now? Were they giving the Stanleys' some tough competition?

Somebody in this town needed to start having some daughters, soon. Considering how pretty and smart Miranda was, Sam figured he and Bertha ought to have a few more just like her. Of course, the way things stood, he didn't think he had much chance of convincing Bertha that this was a good idea.

Gordon Nichols still had his haberdashery, although somebody named Thompson had opened up some competition across the street.

Charlie Carter still ran his barbershop and dentist office. Doc Marsh was still in business. Sam was glad to note these important things. Suppose Bertha got mad enough at him to whack him over the head with a frying pan or poison his oatmeal? He'd need all the medical help he could get.

Fred the Blacksmith still had his smithy set up next to Miss Sadie's. Sam had always wondered if Fred had done that deliberately, but had never had the nerve to ask.

Fred looked up from his forge and out the door. When he saw Sam strolling by, he waved his hammer in greeting. Fred liked to scandalize everybody by working Sundays, no matter what. Then he'd always close shop early the last day of April and disappear onto the prairie all night and most of the next day. Speculation was, he always took Miss Sadie along for a picnic. Sam figured a man as necessary to a farming town as the hardworking blacksmith deserved a vacation at least one day a year, and could pretty much do what he darned well pleased.

Fred had to be pushing seventy, Sam reckoned, but he was in better shape than most men in town who were only half his age. Maybe the heat from the forge had dried him out and kept him preserved, Sam speculated. Or maybe there was something beneficial about being so close to Miss

Sadie and her girls. He didn't know about Fred, but Sam figured he sure could benefit a whole lot from being close to Bertha real soon.

"Hey, mister."

Sam turned around, looking for the source of the youthful voice.

"Hey, mister. Over here."

Sam peered into the alley between the Lonesome Whistle Saloon and Sullivan's Last Chance Saloon. A freckle-faced boy was motioning for him to come closer. Sam looked to either side and in back of him.

"Yeah, you. C'mere."

Frowning, Sam eyed the boy warily. He looked familiar, but different somehow. "Who are you?"

"C'mere," the boy insisted. "I got a message for you."

"A message for me?" Sam asked.

"Gol-dangit, mister! You deef or something? How many times I gotta tell you?"

Now Sam recognized the boy. It had to be one of the Douglas kids.

Allen Douglas and Jimmy Walters used to beat up on the other kids in town when Del was little until, thanks to Tom Pickett's sage advice about keeping his dukes up, Del had walloped them both.

This one must be the youngest. What was his name? Yeah, Maxwell. Last time Sam saw him, he must have only been about three. He'd grown taller and filled out, but he was just as ornery-looking as his older brother. Sam hoped Max and his friends weren't doing the same thing Allen and Jimmy used to do, but he had a sneaking suspicion that was being too optimistic.

Sam pointed into the alley.

"You want me to come in there so you can give me a message?"

"Yeah. Yeah." The freckle-faced boy waved frantically. "C'mon, mister. I ain't got all day."

"Who's it from?"

"I got a whole two bits, mister. I don't want to have to give it back if'n you don't get the message," Max started to whine. "I could really use the money to buy some oranges for my little sister. She's real sick, you know."

The best as Sam could recall, there wasn't any little sister. But he had to admit, the boy was as good a huckster as his older brother. Nobody who went to that much trouble for a lousy two bits should be disappointed.

"So what's this important message?" Sam asked as he strolled toward him down the alley.

Bertha knew there was trouble as soon as she saw Sheriff Duncan approaching.

When the meeting was over, she'd looked for Sam, but couldn't find him anywhere. She started to ask the few people left who hadn't gone over to see the Baldwins' new porcelain tub if they had seen Sam.

"I don't pay any attention to him, Mommy," Miranda told her. "So don't even bother asking me."

"We've been sitting here most of the time," Rachel said. "We noticed him wandering around, but not actually wandering off."

"Yeah, I saw him," someone else said.

"He stopped to say hello and ask about my rheumatiz," Miss Meecham offered. "Such a considerate young man."

"I saw him heading down Main Street," Pops said.

"He's gone again, for good," Widow Crenshaw predicted, shaking her head ominously. "He went down to the train station and got on board for parts unknown. I knew it. I just knew it."

"Poor Janet," Miss Barber sympathized. "It must be so horrible to always be right."

"Naw, you're all wrong. Sam told me he was just going to stroll around and catch up on all the things he'd missed," Pops said.

"What could've sent him away this time?" Miss Barber wondered aloud.

By the way all heads turned to her, it was easy to see that people were always more ready to believe the worst.

Miranda gulped hard, but never said a thing. Very unlike her, Bertha decided.

"Once a man gets a taste of the wanderlust . . ." Widow Crenshaw pronounced with the voice of doom. Then she just shook her head. It was all too horrible even to contemplate finishing the sentence.

"He didn't have that much money on him, I don't think," Bertha offered.

"He didn't come to town with much, either," Widow Crenshaw reminded her. "So I don't see as it would bother him much to travel without it."

"But without his clothes?" Bertha said.

"Oh, you're worrying for nothing," Rachel said. "He probably went for a walk, just like Pops said, and lost track of time."

"He always did keep forgetting to wind his watch," Bertha added hopefully.

Widow Crenshaw shook her head. "How could a man lose track of time with that big new station clock bonging out the hour every hour?" She leaned over the Miss Barber and whispered rather loudly, "I tried to tell Mr. Richardson that thing was way too loud. But would he listen to *me*?"

Bertha didn't give a hoot about the clock, or Mr. Richardson, or Widow Crenshaw's sensitive ears.

"But did anyone see Sam after that?" Bertha asked.

Everyone shook their head.

"He'll be coming back for you, Mrs. Hamilton," Pops said. "I can feel it in my bones."

But she'd been waiting at the church now for almost two hours, wondering where he could have gone. Her shoulders slumped as her hope faded. She walked over and sat on the bench beneath the walnut tree. She was glad when Rachel followed her.

"He'll come back," Rachel assured her with lots of gentle

little pats on her shoulder. "Don't you pay one bit of attention to anything those two old biddies had to say."

Hope had lasted her a while. Then Bertha noticed the sheriff, coming toward her.

"Mrs. Hamilton." He stood there with his hat in his hands, running his greasy fingers along the brim. He was acting a whole lot different than he had when she'd tried to get him to do something about Sam sneaking around her house, spying on her. It was almost as if he really was ready to do something to help her now.

Bertha's heart began to beat more rapidly. She could feel the blood rushing to her head. Damn Sam for doing this to her again!

She was glad that by now, everyone had decided the Baldwins' new tub was more interesting than a missing Sam, and the Baldwins were serving food. She didn't need anyone around looking for the opportunity to hear some good gossip or some bad news.

"Sam's left, hasn't he?" she asked. Her voice sounded small and distant, as if someone else were speaking.

"Left?" Suddenly the sheriff she was used to was back, giving a nasty little chuckle, as if he were enjoying her anguish. "Shoot, Mrs. Hamilton. He ain't going nowhere in the condition he's in. We need you to come with us."

"Come with you," she repeated numbly. She held out her hand to Rachel for support. "Condition he's in?"

There was only one reason he'd want her to come with him. Sam was dead and, as next of kin, she had to go identify the body. It had to be. The sheriff hadn't lied to her. If the condition Sam was in was dead, he sure wasn't going anywhere like that.

She could feel her stomach turning cold and churning wildly. She hadn't eaten since breakfast over seven hours ago. There wouldn't be anything to come up. Then why did she still feel like she was going to empty the contents of her stomach on the sheriff's dusty boots?

"Come with me, little lady."

Bertha looked frantically about.

"Go on," she heard Rachel's voice behind her. "We'll look after Miranda. We'll collect the kids and come by, just in case you need us."

Bertha wondered how she found the strength to walk down Main Street. As they stepped up onto the wooden sidewalk, she was glad for the pole to help support her. Her legs trembled all the more as they approached the building that housed the undertaker, but the sheriff didn't stop there.

All right, she told herself as she started to breathe again. He's not at the undertaker, so he can't be dead. Bolstered with that small consolation, she swallowed hard and continued on.

She tried to keep herself calm as they passed Doc Marsh's office, connected to his house. Maybe Sam was inside, lying on the examining table, mangled, missing eyes and limbs, gasping for breath, bleeding to death.

She squeezed her eyes tight to blot out the horrible picture, but it didn't work. The sheriff hadn't been specific about what was wrong with Sam, so all the worst things possible immediately came to her mind.

They passed Doc Marsh's. Bertha frowned. If Sam wasn't at the undertaker's or the doctor's, where the heck *was* he? By now, she was beginning to figure Sam better be pretty badly hurt to cause her this kind of worry and suffering.

They passed Clarence Carter's barbershop and dentist office, with its red and white pole. Red and white, just like Sam's skin and blood, Bertha couldn't help thinking. But why would he be at the dentist's? Had he gotten into a fight, and somebody punched him in the mouth? Or had he gotten drunk and fallen face first onto the floor?

Now, she decided, they might be getting a little closer to the truth of the matter.

As they passed the barber and approached the blacksmith shop, Bertha's eyes widened all the more. This puzzle was getting stranger with every step she took. She knew darned good and well what was at this end of town, and she wanted to know what the heck Sam was doing here. He'd never been all that friendly with Fred. She hoped he wasn't all that friendly with Miss Sadie or one of her girls. If he was, she'd make real sure Sam really needed Doc or Mr. Carter—or maybe even the undertaker!

"This way, little lady." Sheriff Duncan motioned for her to follow him down the alley between two saloons.

"That's a horrible place," she protested. "I can't go in there."

"Well, little lady, we can't move him."

Suddenly Bertha was struck with the image of Sam, gasping away his last earthly breath, pinned beneath a beer wagon.

"What is Sam doing in the alley?" Bertha demanded.

The sheriff didn't respond. He just motioned her on.

Slowly she approached. Sheriff Duncan was standing over a motionless body. Sam was lying on his back, one arm slung over his eyes. She moved closer to him.

She didn't see any gaping gash in his throat. She didn't see his body riddled with bullet holes or arrows. As far as she could tell, he still had all his body parts. She could see his chest slowly rising up and down with each breath.

The icy paralysis that had wrapped around her heart released. Sam was still alive!

She peered down at him.

"Sam! Sam!"

He didn't rouse.

What did it matter if she had on her best Sunday-go-to-meeting dress? She knelt in the dirt beside him.

"Sam! Sam!"

He lay very still.

Tentatively she extended her hand to touch his shoulder. Suppose seeing his chest moving up and down was just an illusion? What if Sam really was dead? How could she bear to reach out and feel the cold clamminess of death on his skin?

But he was still warm to her touch. She pushed him a few times, trying to rouse him. "Sam!"

He let out a low groan.

She gently moved his raised arm. She breathed a sigh of relief when she saw there were no injuries to his face.

She reached down and pulled up one eyelid after the other, just to make sure both eyes were still in place. All she saw was the bloodshot whites, with the edges of the brown rolled back up into his head. But at least there were two of them in there.

She felt his nose. No blood. No, it wasn't broken, as far as she could tell.

His arms and legs were lying at normal angles. It didn't look as if any of them were broken, either.

No split lips. She gently pushed his lips apart. No chipped teeth. No severed tongue. What could be wrong then? Why was Sam still lying unconscious in the alley between two saloons?

He moaned again. She began stroking his forehead. He wasn't feverish.

She looked around the sea of unfamiliar faces, then looked up at the sheriff. "Where's the doctor?"

"Hey, somebody go get the Doc," the sheriff called.

"Go get the doctor?" she repeated. "Do you mean you haven't sent for him before this? Why have you left my husband just lying in this alley? Can't you see he needs medical care?"

"That's why we sent for the doc, little lady."

Bertha just gritted her teeth when what she really wanted to do was bite Sheriff Duncan's head off with them—in one giant, vicious snap around a greasy mouthful. Then she'd spit him out—real quick!

She clenched her fists tightly in her lap.

"He could have died waiting for you to get around to it!"

"Hey, little lady, don't go getting riled up at me," the sheriff answered. "I walked all the way down here to see what these fellows found in the alley, then I walked all the way over to the other end of town just to get you, then I walked all the way back here with you. That's above and beyond the call of duty. What more can you expect of me?"

"Sheriff, the town's not even half a mile long," she pointed out. "It's not like you had to travel with Lewis and Clark."

"What do they have to do with this?"

Just as she was about to sigh with exasperation, Sam groaned again. Her husband deserved all her attention, not this addlepated sheriff.

"Sam! Sam! Talk to me."

But he didn't say a thing.

She rose quickly. "Please help me," she tried to order some of the men who were milling around. "At least let's get him out of the dirt."

They just stood there, staring at her. She blinked. She didn't know these men or their families. She didn't know too many of the people who lived on this side of town, or who spent their Saturdays and Sundays in saloons. She didn't think she wanted to.

"Please. Can't you see—?"

"Can't do that, lady," someone said.

"Can't move him 'til the doc gets here."

"Why not?" she demanded.

"Well, there might be broken bones and stuff. . . ."

"Yeah, a broke rib could've gone through a lung, and he'll drown in his own blood."

"Ruptured guts."

"Yeah, stomach fever. Takes 'em a week or so to die. Real gruesome to watch."

They were all just full of marvelous suggestions now about why they shouldn't bother moving Sam.

"You're all having a lot of fun with this, aren't you? Oh, why don't you all just go back to your drinking!" she cried angrily. "On Sunday afternoon, of all days! I hope you all have darned good hangovers tomorrow morning, the kind that feels like somebody's driving a ten-penny nail right through the middle of your foreheads, and coating your tongues with moldy felt."

She surprised herself. She wasn't usually a vindictive woman, but, yeah, that would suit all those lazy good-for-nothings just fine.

"Oh, Sam," she murmured softly. "You've just got to be all right. What would I do without you?"

"So what's the problem here?" Doc Marsh demanded as he pushed his way through the crowd.

"Sam Hamilton," Sheriff Duncan replied, nodding toward him.

Bertha scrambled to her feet. "Please, can you do something? Anything?"

Doc Marsh pointed to several of the men. "For crying out loud, fellows. Come on. Let's get him out of this mud and over to my office."

This time the men sprang to work immediately. Broken ribs or no, they lifted Sam like a sack of meal and hauled him off to the doctor's office.

Bertha pursed her lips and tried very hard only to think of being thankful that Doc Marsh was now giving Sam the proper care he needed. She tried not to think how men only seemed to listen to orders given by someone else wearing trousers, too.

"So, what happened here?" Doc asked.

Sheriff Duncan reached up and scratched his head. "Somebody found him out here, unconscious. We thought he was just drunk at first, but after a while, we figured he didn't smell like he'd been drinking, so we just left him there 'til we could find you and his missus."

"Yeah, real fast work there, Sheriff," Doc grumbled.

"You bet."

Doc just turned away. "Come with me, Mrs. Hamilton."

Bertha walked beside him to his office. The sheriff followed.

"The men'll have your husband to my office and Mrs. Marsh'll have him situated in my examining room by now,"

Doc told her. "I'll examine him and let you know what I've found as soon as I can."

Bertha sat in the empty waiting room, twiddling her thumbs and tapping her feet. She was glad there wasn't anybody else in the waiting room. She didn't feel like sharing her anxiety with a bunch of nosy townspeople.

But she wished she had Rachel here to worry with her. She wished she had Miranda here to keep her busy so she wouldn't have to think about all the painful medical things Doc might have to be doing to Sam just to make him better.

Maybe they were the same things he'd tried to do for Reuben Taylor—and look what had happened to him! Sam wasn't dead yet. He couldn't be. How could he manage to survive this long just so he could die now? He just couldn't!

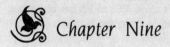 Chapter Nine

The little shuttered window in the wall between the waiting room and the examining room squeaked open.

"Mrs. Hamilton?" Mrs. Marsh, who served as her husband's nurse when she wasn't raising their six children, called to her.

Bertha's feet stopped in mid-twitch. Her hands gripped each other. What would she do if Mrs. Marsh told her the Doc wanted her to see him, not Sam? Did that mean that Sam was still unconscious? Or did that mean he was dead?

"You can come in now, Mrs. Hamilton."

"How's . . ."

Before Bertha could finish, the window closed. She tried to stand on quaking legs. Mrs. Marsh was usually so friendly and talkative. It wasn't like her to just close the door without some kind of comment. Something must be very wrong.

She tried to recall each of the few words Mrs. Marsh had said, and the exact tone she'd used for each of them. Maybe then she could figure out what was going on. But there wasn't much to be gleaned from five words.

Slowly Bertha stood. She made sure she had her balance before she tried to make it to the door. No sense fainting and falling and injuring herself, too. Then what would happen to Miranda?

She slowly opened the door into the examining room. In a trembling whisper she called, "Doc?"

Doc lifted his head from the large, leather-bound book he was making notes in at his big wooden desk. He flashed her a bright smile.

Sam was lying on the examining table, his head wrapped in a white bandage. He didn't seem able to lift his head, but he did manage to raise his hand a little and signal he was all right.

"Oh, Sam! You're alive!"

She rushed to his side and grabbed his hand. She pressed her lips together to keep them from trembling. There wasn't much she could do about the tears of joy that trickled down her cheeks but brush them away with the back of her hand.

She couldn't help but laugh in nervous relief. "You look like a Hindu swami or something," she told him.

"That's because I'm so wise."

"Wiseacre is more like it."

Sheriff Duncan was standing in the corner of the examining room, going through Sam's suitcoat pockets. What in the world was he looking for? Loose change or something edible?

"What happened to you out there, Sam?" Doc asked.

"I was unconscious," Sam replied hoarsely. "I was kind of hoping somebody'd be able to tell me."

"Well, somebody bashed you on the back of the head pretty hard," Doc said.

"Is that a medical term, Doc?"

"I see it didn't injure your funny bone any. Anyway, you're going to have a whopper of a goose egg for a while, and some awful headaches. Don't be surprised at some dizziness, too, when you try to sit up."

"Worse than a hangover?"

"Definitely. No hair-of-the-dog to try to make you feel better. In fact, I don't want you drinking any strong liquor for a few days. And, Mrs. Hamilton, not to be too indelicate, but when your husband sleeps, I want you to check on him every once in a while to make sure he's still breathing."

"Good gracious!" Bertha exclaimed.

She hoped she didn't sound like she was too alarmed. She'd already planned to check on Sam constantly. What really bothered her was that Doc automatically assumed she and Sam were sleeping together, in spite of the stories to the contrary that must be circulating. What had Sam been saying in his delirium?

"Did you see who did this to you, Sam?" Sheriff Duncan asked.

"No." He started to shake his head.

Bertha could see his eyes start to roll and lose focus from the motion. He closed his eyes and held his head very still, and continued to answer.

"I was hit from behind. It was probably just some lazy drifter looking for a way to make a quick buck. This town is full of strangers now."

"They might be strangers, but they sure ain't dumb. No offense, Sam, but who'd want to rob a dirt-poor farmer like you, anyway?"

"Oh, no offense taken, Sheriff. Do you have much trouble with thieves in town?"

"None that I don't catch soon enough."

"Well, I think you're running behind schedule on this one." On the other hand, Sam speculated, he didn't think the sheriff could do much running anyway.

"Oh, he won't be on the loose for long," the sheriff stated confidently. "He's not a very good thief."

"How do you figure that?" Sam asked. He slowly and carefully tilted his head as he watched and waited for the man's reply.

Sheriff Duncan held Sam's suitcoat out so Sam, Doc, and Bertha could see the inside.

"Well, your billfold's been pulled out of your breast pocket just far enough to see it's been fooled with, but not far enough to get anything out of it."

"Why would the thief do that?" Bertha asked. "I mean, it's not like he didn't have the time to rob my husband. Sam *was* lying in that alley long enough."

Sheriff Duncan made no comment.

"Maybe they were stopped in the middle of trying to take it out," Doc suggested. "Somebody's always coming and going through those alleyways."

"How do you know they weren't putting it back in?" Sam asked.

"'Cause nothing's missing, is there?" The sheriff handed Sam's billfold to him.

Sam carefully opened it and counted the few notes. "No."

"There were some loose strings from the material still running up the seam, like the billfold was coming out—not going in, like it had been put back. Anyway, usually, once they get the billfold, they either take it, too, or they throw it on top of the nearest garbage heap."

"That's amazing, sheriff," Bertha said. What really amazed her was that Sheriff Duncan could be so observant about anything besides food. Her estimation of him rose considerably.

"What did you think I do all day? Just sit around eating?"

Bertha refrained from telling him that's exactly what she, and the rest of the townspeople, thought.

"I get a lot of reading done, little lady," he boasted.

"Then maybe you can tell me who'd be so desperate they'd even try to rob my husband?" she demanded incredulously.

"He sure hit you a wallop, Sam," the sheriff said instead.

Sam reached up to gingerly finger the bandage around his head. "That's for sure."

"What's that got to do with anything?" Bertha demanded.

The sheriff scratched his head ferociously as the puzzle seemed to grow more complicated. "Who'd go to all that trouble trying to rob you, not take a darned thing, but hit you hard enough nigh on to kill you?"

"Somebody who was more concerned with the hitting than with the robbing," Doc replied.

"Do you mean somebody *wanted* to hurt Sam?" Bertha exclaimed.

"Shoot, Mrs. Hamilton, a blow to the head like this—well, if they'd hit him a little harder, they'd have probably killed him."

Bertha could feel her fingers growing numb and her heart beating in her ears.

"But they wanted to make it look like it happened while somebody was trying to rob you," the sheriff continued. In the silence that followed, he looked from Sam to Bertha and back. "Who'd want to kill you, Sam?" he finally asked.

Her estimation of the sheriff returned to its original level. How could he come up with something so preposterous?

Everybody liked Sam. Everybody but herself and her daughter. And everyone in town knew she hadn't been exactly cordial to her returning husband.

Oh, no! What would she do if anyone even began to suspect that she might have something to do with this?

No, no. She'd been at the Ladies' Charitable Aid Society meeting. Everyone there would tell the sheriff so. And Arthur had seen her.

Oh, no. This was getting worse, she thought anxiously. There was Arthur, too, she had to suspect. She wouldn't put much past Widow Crenshaw or Miss Barber, either, although she didn't think they'd be sneaking around in alleys. Who else in this town wasn't too happy to see Sam return?

This was growing more and more ridiculous. Here she was, accusing her friends—and even herself! She had to stop and inject some sense into this conversation.

"You've got to be mistaken, Sheriff."

"Nobody'd want to kill me," Sam agreed insistently. "Why, I'm one of the most likable fellows you'd ever want to meet."

There was a knocking at the office door. Mrs. Marsh answered, then admitted Tom, Rachel, and Miranda. Miranda ran right up to the examining table.

"Wow! What happened to you? Where's the blood?" she demanded as she circled the head of the table, examining Sam's bandage. "Why isn't there more blood?"

"I think I left most of it back in the alley."

"Did any brains come out?" she eagerly demanded, tipping her head in an attempt to see under his.

"I don't think so."

"Don't worry. You wouldn't miss them if they did."

Cautiously she extended her index finger and brought it up to Sam's head. She never actually touched him, but continued to run her finger around barely a quarter of an inch from the bandage.

"Does it hurt?"

"Yes, of course."

"Good. Who hit you?"

"I don't know. I never saw—"

"Will they do it again?" she asked even more eagerly.

"Miranda, don't bother your father," Bertha admonished.

"Go away," Sam told her with a weak chuckle. "Del was right. You *are* a little pest."

"We heard Sam was all right," Tom explained. "But we figured you still might need a little help getting him back home."

Sam was deliberately growing weary, Bertha noticed. "Thanks. I think that's the best idea. . . ."

"Hey." Sam snapped his fingers clumsily. "I'll bet that kid would know who hit me."

"What kid?" the sheriff asked.

"This kid—lots of freckles. He told me somebody had given him two bits to give me a message. He called me into the alley. The next thing I knew, somebody hit me from behind."

"Lots of freckles? About yea high?" Tom held his hand out, palm down, level with his chest. He turned a questioning glance to Rachel. "Got to be Max Douglas, the little—"

"Now, now, Tom, not on Sunday," Rachel scolded.

"Little troublemaker," Tom revised with a benign smile. "Come around tomorrow and I'll tell you what I really think of him."

"Max Douglas. I kind of figured that's who it was," Sam said. "Yeah, that's got to be him."

"Max Douglas is a skunk!" Miranda exclaimed, turning up her nose.

"He could tell us who gave him the money," Sam continued.

The sheriff nodded. "It's worth a try."

"He won't tell you," Miranda insisted. "He's mean to everybody. I hate him."

Bertha held her breath and hoped they wouldn't find Max for a while. She had an awful, sneaking suspicion creeping up her back like snakes slithering up a rock, just exactly who had hit Sam. And she didn't like what she was thinking at all.

"Oh, my goodness! What happened here?" Bertha exclaimed. "My house, my house!"

Rachel rushed in behind her.

"It looks like a tornado went through here," Tom said.

All the chairs had been overturned. The cupboard was open and all the contents pulled out.

Tom was trying to hold Sam upright, but it wasn't easy. Sam's legs kept giving out from under him and he was too dizzy to stand by himself.

"Miranda, put that chair back upright," Tom told her.

Miranda rushed to the rocking chair and hauled it back into place.

Bertha rushed into the parlor. She stopped at the doorway and breathed a sigh of relief.

"Oh, thank goodness Great-aunt Sophie's lamp is all right."

"Is that all you're worried about?" Rachel asked.

"Of course. It's the only thing of real value in this house, even if it is mostly sentimental," Bertha answered. She gave a nervous little laugh that was more a release of the tension she felt than of actual humor.

"What about the bedroom?" Rachel asked.

"Who'd want Sam's clothes? Or mine?" she added quickly.

"Geez!" Miranda came stamping out of her bedroom. "Whoever did this is in for a good smack. They upset my mattress and pulled all my clothes out of the drawers. It's going to take me hours to put it all back again!"

She started to stamp back into her room, but turned around and looked at Bertha. "You can put your own clothes away."

Bertha dashed into her own room. Sure enough, the mattress in there was overturned, too. The drawers of the chest were all pulled open and the contents dumped on the floor or on the bed. She just hoped nobody noticed they were all Sam's clothes and wondered where hers were, and hadn't taken any notice of Miranda's complaints.

"Come on, Mrs. Hamilton," Tom said. "I'll help you get the mattresses back on straight. Then we can put Sam to bed proper like. You and Rachel and Miranda can fix the clothes and the cupboard."

"Who could have done this?" Rachel asked.

"Probably those rotten Douglas kids," Tom answered.

"But they just tip over outhouses on Halloween," Rachel protested. "This isn't the kind of thing they'd usually do."

"Well, maybe they're branching out."

Bertha was silent all the while Tom helped her with the mattresses and Rachel muttered about the mess. It had to be the person who had been sneaking around her house the other night. But if that were true, then it couldn't possibly have been Sam who was spying on her, because all this mess would have happened while he was lying bleeding in the alley and in Doc Marsh's office.

Bertha swallowed hard. That meant that someone else was spying on her. It couldn't be Arthur. While Arthur didn't like Sam, she was pretty certain he'd never hurt her.

She didn't know who could be spying on her, and that made her more than angry he'd ransacked the house, and more than nervous. It made her afraid.

* * *

"Okay, okay, Tom," Sam muttered after they'd gotten him situated in bed. "The joke's over. Stop spinning the bed."

"Just put out your foot and stop it," Tom advised with a chuckle.

"Very funny."

"Are you sure he's going to be all right?" Rachel asked quietly.

"That's what Doc said."

Bertha folded the last of the clean bandages and laid it on the dresser next to the little blue bottle of laudanum Doc had given her for his pain, and the smelly jar of green-flecked salve Mrs. MacKenzie had brought over, although how she knew about Sam's injury so fast, Bertha couldn't figure out.

"Of course," he said the same thing about Reuben Taylor."

Sam placed both palms on either side of his head and groaned. "Oh, thanks for reminding us once again."

"Naw. The man's got a head like a rock," Tom stated. "Of course he's going to be all right."

"Are you sure *you're* going to be all right?" Rachel whispered so that only Bertha could hear.

"I wasn't the one hit in the head."

"I mean taking care of him and all."

"Sure. I nursed Miranda through the measles. I can take care of Sam."

"He's a little bigger to try to move around."

"Oh, don't worry," Bertha assured her friend. "He's not going anywhere." Not if she had anything to say about it. She was going to do everything in her power to keep Sam around.

Tom nudged Rachel and nodded toward the doorway. "Well, I guess it's time we were going, though."

"Thanks for helping me," Bertha said as she led them through the kitchen. "As for that mess, well, cleaning that up was friendship beyond belief."

"Easy as pie," Rachel said, brushing her hands one against the other.

"And I never could've gotten Sam in or out of the wagon without you, Mr. Pickett."

"But you could've gotten me into bed all by yourself," Sam called. He let out a low moan. "Oh, my head."

"Serves you right for saying such things in front of the neighbors," Bertha scolded.

"No sympathy." He groaned. "Tom, come back. You're the only friend I have left in the world."

But Tom hadn't followed the ladies too far. He hung back by the bed.

"You ladies go on out," he told them. "I just want a few words with Sam—man to man, you know."

Bertha and Rachel grinned at each other and continued outside.

"How are you doing?" Tom asked, leaning against the wall by the bed. "Has the bed stopped spinning yet?"

"Tom, if . . . if the bed *doesn't* stop spinning . . . I mean, if, well, you know . . . if the worst should happen . . ."

"Don't even think that way!"

"But Reuben Taylor died from—"

"Will you stop constantly resurrecting him? You're a sight younger that he was—and too darned ornery to die yet."

"But if I should . . . will you take care of . . . ?"

"I've been keeping an eye out for Bertha and Miranda since you've been gone," Tom told him. "Helping with the cattle. Doing little repairs."

"Quinn said the place was a shambles. That he had to do all kinds of repairs."

"You should know me better than that. I wouldn't leave them alone. Anyway, it was Bertha did most everything around here until she could afford to hire a hand, then two."

"She did?"

"Oh, I suppose she could do anything she set her mind to."

"I suppose so." Sam also supposed he should have some pride for his wife and her abilities and accomplishments in his voice, but right now it was a little hard to muster.

Then Tom started to laugh.

"The only thing Quinn ever did was nail a few shingles back on the roof a couple of weeks ago. He nigh onto fell off and broke his neck in the process. I know because I watched the dang fool from the top of the rise. Darn near wet myself laughing."

"Promise me you won't let that damn Quinn—"

Tom reached up and rubbed the back of his neck. "Well, now, Sam, Mrs. Hamilton's a grown woman, making her own decisions. I can't hardly lock her in her room like a wayward child."

"Just don't let that damn Quinn—"

"What've you got against the man, Sam? He's got a good livelihood. He's a temperance man. A churchgoing Democrat. And after all, Bertha did think you were really dead, and he waited 'til she came out of mourning before he started calling."

Sam raised his hand and gingerly touched the bandage as far back as he could reach with his head resting on the pillow.

"This is what I've got against him."

Tom stared at him.

"You think Quinn hit you? You're joking."

"You know me. I don't joke about things like this, Tom."

"What makes you think he did it?"

"He's got the ready cash to pay that kid to lure me into the alley."

"The kid told you he got two bits. Thunderation, Sam. Del carries that much around in his pockets."

"Quinn's tall enough and strong enough to have hit me from behind."

"So are a lot of other men in town, and a couple of the women, too."

Sam chuckled.

"Anyway, I thought you said you didn't see who hit you."

"I didn't have to. Who else around here would want me out of the way?"

"Miranda?" Tom offered with a teasing grin.

Sam grinned in spite of himself.

"She'd know the boy from school."

"But she couldn't reach up that high," Sam protested. "And where would Miranda get the money?"

"She doesn't need money. She'd just plain nag him 'til she plum wore down his resistance, and then he'd do anything she asked just so she'd leave him alone."

"Women. They sure learn early, don't they?"

They nodded their heads in universal agreement.

"Anyway, Miranda wouldn't have ambushed me from behind. I think the little whippersnapper would take a lot of pleasure in letting me know it was she—and she alone—who bashed me."

Tom nodded. "You might have a point there. Do you think you ought to sleep with a loaded pistol under your pillow?"

"No. With the luck I've been having lately, I'd likely blow my own brains out."

"What about the boy, Max? Didn't he say a man had paid him?"

"Sort of."

"Then all we got to do is get Max to tell us what the man looked like. If it's Quinn, then we've got him. If it's not—"

"Then we've got a bigger problem."

Tom frowned. "What do you mean?"

"Nothing. Nothing. Just getting a little tired, I guess." Sam let out an exaggerated yawn.

"Yeah, well, if you decide to take a nap, do me a favor. Make sure you wake up."

"That's my number-one priority, Tom."

"Well, if you or the missus need anything, just let us

know." Tom pushed himself off from the wall and headed for the door. "I'll stop by again tomorrow."

"Thanks, Tom. Thanks for everything."

Sam settled back against the pillows. He knew he ought to close his eyes and rest. It was the only way to stop the room from spinning and his head from aching. Now if only he could find something that would set his mind at ease.

He hadn't been able to bring himself to mention it to Tom, his best friend. He didn't even want to mention it to Pops, who didn't seem shocked by anything.

Quinn was a definite suspect as far as he was concerned. He'd only been joking about Miranda's open hostility. But there was one other person in town who'd be happy to see him again.

Max hadn't said a man had given him the money. He'd just said "somebody," and everybody, even Tom, supposed it was a man. But that didn't necessarily have to be so.

Sam didn't want to believe this could possibly be true, but the nagging thought kept running through his mind. Had Bertha really been at that church meeting this afternoon? Or had she followed him into town?

It was too impossible to believe, but everything seemed to fit. She'd made a new life for herself. She had the wealthy Arthur Quinn all lined up and waiting to go as her new husband. She had no legal means to get him out of the house, and he'd made it pretty darn clear to her he wasn't going to be leaving any time soon. Getting a divorce might be possible, with that conniving Arthur's help, but it wasn't exactly well-accepted. There really was only way she could get rid of him—kill him.

Sam's heart ached even more than his head. He couldn't decided if it was his headache that was making him so nauseated or the idea that Bertha hated him that much.

It was too much effort to roll over onto his side, so he just laid there, staring up at the white ceiling that continued to wave overhead. He watched the shadows dance across, and the light begin to fade.

Bertha came into the room, carrying a small tray.

"Sam," she whispered.

He lay on the bed, flat on his back. His eyes were closed. He looked so pale against the white sheets, she was almost afraid he'd died in his sleep.

"Sam, are you awake?"

He opened his eyes.

"Good." She breathed deeply. In a voice that was just a bit louder, and a whole lot more cheerful, she said, "I didn't think you'd feel like doing a lot of chewing, so I've got some chicken broth for you."

"Thanks. Is it the same stuff I wanted to serve Quinn?"

"What are you talking about?" Her fingers tightened around the edge of the tray. "You never wanted to give Arthur soup."

"No. It was coffee with sugar."

Oh, no. Sam had gone delirious on her. Should she send for Doc Marsh or Mr. Pickett?

She lowered the tray so he could see the full bowl and spoon. She half expected him to tell her chicken broth was his favorite meal.

"It's just soup, Sam. See?"

He just looked at the tray and blinked.

"I don't think I can eat two bowls."

"Oh, dear. I'll bet you can't find either spoon, can you?"

"Probably not."

"Do you want me to help you . . . feed you?" she offered.

"No, thanks."

"Should I just put the tray down on the table?"

"No, thanks."

"Miranda's eating out in the kitchen. Do you want me to stay here with you?"

"No, thanks." He turned his head away from her.

"You've had a rough day." She tried to sound as sympathetic as she possibly could. "Why don't you take a nap?"

"Yep."

"You'll call me if you get hungry?"

"Yep."

"I'll be looking in from time to time during the night, so don't be startled if you hear me," she warned. She hoped to get some kind of response from him other than one syllable grunts. "I'll try not to wake you."

"Fine."

Carefully balancing the tray in one hand, she closed the door behind her.

He wasn't feeling well at all. That had to be the reason for his lack of humor and his short answers.

She stared down at the uneaten soup. No sense letting good food go to waste. She carried it all back into the kitchen, sat down beside Miranda, and started to eat.

What in the world had Sam been babbling about? she wondered. Coffee with sugar. Suddenly she recalled Sam's words. "Does he take sugar or rat poison?"

Bertha put down the spoon and stared at the soup. Is that what Sam thought was in it? If so, there was only one person he could suspect of doing it. Did he also think she was responsible for the bump on his head?

No. He was still dizzy and disoriented from his injury.

She started to eat the soup again. She was glad Sam hadn't eaten it. It really didn't have much taste at all.

Bertha stood in the darkness at the side of the bed. Enough light from the full moon came in through the window so she could see Sam, a darkly outlined shadow on the white sheets. Miranda had been fast asleep when she'd risen from the big double bed they shared. But Bertha was still wide awake. She hadn't been able to sleep a wink all night.

Doc had assured her Sam's problem with dizziness and double vision would clear up soon. He hadn't started to run a fever. That was always a good sign.

Still, she worried about him. Doc had told her to get up and check to make sure he was breathing. He hadn't told her how often. If she were really brave, she'd have climbed into bed beside him and lain there the rest of the night, listening to the comforting sound of his steady, even breathing.

What a shame she was such a coward! She was getting used to having Sam around again. She was even beginning to feel glad to see his smiling face across the table from her at breakfast, and hear him humming and rocking as she finished up the dishes at night.

She hadn't gotten him back after all these years just to lose him again, she silently protested. Just let him get better, she prayed as she stood by his bedside. That's all I'll ever ask.

As she left the bedroom, she was surprised to see Miranda sitting in the rocking chair by the fireplace.

She rarely did that anymore. When she was younger, she used to do it a lot. She'd climb up on Bertha's lap whenever she'd fallen and scraped her knee or elbow, and needed to cuddle. But she was sitting there alone now, rocking herself like a big girl. Bertha marveled at how fast kids grew up.

"What are you doing up?" Bertha asked.

"I couldn't sleep," Miranda sniffed.

"You don't do much sleeping sitting up in a chair. Why don't you come back to bed?"

"Yeah." She sniffed again and didn't move from the rocker.

"Your throat sounds scratchy. Are you coming down with a cold?"

"Nope."

Miranda never admitted she was coming down with a cold. That meant a dose of Hostetter's Celebrated Stomach Bitters. Miranda would rather eat bait.

Bertha moved around the rocking chair to face Miranda. Her eyes were red and puffy. She was still sniffing.

"You *do* have a cold."

"Nope."

Bertha dropped to her knees in front of the little girl.

"Miranda, you've been crying."

"Nope."

She reached up to take the little girl's rounded chin in her hand. "Don't fib to me, young lady. What's the matter?"

"What's the matter?" she repeated. Her fists were clenched into tight little balls in her lap. "Can't you see what's the matter? He's going to die."

"No, he's not. He's getting better, just like Doc said he would."

"I just don't want him to die."

"I thought you didn't like him. I thought you wanted him to leave."

"Well, that was in the beginning." Miranda sniffed again. "Now I'm sort of used to him, like a wart on the back of your hand. It's a bother, but after a while, you miss it when it goes away. It's . . . it's kind of . . . well, interesting having him around."

"But you say such horrible, insulting things to him."

"But no matter how much I pick on him, he always comes back with something kind of funny. No matter what I say, he never gets mad, except . . ."

"Except what?"

"Never mind."

"Did he get mad at you?"

"Yeah, but . . . but, well . . ."

"Did you deserve it?"

"Probably."

Bertha reached up to smooth down the hair on the top of Miranda's head. "I know. I don't want him to die, either. I'm starting to like him being around, too."

Miranda pulled open the curtain, admitting the bright morning sunlight. Then she jumped up on the bed.

Sam blinked and kept his eyes squinted. Bertha couldn't be sure if it was from the pain or from any problems he might still be having with double vision, even after a night of rest.

"Can I watch you change his bandage?" Miranda asked.

Bertha stopped unwrapping Sam's head and stared at her daughter. "Why do you want to watch something like that?" she asked with a grimace.

"'Cause I missed all the blood the first time."

"Why in heaven's name do you want to see blood?"

"Not just any blood. *His* blood."

"Would it help if I just opened a vein here?" Sam asked.

"Would you?"

"I thought little girls were supposed to play with dolls, and think blood and bugs were icky."

She bounced on the bed again. "Nope. Not me."

"I should've figured."

"Just be quiet then," Bertha warned. "And for heaven's sake, sit still!"

"Yes, ma'am," Sam and Miranda both answered.

Actually, Bertha was glad to see Miranda. Seeing Sam lying in bed in front of her was making her hands shake and her palms perspire. Standing so close to him made her heart beat unbearably fast. Every time she looked down at his face, she could remember the feel of his warm breath against her cheek and the passionate pressure of his lips against hers. She looked forward to feeling those sensations again, just as soon as Sam had recovered.

Of course, little things like a seven-year absence or a knock on the head wouldn't stop Sam. At any moment she expected to feel his hand easing around her waist, drawing her down on top of him. Her throat tightened and her body ached with the thought, and the longings the thought fed.

Thank goodness Miranda was here. Sam would behave himself in front of her. So would she. But that didn't mean she couldn't be disappointed not to feel his tentative, loving touch.

As soon as the last bandage fell, Miranda bounced across the bed to examine it. Sam groaned.

"Darn, no blood."

"Someone hit me on the head. They didn't shoot a hole through it."

She romped over to look at the back of Sam's head.

"Wow! What a goose egg! It's a shame you can't see it," she told him. "You'd be really impressed."

"Thank you."

"You want me to get the hand mirror?" Miranda bounced off the bed and headed for the dresser.

Sam gave an audible sigh of relief as the bed stopped shaking.

"No, thanks. I'll just learn to live with the mystery."

Miranda shrugged. "Well, golly, it sure has made me hungry," she said as she skipped off for the kitchen.

Now Bertha was faced with the task of wrapping clean, new bandages around Sam's injury. She could handle that. But she was leaning close against him in order to reach around behind his head. She could feel his shoulder pressing against her side.

Then, as she moved back and forth, she could feel his shoulder moving against her breast. She could barely breathe with the fear that he would reach up to caress her. Or was it with anticipation that he would, and the fear that he wouldn't?

She swallowed to make it easier to speak. "There." She swallowed again; this time it was her pride. "There, all done." She stepped back from the bed.

He hadn't laid a hand on her the entire time, even after Miranda was safely out of the room. He hadn't even made any of his usual playful, suggestive comments.

What had she done wrong? She'd fed him well—perhaps even better than usual since he was recuperating and needed to regain all his strength. She'd made sure he had hot water to wash and shave with. She'd made sure his sheets and clothing were always clean.

And he'd only said thank you. He hadn't tried to touch her. He hadn't invited her into his bed, even in jest. She realized—and probably so did he—that he really wasn't in much condition to do anything right now anyway. But at least she could have kept him warm and comforted him.

Suddenly she was seized with a terrible worry.

What would she do if she discovered he had decided, after seeing her and spending time with her again, that he really didn't love her anymore? What if he'd finally believed all her refusals and decided he'd never be able to change her mind? What would she do if, as soon as he was completely recovered, he left—never to return again?

She couldn't blame him. Miranda had been—and still was—awful to him, but in a different sort of way.

She hadn't been so kind to him herself, she reluctantly admitted. She'd loved Sam since the first time she'd met him back in Ohio the day her cousin, Adelaide, had married his cousin, Joshua.

She had missed him so much all the while he was gone. She could have been more forgiving, she admitted. Maybe it wasn't too late. Maybe, just as Sam had said as they were driving into town Sunday morning, sometimes you have to start all over again.

Maybe this would be a good time to start.

She picked up the used bandages with shaking hands.

"Let me get rid of these. Then I'll bring you breakfast. A good breakfast. Really good." She realized she was babbling in her nervousness and was helpless to stop herself. "Your favorite."

What was his favorite? she frantically tried to recall. He'd complimented her on all of them so much, she couldn't remember now which was his *real, original* favorite.

"Thank you."

That was all. Bertha really wished there'd been more.

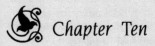# Chapter Ten

It had been raining steadily all day. Bertha had busied herself with the mending, leaving Sam to lie alone in his room. He'd been so silent since his injury, she worried. It wasn't like Sam at all. Even when he'd sprained his ankle very badly the first year they were married, he'd joked about it as he hobbled around on his homemade crutch. He hadn't been so morose and withdrawn.

She decided it would be better to leave him in peace rather that to pester him to be sociable. That might just make him withdraw more—so much so that he might decide to leave. If she had a choice, she'd take Sam, silent, to Sam, gone, any day.

For his part, Sam knew he was feeling better all the time. He could move around without keeling over or bumping into things. He was only seeing one of everything, but he still couldn't focus well enough to read.

Miranda had wandered petulantly around the house all morning. He could tell she was brewing for something. All he had to do was wait for the explosion.

Finally she marched into his bedroom. She stood at the bedside, feet planted firmly apart and hands on hips, and glared at him.

"Geez, I'm getting sick of watching you staring at the ceiling."

"Well, geez," Sam shot back. "I'm getting sick of watching you staring at me."

175

Miranda eyed him sternly, but he could detect just the hint of a twitch at the corners of her mouth.

"Watch out. You're going to smile," he warned her. He pointed his finger at her mouth and made little curlicue motions.

"No, I'm not," she replied quickly. She pulled her face into such a ferocious frown, Sam had to laugh.

"You're lucky it's almost summertime and you don't have to worry about your face freezing that way."

"I have a very pretty face 'cause I look just like my mommy, so I don't mind one bit if it freezes this way."

Sam leaned a little closer to her and was surprised when she didn't back away. He whispered, "I think you and your mommy are both very pretty."

He was hoping she'd giggle or smile, or do some cute little girl thing. He didn't know much about kids, but weren't daughters supposed to do cute little girl things? He should have figured any kid like Miranda, who went looking for blood, wouldn't giggle.

"Are you just going to lay there and stare at the ceiling the whole time you're in that bed?" she complained.

"There's not much else to look at in here. The quilt, the dresser—"

"Yeah, I'd be real depressed if I were you and stuck in a room with just a mirror to look at, too."

Sam knew it wouldn't be a good idea to tell Miranda that if Bertha were in here alone with him, he wouldn't even notice if there was a roof on the building. On the other hand, if Bertha were in there with him, she might just decide to do him in right this time. Maybe he should have taken Tom's advice about the pistol under the pillow.

Miranda heaved a big sigh. "Wait right there," she told him as she walked out of the room.

"I'm not going anywhere."

In a few moments she returned carrying a small, long, narrow wooden box.

"What's that? Your pet snake's coffin?"

"Dominoes," she announced, holding up the box like a trophy.

Oh, geez. Why'd she have to bring them out? Didn't she know every time he even thought of black with white dots he could just picture Quinn playing the game with Bertha, and he wanted to shout and hit something? Maybe she did, and just wanted to see his head explode, seeing as how she'd missed the blood the first time. He wouldn't put it past Miranda.

He had to get out of this.

"I don't know how to play."

"Me, neither."

She knelt by the side of the bed and dumped out the box of tiles. He watched her nimble little fingers quickly sorting the black rectangles into piles.

She leaned her head to one side. "I mean, I sort of do, 'cause I've watched Mommy and Mr. Quinn every time they played."

Sam was glad to hear that. Miranda probably made a great chaperon.

She leaned her head to the other side. "But then, I sort of don't, which is good, too, 'cause now we can play any way we want and there isn't anybody to tell us we're wrong."

He nodded. "You've got a good point there."

"We can't let Mommy play, though."

"Why not?"

"'Cause she knows how. She's real good at it. She used to beat Mr. Quinn all the time, and I was glad."

"Me, too."

"But if we let her play with us, she'll try to tell us all the right rules."

"Mothers are like that."

"Yeah, I guess so, but it sure takes all the fun out of a game."

"We can't have that."

"Nope."

"So, it's just you and me?"

"Yep."

"We'll make up the rules as we go along?"

"Yep."

"And in case of a tie, you win?"

"There won't be a tie. I *will* win."

"You're pretty confident, aren't you?"

"Yep. Now, you put the same number of dots together like this. See?" she told him, arranging two tiles end to end. "Or sometimes, you can do it this way." She placed one tile at a right angle to the other. "Don't worry. It's real easy. Even you can learn."

"Only if I have a good teacher like you."

"Don't try to sweet-talk me, Sam," she told him.

"You're getting more like your mother every day," he mumbled.

"Good."

"On the other hand, your mother's never offered to play dominoes with me."

"Nope. Now you've got *me*."

He had to admit, Miranda was being a lot nicer to him than she'd ever been. Was it the rain? Was it sheer boredom? If she couldn't play with the Picketts, was he the next best thing to nothing?

Maybe it was all just a clever trick to lure him into complacency. Then she'd turn into the old Miranda and finish the job somebody had started in the alley. Maybe, just to be on the safe side, he ought to let Miranda win at dominoes all the time.

But while she seemed to have such goodwill and charity with him, he thought he might just take another shot at building a closer relationship with his own daughter.

"Say, Miranda, do you think, instead of Sam, you could call me Daddy?"

"Nope."

"Not even while we're playing dominoes so nice?"

"Nope."

"Not even when nobody else is around but your mommy?"

"Nope."

"Why not? It would make me happy."

"Well, now, mind you, I don't have anything in particular against making you happy, Sam. But I can't call you Daddy 'cause I just don't *feel* like you're my daddy. Do you understand?"

No, he didn't think he did.

He watched as her little fingers picked up and arranged each tile with great precision.

"Now, shut up and play, Sam."

Ah, well, Sam sighed in defeat. So much for that attempt. Maybe the other children he and Bertha might have someday would call him Daddy, if she didn't kill him first.

At last Bertha appeared in the doorway. "I think you two have had enough dominoes for tonight."

"Oh, but I was winning," Miranda protested.

"You've won *every* game," Sam complained. He regretted his hasty sentimentality in thinking he'd let Miranda win. He needn't have bothered. The little minx was clever.

"Just one more game, please."

Sam leaned over and whispered, "Listen to your ma."

Miranda started packing the tiles neatly into the box.

Bertha watched with surprise. It usually took her several tries, a little arguing and cajoling, and once or twice on a really bad day, even the "mother's look" to get Miranda into bed.

What a change Sam's illness had made in Miranda. She wasn't even asking to see him bleed anymore.

What a change Sam's illness had made in him, Bertha lamented as she stood at the side of the bed. After Miranda disappeared into her own room, Sam just laid back against the pillows and stared at the ceiling again.

What could she do or say to bring back the Sam she'd fallen in love with all over again?

* * *

The next morning dawned clear and bright.

Miranda had gone to play at the Picketts. After a whole day of deprivation, Bertha had promised she could stay from right after breakfast clear on to suppertime.

Sam hoped she was having fun with Sally and Alice, and not pestering the living daylights out of poor Del. For himself, he was glad to see her go. Even though she still refused to call him Daddy, at least she wasn't insulting him anymore. But he didn't think his manly pride could suffer any more losses at dominoes to a six-year-old girl.

Bertha was out back, probably still hanging clean laundry on the line that she hadn't been able to do yesterday, when Sam heard the buggy pull into the drive. Who could that be?

It couldn't be Tom or Rachel. They would just walk on over the hill if they wanted something.

Quinn wouldn't dare set foot in this house again. If worse came to worse, in his death throes, Sam was determined he'd set this place on fire just so Quinn could never live here. Oh, all right, maybe he was being a little melodramatic, he had to admit, but by golly, he did hate Quinn!

It might be Doc Marsh, he realized, come to check on him, and tell him everything was all right. Then he'd be his old self again. He'd be able to get out of bed and find Max. Then he'd find out who'd paid the boy to set him up, and who'd really hit him on the head.

And if it wasn't Bertha, he'd be his old self again, and really set about to courting her. He'd win his wife back again if it killed him!

And if it *was* Bertha who'd hit him? Well, he sort of figured the news would kill him, too, if people really could die of a broken heart.

Who'd let Doc in? Sam wondered as he sat in his bed in his union suit and listened to the footsteps coming up the front walk and onto the porch. At least he didn't have any close neighbors to peek in and see him padding across the floor in his underwear. But he figured Doc would have enough sense just to knock and let himself in.

Sure enough, there was an insistent tapping on the screen door.

"Yoo-hoo!"

Sam cringed. "Sweet Jesus! It's Widow Crenshaw and Miss Barber," he muttered. "Dang, I hate that yoo-hoo yelling"

What were they doing here? The last thing he wanted to do was talk to those two old biddies. Where the heck was Bertha when he needed her to protect him?

Their tapping grew more insistent. "Yoo-hoo, Mrs. Hamilton! Where are you, my dear Bertha? Are you home?"

The tapping stopped. Sam breathed a sigh of relief. Maybe now they'd just go on their way.

With a feeling of horror overtaking him like syrup running down a stack of pancakes, he heard the screen door open. Thunderation! They were just walking right into the house like they owned the place. Right about now, Sam wished he owed the biggest, loudest, meanest dog in the county.

"Mrs. Hamilton, are you home?"

"Yoo-hoo! Bertha?"

If they had minded their own business and stayed outside, he could have pretended he wasn't home. But once they went nosing through the house, they couldn't help but notice him hiding under the covers. He might try to pretend he was sleeping, but who could sleep through their loud caterwauling?

If he tried to keep his eyes closed through their calling, they might mistakenly think he was dead. If he just laid there, would they run back to town and send the undertaker for him? Better yet, he could jump up and yell *Boo!* He started to chuckle at the thought of scaring the bejesus out of those two busybodies. It would serve them right for coming in uninvited.

"Yoo-hoo!"

They were drawing closer. Sam felt like a man tied to a fence post in the path of an oncoming tornado. There was nothing he could do but grin and bear it.

"Ladies! What can I do for you?" More frantically, he called, "Bertha! Bertha, we've got visitors!"

He tried to sit upright in bed. His bandage had gone askew on his head. He managed to pull the covers all the way up to his neck to hide the fact that he only wore his union suit.

"Bertha! Where are you?"

"Mr. Hamilton, you poor man," Widow Crenshaw said. She stood there shaking her head and clucking her tongue.

"What a horrible shame," Miss Barber agreed.

"That this should happen to you when you've so recently returned to town."

"What a blot on the name of our fair city," Miss Barber lamented.

"I'd say it made a bigger blot on my head," he told them. "Now, to what, besides my sore head, do I owe the honor of your call?"

"Why, we want to make sure you're recuperating properly," Widow Crenshaw answered.

"Much obliged."

"We want to make sure she's feeding you right."

"Very well, thank you." He tried to pat his stomach through the sheet.

"We want to make sure the person responsible for this gets his—"

"Or her," Miss Barber interjected.

"Just desserts."

"Well, offhand, I'd say the sheriff, and not the sick man in bed in his underwear, would be the one to talk to about that."

Both Widow Crenshaw and Miss Barber let out a disdainful laugh. "What can the sheriff do?"

"Oh, I'd say he'd been a bit of a help to me."

"Not at all," Widow Crenshaw contradicted. "If that were

true, he'd have your attacker behind bars this very minute."

"Well, we have to find him first."

"Him?"

"I don't think I was hit by a vengeful cow."

Widow Crenshaw and Miss Barber twittered behind their fingers, then grew extremely serious again.

"Not precisely, no, Mr. Hamilton. However, have you thought of the various people in town—the *suspects*, as it were—who might be happy to see you leave?"

Oh, my goodness! They'd been reading too much Edgar Allan Poe and Wilkie Collins again at the public library. Why didn't old ladies read uplifting sermons in their spare time anymore?

Sam gave a weak laugh. "I haven't been back in Grasonville for all of two weeks yet. How could I have any enemies?"

"Perhaps it's someone who's harbored ill will against you for a long time," Widow Crenshaw suggested.

"But even if it was someone I'd offended before I left, you'd think in seven years they'd have kind of forgotten. If not, they really need to take up some kind of worthwhile pastime."

But not reading gothic novels, he silently added.

Widow Crenshaw cleared her throat. "Mr. Hamilton, we hate to be the ones to bring this matter before you—"

"Oh, don't underestimate yourselves," Sam said. He knew they just *loved* to bring this sort of matter before anyone.

"Thank you, Mr. Hamilton, but we feel it's our duty as law-abiding citizens to see that justice is done."

"Have you talked to Mr. Martin about this, too?"

"This matter doesn't pertain to civil law. *This* is a criminal matter!" Widow Crenshaw's wrinkles stretched as she widened her eyes with horror.

"Criminal?" Oh, brother! They really shouldn't let these two read Poe.

"Yes, indeed. Attempted murder is a crime."

Sam nodded. "Always has been. Then I suppose you should talk to the sheriff. And Max Douglas. He saw whoever hit me."

"Oddly enough, Max can't be found."

Sam's eyes widened. "Is the sheriff still looking for him?"

"Probably not. But *we* are."

At first he didn't think that was very much help. Then he figured, if anybody knew anything about anybody else in town, and where to find them, it would be these two.

"You don't think anything's happened to the boy, do you?"

"Oh, he'll turn up. Boys will be boys, you know," Miss Barber said lightly.

Widow Crenshaw pursed her lips and jabbed Miss Barber in the side with her elbow. Very seriously she replied, "Right now, we'd rather not say."

Oh, brother! Maybe these two should start writing penny dreadfuls themselves.

"It's not really that we need the boy to identify anyone anyway," Widow Crenshaw continued. She leaned forward and whispered, "*We* know who did it."

"You do?"

Drawing herself up pridefully erect, she stated, "To be blunt, Mr. Hamilton, we suspect that your wife tried to murder you."

Sam eyed them cautiously. It was one thing to have his own doubts about Bertha. It was a completely different matter to hear other people voicing these same doubts. It was drastically serious when the other people were the two worst troublemakers in town.

Still, some perverse doubt inside made him want to hear more. But he had to go about it carefully, so they wouldn't suspect that he placed any belief at all in them or their claims.

Very calmly he looked Widow Crenshaw in the eye and asked, "What in the world would make you think that?"

"Well, it's common knowledge she had to be forced by

legal means into accepting you back into your very own home," Widow Crenshaw readily supplied.

"I don't think Mr. Martin standing in front of the sheriff's office on Main Street telling her that my name was still on the property deed would be considered really *legal* means."

"Nevertheless, she didn't do it of her own free will."

"But I *am* living here with my wife now—very happily, too, I might add."

He wisely neglected to mention that he was cautiously eating everything she gave him, and wishing there was a lock on the bedroom door each night.

"Then, of course, there are the difficulties with your daughter . . ."

"My daughter and I are getting along just fine, thank you," he snapped.

"And, to top matters off, there was that little public incident in the church immediately before your mishap."

"Wouldn't that sort of point more to Miranda being the culprit?" he asked with a skeptical lift of one eyebrow. Their suppositions were growing wilder with each passing moment. "Anyway, my wife was at that ladies' church meeting when all this happened."

"Was she?" Widow Crenshaw turned to her partner. "Catherine, did you see her there?"

"Why, Janet, I do not recollect whether I did or not."

"Miss Barber, you couldn't see Jesus and all his angels if they were sitting in the pew in front of you," Sam snapped.

"However," Widow Crenshaw continued, unfazed by his less than flattering evaluation of Miss Barber, "I did see her, immediately before the meeting, in a rather secluded section of the church, having a tryst with a certain Mr. Arthur Quinn." She beamed at Sam triumphantly.

"What . . . what does that have to do . . . ?" Sam began but couldn't even finish his sentence.

His feet were numb and the rest of him felt as cold as a winter pond. It couldn't have been any harder for him to breathe if Bertha had stabbed him in the chest instead of bashing him over the head.

"Obviously your wife is still involved with the man, Mr. Hamilton."

"I'm still not convinced that any of this is reason to kill me."

With a smug smile of her face, Widow Crenshaw turned back to Sam. "Of course, with these kinds of charges against her, having Mrs. Hamilton remain here with you and your daughter is completely out of the question. And *that* is reason enough."

Some of the warmth was coming back to Sam. Anger was a very efficient fuel. The more these two talked, the angrier he was becoming.

"I've never once mentioned to Bertha that I wanted to take Miranda away from her. I told you both when you first brought this up, I'd never do such a thing."

"Well, that may not be your decision to make," Widow Crenshaw pointed out. "Some things the courts must decide."

Sam stared at them both as coldly as he possibly could. It was easy when he kept in mind how much the two of them reminded him of rattlesnakes.

"I think it would be a good idea if you two left now."

"But, we're not done discussing—"

"Oh, yes, you are. Now out!"

Sam dropped the sheets to his lap and pointed toward the door.

The ladies gasped and began to back up.

"Is there some part of what I'm saying you two don't understand?"

He grasped the edge of the sheet and threw it back, exposing his legs and bare feet.

"Do I have to get out of bed and show you the door?"

They gasped again. Widow Crenshaw turned and headed for the door. Sam could hear her stomping all the way across the kitchen floor so hard the house fairly shook.

"Oh, Janet, wait for me!" Miss Barber cried. Without Widow Crenshaw's guiding hand, she managed to collide with the rocking chair and the table before she found the door.

After he heard the screen door slam shut, he leaned his aching head against the headrest and sighed. He was so angry he wanted to spit. He could just be thankful Bertha hadn't heard them.

If he truly suspected her of trying to murder him, why had he gotten so angry when someone else did, too? Probably because, deep down inside, he knew Bertha couldn't possibly harm him. He didn't care what facts—or even wild suppositions—other people could offer him that might point to her guilt, he knew in his heart that she still loved him as much as he loved her. He just had to get her to admit it.

"Goodness gracious!" Bertha exclaimed when she entered the kitchen. The empty wicker laundry basket she carried dropped to the floor. "What happened here?"

The rocking chair was sitting skewed toward the doorway. The little table had toppled over. It looked as if somebody had been in here fighting.

Either that, or—Bertha froze in her steps and looked about her. Had whoever ransacked their house the first time come back? If so, what were they still looking for? And why had they only knocked over a table and misplaced a chair this time?

Had whoever hit Sam in the alley came back to finish the job? Had they succeeded? Why had she left him alone? Chill fingers of fear swept up and down her back.

"Sam! Sam! Are you all right?" she cried frantically.

She ran to the door of the bedroom. When she saw Sam, she stopped and clung there in relief.

"Sam! Oh, Sam, are you all right?"

This time he wasn't lying down, staring up at the ceiling as he usually was. He was sitting up at the edge of the bed, resting his elbows on his knees. His hands were clasped in front of him and his head hung down.

She couldn't just grab him, throw him back on the bed, and tell him how much she loved him, and how glad she was to see he was all right—no matter how much she wanted to. He didn't seem all that interested in her anymore anyway.

"Sam, are you all right? Who did this to you?"

She sank down on the bed beside him, something she swore she'd never do. But she was too concerned for his health and well-being now to worry with any false pride. She was too glad to see he was still alive and in one piece. She inspected his head for more bumps. Finding none, she gently pulled his hands away from his face.

"I'm fine." He pulled away slightly.

"I'm sorry. I thought you were hurt."

He looked up at her. "Nope."

"I'm glad you're not. Were you praying? I'm sorry I interrupted."

"No. I was just thinking."

"About what?"

He shook his head. "I don't think you want to know."

Yes, I want to know! she silently cried. I'm your wife. Instead, she just jerked her head back toward the kitchen and asked, "What happened out there? Who did that? Did they hurt you?"

"No, of course not. It was just Miss Barber, running into things, as usual."

Bertha wanted to scream with horror. "Miss Barber *and* Widow Crenshaw were here?"

"Of course. The only place they go without each other is the outhouse."

Bertha wanted to laugh, but she didn't think Sam thought it was really funny.

"Oh, no. They were here in this house and I wasn't. I didn't see them come. When . . . Why didn't you call for me?"

"Did you really want to see them that bad?"

She gave a bitter laugh. "I don't want to see them at all. But without supervision, they tend to kind of snoop around a person's house. I caught them once, going through the drawers upstairs, at a party at old Mrs. Newcomb's."

"Well, they snooped their way right in here to see me. I called, but apparently you didn't hear me."

"I'm sorry. Still, I suppose it was nice of them to stop by," she reluctantly admitted.

"I guess so."

She didn't think he sounded too grateful. She also didn't think he sounded too convinced of the sincerity of their visit. Neither was she.

He looked up at her. "Bertha, why did you get so upset when you saw the chair out of place and the table knocked over?"

"Well, good furniture is hard to come by out here, and right now I can't afford to buy more." She gave a little laugh. "Do I still sound like Miranda?"

"You wanted to know who'd done it," he said instead. "Why didn't you think maybe I'd done it trying to walk around?"

"Because you're not that clumsy or dizzy anymore. If you'd felt well enough to walk, you'd have put things back to rights again. And if you were so ill you'd knocked the things over when you fell, you'd probably still be lying there."

"Geez, you ought to talk to Widow Crenshaw and Miss Barber about their choice of reading material."

She frowned at him. "What's that supposed to mean?"

"Nothing," he answered quickly.

"Did that bump on the head knock out more of your senses than we'd thought?"

"No, no. It's nothing."

"Well, I'm glad you're all right. But I've got work to do." Bertha rubbed her hands together and prepared to stand.

"Bertha?" He laid a hand on her arm, preventing her from

rising. "You wanted to know if I was all right. Why were you so sure someone else had been here?"

"Because it happened before."

He frowned. "When?"

"You wouldn't remember. It was the day you got hit. The Picketts and I took care of it all."

"Did you tell the sheriff?"

"Why? He wouldn't have helped."

Sam chuckled. "I guess not. He'd have claimed it was too far to come out to do anything. But, why were you so sure they'd hurt me?"

"I . . . I guess because it's happened before, too."

"Most people seem to think it was just a botched robbery, a one-time thing. Why would you expect it to happen again?"

"Well, I . . . I . . ." Suddenly she frowned in frustration and annoyance. "I don't know why you're asking me questions like these."

"Then let me ask you this. If I hadn't come back from Nevada, what would you be doing right now?"

"Right now?" she stressed.

"Yep."

"Standing here talking to myself when I should be finishing up the laundry." She gave a little laugh. "That rain put me way behind in my chores."

Sam wasn't laughing. "No, seriously. What would you be doing?"

"The laundry."

"Yours."

"Sure. And Miranda's," she added.

"And Quinn's?"

"What?" She stared at him in disbelief. "Why are you still so worried about Arthur?" Before he could reply, she held up her hands and exclaimed, "No! No, I haven't had to resort to taking in other people's laundry yet, and I hope I never do. I wouldn't be doing Arthur's laundry because Arthur is not my husband."

"But if I hadn't come back, he would've been, wouldn't he?"

"I don't know." She shook her head. Why was he still asking her silly questions about Arthur? "What difference does it make now anyway?"

"It makes a difference to me. Would you have married him?"

"Maybe. I still don't see what difference—"

All her hemming and hawing was getting on his nerves. He had to be blunt.

"Have you already been a wife to him, Bertha? I mean, without bothering with any of the legal stuff?"

She stared at him. "What kind of question is that?"

"Have you?"

"Are you out of your mind? Of course not! I'm your wife."

"But you thought you were my widow, and—"

"I still wouldn't . . . I mean . . . no! How could you even ask such a thing of me?"

He looked at little relieved with her answer, but not completely. There was still something hagriding him that he needed to pursue.

"What if I had died in that alley?"

"But you didn't, thank goodness. So let's just be grateful—"

"What if I had? Would you marry Arthur then?"

"No. I mean, maybe in a couple of years, but—"

"What would you do so that he could be your husband?"

"What?" She glared at him. "That bump on the head *has* made you crazy."

"You heard me. I'm here, but you want Quinn for your husband. What do you do?"

"Will you forget him? I *don't* want him for a husband. I thought I'd made that perfectly clear."

"Would you hit me over the head?"

"I'll hit you over the head now if you don't shut up about him." She tried to give him a playful push, to get him out of this morose mood. But Sam was watching her, his dark eyes deadly serious.

Bertha's heart skipped and her fingers turned numb. She could feel the blood roaring in her ears. She regretted her hastily spoken, teasing remark. Sam could misinterpret it so easily. Her throat tightened and tears began to fill her eyes.

In a voice barely above the whisper, she said, "You're serious. You really think I did that to you."

"No, I . . . I just need to know—"

Never taking her eyes from him, she slowly raised her index finger and pointed it at him, moving it up and down with forceful strokes with each point she made.

"I bear and raise our child alone. I worked this run-down, debt-ridden farm until it's holding its own, and even supports two hired hands. I waited for you for seven years. I'll admit I was a little less than happy to take you in. But when I did, I cooked for you, did your laundry and mending, cleaned up after you. I turn away the only man who wanted to court me. I took care of you when you were hurt, and prayed you'd get better because I couldn't bear to lose you again."

She lowered her hand and glared at him.

"And now you want to accuse me of being the one who hurt you?"

"I only asked—"

In frustration, she stamped her feet on the floor so hard it hurt. It was nothing compared to the pain in her heart.

"You have got to be the *dumbest* creature that walks, swims, or crawls on the face of the earth!"

"I mean, it might have been—"

"Who? Miranda? Pops? Rachel Pickett?" She ticked them off on her fingers. "Who else did we miss as being the most unlikely candidate? Reverend Knutson? Miss Meecham?"

"See, it's not just you."

"I don't care if you suspect every other person in town. How could you include *me*?" Her voice broke, but she swallowed hard and fought back the tears.

He moved so close Bertha could feel the heat of anger emanating from his tense body.

His eyes were very dark, and his voice was very low when he said, "You forgot someone else. Arthur Quinn."

Bertha sat there, watching him, waiting for him to continue.

"Aren't you going to jump to his defense? Aren't you going to tell me I'd accuse him of any foul deed just because I'm jealous?"

Very quietly she answered, "No."

"No?"

He was staring at her. She could see the uncertainty in his eyes, as if he were waiting for her to give him another flimsy reason for accusing Arthur.

"Why not?" he asked.

"Because . . . I think you may be right."

"I'm right?" His eyes lit up with disbelief.

"I'm not saying you're completely right," Bertha amended, turning away from him. She couldn't be this close to him and still think as clearly as she needed to in this new situation. "I'm just not saying that I think you're completely wrong."

"Do you know something about this that I don't?"

"No, of course not. Arthur and I didn't put a plan together or anything, if that's what you mean. And I wouldn't be surprised if you did."

Feeling guilty from listening to those two old busybodies, he quickly assured her, "No, no. I'm so sorry I ever said anything about you. But what makes you suspect him?"

"I'd really rather not go into that right now, if you don't mind." If she told him the truth, he'd only hate Arthur more.

He reached out to hold her by the arms. Gently he pressed against her until she turned and looked into his eyes.

"We can't have any more secrets between us, Bertha. We've got to trust each other, even if we don't think we can trust anyone else. If the man really tried to kill me, I've got to know."

"It'll only make you angrier with him," she warned.

"I'm already getting pretty perturbed playing twenty questions with my wife. I'd rather be mad at him. Now, tell me what you know."

She disentangled herself from his grasp.

"After church he talked again about helping me to divorce you."

"So that's what they saw," Sam muttered.

"What?"

"Never mind. Just tell me what Quinn said to you."

"I told him I didn't want a divorce. That's when . . ."

She breathed a deep sigh and flung her hands down into her lap.

"Oh, this is the part that's really going to sound bad for Arthur."

"I don't care about Arthur sounding bad. What did he say? Or do?"

Bertha still hesitated a few moments. This was not an easy thing to relate to a husband.

"That's . . . that's when he said he wished there was some way he could make me change my mind. And then he ran off in a huff."

"And that's when he came and hit me."

"We don't know that for sure," she reminded him.

It sounded so awful for Arthur, and he had been good to her for a while. She had to inject some kind of softening influence into this very dangerous conversation.

"Well, I don't think he ran off to find his great-uncle the judge," Sam said.

"I wouldn't want him to, even if his uncle would do it for free. I tried to tell him very firmly, but he wasn't listening. I told him I didn't want to marry him."

"Why not?"

"I told him . . . I didn't love him."

"You don't?"

"Of course not!"

"Do you love *me*, Bertha?"

She drew in a deep breath and swallowed hard. How

could she admit she loved him now when she'd been so horrible to him in the beginning? And he had been just as horrible accusing her of trying to kill him?

"Do you love me, Bertha?" he repeated.

Sam's hands glided down her arms, across her wrists, to take her by both hands. Gently he pulled her closer to him.

Looking her directly in the eyes, he asked one more time. "Do you love me?"

"Yes, Sam. I love you. Yes, I love you," she repeated.

Once it was said, it was much easier the next time. It felt so good to say it now, again and again.

He pulled her to him completely. His lips met hers fiercely. She joined him with equal passion. He had waited so long. Their first kiss had been a wonderful fulfillment of all his patience. Now there was no longer any time for patience.

"I never stopped loving you," she gasped into his ear. "I was really mad at you, but I always loved you. Thinking you didn't love me was what made me even more angry and frustrated with you."

"No more anger, my love. No more frustration," he murmured against her soft cheek.

His hungry lips never left her warm, smooth skin. Stretching out his leg, he gave the bedroom door a shove with his foot. Helped along by the strong breeze wafting through the house, the door slammed shut.

"This afternoon was made for us," he told her.

He reached up to stroke the few strands of her fair hair that had fallen into her face when he pulled her down on the bed. She closed her eyes for a moment. The dark lashes lay against her creamy skin like tiny curtains. When she opened her eyes again, it was as if the curtains had risen, revealing the light in her eyes.

"There's a fire in your eyes," he told her, continuing to stroke her hair.

She held his face in her hands, savoring the feel of the rough stubble of his beard against her palms.

"I'm beginning to feel sort of warm all over," she admitted.

"Lady's fire, that's what Pops called it."

"He's a wise old man."

"It's shining in your eyes now."

"It's shining for you, Sam. Only you."

His fingers gently traced little circles on her cheeks, around her eyes, and down her nose—the little game they'd played when they were first married.

She giggled. "You remember."

"I could never forget," he responded in a hoarse whisper.

His fingertip tickled the edges of her lips and the corners of her mouth. She kissed his fingertip. He slid his finger down her chin, down the softness of her throat.

He meandered to the sides of her neck. She squeezed up tight and squealed.

"Stop! That tickles."

"You haven't changed a bit."

He traced the ridge of her collarbone, then stopped when confronted by the buttons of her bodice.

"Aha! A barricade. Captain, we'll have to smuggle the goods past the blockade."

Laughing, she demanded, "What sort of contraband are you carrying, mate?"

He pressed his body closer to her.

"Sausage."

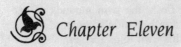 Chapter Eleven

"Tell me I've reached my home port, Bertha," he whispered in her ear. "Tell me, after all the time I've been away, after all the troubles we've been through, that I've finally come home."

She reached up and wrapped her arms around the back of his neck. Her fingers toyed with the fringe of hair that curled against his tanned skin, then moved upward to run through his auburn waves.

"Welcome home, my love. I should've told you this a long time ago."

"I'm home now, and I'm staying home." His fingers fumbled with the buttons on her bodice. "You can tell me that every day for the rest of our lives. I'll always be around to hear it."

"I'm glad we're going to have the rest of our lives together, Sam. I can't tell you how much I missed you."

"You don't have to. I missed you just as much."

"I missed you more," she said tauntingly.

"No, I missed you more."

Then held their foreheads close as they laughed at their private joke. Then the laughter stopped as their lips met once again.

Then he grew more serious and laid his hand upon her stomach. "I missed seeing you carrying our daughter."

She smiled. "We'll have chance for many, many more."

"I promise, I'll do my best."

Slowly he unfastened the rest of her bodice and pulled the fabric loose from her skirt. He ran his finger across the edge of the tiny white lace bordering her chemise. The lace was warm from being next to her body, but nowhere near as warm as her soft, delicate flesh, the twin mounds of her pliant breasts. Her own warmth couldn't compare to the warm tightening he felt in his own loins for her.

He moved to the fastening of her skirt.

"That tickles, too!" She cringed and giggled.

"You are so ticklish. I wonder how I ever managed to touch you at all."

"Very carefully," she told him, pulling his face down so she could kiss him once again.

"Very happily," he amended.

As he lifted his head, her hands drifted down his neck to the opening of his union suit. She felt the soft nubs of the knitted fabric as she unfastened each tiny button. She ran her finger across and up and down his chest. The softly twining hairs slid between her fingers.

He bent down and placed a fierce kiss on her lips.

"Don't move. I'll be right back."

Pushing himself quickly from off the bed, he pulled the shirt from his body. It hung down behind him as he grabbed the sides and pulled them apart to encircle his lean hips.

Bertha watched him from the bed.

"I've waited so long for you."

"I won't keep you waiting a moment longer."

Releasing his grasp on the bunched-up fabric at his waist, he pushed the garment past his hips, and let it fall to the floor. Quickly he joined her in bed to lay beside her.

He reached out to stroke her softly rounded breasts while she placed a hand on his smooth, lean hip and let it rest there. He kissed her again and again. Like a starving woman, she hungrily accepted them all and begged for more.

Lying beside her, he moved his hands over her, exploring every facet that he had missed for so long. Her nipples were larger, darker, her waist a little thicker, her stomach a little more rounded—not the body of the young woman he'd left so long ago, but the sensuous, generous, receptive body of a woman in the full bloom of her life. A woman ready to love a man with every fiber of her being.

Gradually her hand slid downward to toy with the curling hairs of his loins. Her fingertips brushed against the heat of his passion. He moaned with longing.

She moaned softly in response.

"I must have you now," he told her.

"Yes, you must."

He drew in a deep shuddering breath of anticipation and moved to cover her with his body.

Slowly, gently, holding in the enormous force of the passion he felt for her, he entered her. She clasped him tightly to her, enjoying the feel of his weight, and heat, and manhood moving over her, and in her, and through her.

She sighed with contentment just to have him once again within her. He had always been a part of her, even though they were separated by half a country. He always would be, now and forever.

The creak of the rope supports, the squeak of the wooden bed frame, the white cotton curtains billowing out on the cool, late spring breeze in rhythm to their lovemaking. The scent of the new mown grass, the plowed earth opened to receive the seeds of new life, the musky masculine scent of Sam himself as he throbbed above her. Her own all-absorbing reception. She would remember these always, now and every time they made love. Every time they were apart, these memories would recall to her Sam and the undying love between them.

The fiery explosion of his passion whirled her over the edge into a starlit chasm. They came to drift together like leaves in autumn floating to the mirrored surface of a still pond, gently cradled in each other's arms.

* * *

"What do you mean, there's no supper?" Miranda complained.

"Well, Mommy got sort of busy—" Sam started to explain. He reached up to smooth down his hair.

"With the laundry," Bertha quickly added, scooping up the fallen laundry basket and storing it beside the washtub and scrub board.

They'd lain there so long together, they'd barely had time to dress when they heard Miranda stomping up the front steps. Thank goodness she wasn't, and never had been, a quiet child.

Bertha hadn't had time at all to turn the rocking chair back facing the fire, or put the table upright, or put the laundry basket back in its place.

"So she didn't have time to cook," Sam finished.

"What are we going to eat?"

"Pancakes?" Bertha suggested, picking up the griddle.

"Breakfast for supper?" Miranda demanded in disbelief.

"Sure, why not?" Sam said.

"My stomach'll get all mixed up with morning food at night and think it's supposed to stay awake. Then I'll be up sick all night. You wouldn't want that, would you?"

"No, but I think I know how we can fix it."

"Not Hostetter's Celebrated Stomach Bitters!" Miranda stuck out her tongue and gagged.

"No, but there's a little apple pie left," Bertha said. "You can have the last piece. Your stomach will think it's dessert, and go right off to sleep."

"Oh, okay. Then it's safe to eat pancakes. But no burnt ones."

"I'll try to keep an eye on them," Bertha promised. She started getting out of the cupboard all the things she'd need to mix the batter.

"Hey, Sam! You're not in your underwear anymore," Miranda remarked as she headed for her bedroom.

"Uh, well, no. I thought I needed a change."

Just before she closed the door, she stuck out her head. She was holding her nose. "You sure did!" She slammed the door shut.

In only a few moments she opened it again. Sticking her head out the door, she called, "Mommy, where's your clothes?"

"Oh, oh, well, I knew how much you didn't like sharing a room, so . . . so I decided I'll share with your daddy instead."

Miranda eyed Bertha. "Yeah, well, okay." Then she turned to Sam. Giving him a conspiratorial wink, she whispered loudly, "You won't like it. She snores."

"Thanks for the warning." Sam smiled at her and nodded. "I think I can put up with that."

"Miranda was right," Sam told Bertha that night as she dampered the stove and turned down the wick.

"That I snore? How do you know?" she asked as they entered the bedroom. "We haven't actually *slept* together for seven years."

He closed the bedroom door tightly behind him. She turned down the wick of the lamp on the dresser. The moon had waned to a silvery crescent. It didn't afford much light, but the stars added to the shimmer of the satin sky.

"No, I mean about the pancakes making your stomach think it was morning."

Bertha turned around and laughed.

"That girl can come up with a thousand tales to keep from having to go to bed. You didn't actually believe her childish ideas, did you?"

With one swift motion Sam enveloped her in his arms. She responded immediately, reaching around his waist to hold him tightly to her. She breathed deeply the scent of syrup that lingered on his lips as he kissed her with increasing passion. She pressed closer to him to enjoy the heat of the elongated bulge of his manhood against her stomach.

At last he slowly backed away just enough to whisper, "Of course not. But I can come up with a thousand and one tales to keep us up all night."

"I'd like to hear each and every one."

He lifted her in his arms and placed her on the bed.

"Chapter one, page one . . ." he began.

The rope supports swayed as he knelt beside her.

He was a dark silhouette in the shadowy room, outlined by the lights of the night outside. His hair, his cheekbones, his lower lip. He moved closer to unfasten the buttons of her dress.

He made no teasing comments now. There was none of the tentativeness that surrounded their first lovemaking in many years. They were man and wife again—comfortable with their familiarity with their own body and with each other's, eager without hesitation for the pleasures they could both give and receive.

They knew what they wanted with an intensity that defied mere words.

Night shadowed his features, but his dark eyes seemed to come alive with inner fires of passion. He watched her body as she lay naked in the bed. Was her body outlined, too, with the silver fire of distant starlight? she wondered as she watched him undress.

The moonlight glided along his shoulders and down his muscular arms. It shone on the edge of his hip, and the indentation before his leg. He turned to her, the shafts of moonlight outlining his arousal.

She stretched out her arms to beckon him.

"Come to me now, my love," she whispered. "I can't wait another moment."

He hung above her, burning with longing. This afternoon hadn't satisfied their passions. It had only fed the fires with fuel that burned but was never consumed.

Their desires rose to fevered pulsations that at last exploded to leave them gasping and smiling, slightly groggy with the enveloping cloud of warmth.

They lay side by side. She nuzzled her cheek against his chest as he wrapped one arm about her shoulder. She curled her leg over one of his and snuggled closer.

"This is the way we always meant it to be," she said.

"This is the way it will be, from now on," he promised.

Bertha sighed with contentment. This was all she had ever wanted—her beautiful child, the productive farm, her tidy little home, enough to eat, a little money put by for a rainy day, good friends like Rachel and Tom, and most important of all her loving husband back to stay.

If her life truly were one of those silly melodramas, this would be the happy ending everybody cheered for.

Once Arthur realized that she and Sam were together again as man and wife, and intended to stay that way, he'd have enough sense to leave them both alone. Then they'd never have any more problems.

Somewhere in the distance, a dog howled. The curtains billowed as the breeze outside picked up slightly. The branches of the small maple trees growing near the house, full of new young leaves, swished in the breeze. The lilac bushes closer to the house rustled, too—a little too much.

Bertha sat up with a start.

"What's the matter?"

"Shhh!"

"What?"

She clapped her hand over his mouth. Her throat tightened as her ears strained to hear the sound again.

Sam reached up to cover her hand with his own. He pulled her hand away from his mouth, then sat up, too.

"In the bushes," she whispered. "There's someone out there. You weren't just making up stories to get me in trouble."

"Of course not. But—oh, my goodness! If it wasn't you, who is it?"

The rustling moved around the house until they could hear the distinctive sound of footsteps on the front porch, pacing back and forth. The footsteps descended the porch steps. The scuffling down the brick walk was followed by a moment of silence.

"Do you think he's gone?" Bertha asked.

Before Sam could answer, they heard the rustling in the bushes again.

"He's circling the house," Sam told her.

"Is he trying to get in?" She clutched the sheets to her bosom.

"It would be easy enough, since the doors aren't locked and most of the windows are open."

"But I haven't heard him even try the doorknobs."

"So I guess he doesn't really want in."

"Does he just want to scare us?"

Sam shook his head.

As the rustling in the bushes continued, Bertha said, "It's almost as if all he's trying to do is peek in all the windows."

"For now."

Sam slipped out of bed. He dropped to his knees, trying to find where he'd flung his trousers in the darkness. Bertha could hear him pulling them on, then slipping on his shoes.

"Get dressed," he told her. "Then go in and stay with Miranda."

"It's you he's after, not us."

"How do you know?"

"Well, it's . . . it's Arthur, isn't it?" she finally managed to say.

"Probably." He didn't seem the least bit surprised.

"He wouldn't hurt Miranda or me."

Sam didn't answer.

"Would he?"

"I don't know. Anyone who goes sneaking through the bushes peeking in people's windows isn't acting like a rational man. He may take it into his head that if he can't have you, no one else can, either."

She gasped.

"We don't want Miranda getting caught in a cross fire."

"Oh, my God! Can't you think up something reassuring to tell me?"

Sam stood there for a moment, his brows drawn together as if he were pondering what to do next. Then he breathed a sigh of resignation and moved toward the chest of drawers.

"I think I need to go put a little fear of the Lord, and common sense, into Mr. Quinn's head," he said instead.

He reached down behind the chest of drawers and withdrew his old carpetbag.

"What are you going to do?"

"Nothing. If I don't have to."

Bertha heard a metallic click and saw the moonlight glinting off the barrel of a revolver. Her eyes grew wide, trying to take it all in.

"What in heaven's name are you doing with that?" she demanded. "You never had one of them before. You just used the shotgun for hunting—and you weren't that good, I'm sorry to say. Why do you have one of them?"

"Out West a man needs one of these," he explained.

She could hear the click as he slid each bullet into the chamber, then rolled the cylinder to add one more.

"This is not out West."

He tucked a few extra bullets into his shirt pocket. Then he rose and replaced his carpetbag behind the chest of drawers.

"But sometimes, a man still needs one of these."

"I hope you know how to use that thing—better than the hunting gun."

"Don't worry. Unfortunately, I do."

"Be careful, Sam," she whispered as he opened the bedroom door and moved out into the kitchen. "I can't lose you now."

Bertha slipped into her dress and buttoned the front in such a hurry that she mismatched the buttons and button-holes. She had no time to redo it. It would just have to stay that way.

Ducking her head, waiting any moment for the gunfire to begin, she crept into Miranda's room. Slowly and quietly, so as not to awaken Miranda, she sat on the edge of the bed.

"Huh? Mommy?"

"I'm sorry I woke you," she whispered. "Just go back to sleep."

"So he kicked you out for snoring too loud, huh?"

Bertha smiled and caressed Miranda's head. "Something like that. Go back to sleep."

Miranda turned to her side, cuddling her doll. "I will as long as you don't start snoring."

Bertha watched Sam through the open doorway. She knew it would be safer for Miranda if she closed the door tightly, and maybe even wedged a chair under the doorknob. But she couldn't stand not knowing what was happening to Sam, so she left it open.

He held his gun pointing up. At least he wouldn't shoot himself in the foot, she thought. He pressed himself along the darkened walls, moving toward the front window. He looked as if he knew exactly what he was doing. Obviously Sam had done some sneaking up on people while he'd been away.

Sam made his way in the dark toward the sound of the footsteps on the front porch. He looked at the dark sky through the window. Why couldn't there have been a full moon tonight? It was going to be hard to tell who the prowler was, although he had a fairly good idea it was Arthur. But he needed proof, not suspicions, before he went to Sheriff Duncan.

He pressed his back flat against the wall and reached for the door handle. He turned the knob as quietly as he could, then quickly flung the door open. When a barrage of bullets didn't hit the front door, Sam slowly peeked around. He was just in time to see a pair of boots disappear off the other side of the front porch.

"Damn!" he muttered.

Carefully staying low, and keeping close to the side of the

house, he ran to the edge of the porch. He couldn't see a thing in the darkness. He couldn't hear a thing above the swishing of the branches of the bushes.

He turned quickly to watch the front door. He couldn't let the low-down, sneaking skunk double back and go in the front while he was watching for him around back.

He waited a moment longer, then ducked back inside the house. Quickly he made his way across the kitchen to Miranda's room.

"Are you okay in here?" he whispered.

"We're fine," Bertha responded.

She stood and hurried to his side. He wrapped his arm protectively around her shoulder and began to guide her back to the bedroom.

"He's gone for now, I guess. First thing tomorrow I'm going into town to talk to the sheriff."

"I'm coming to town with you," Bertha told him. She was standing by the door, putting on her bonnet and shawl.

"I'm going with her," Miranda told him.

"We drank the last of the coffee this morning," she explained. "Having two people drinking it uses up what I had stored a lot faster than just one would."

"Even if I had to survive on only bread and water, it would be worth it just to be with you again," he told her. Leaning over, he planted a gentle kiss on her cheek.

"Oh, geez!" Miranda exclaimed. "Hey, you two, there's an innocent little kid in here."

"Where?" Sam looked all around, specifically avoiding glancing at her.

"Very funny. I think it was better around here when you two were fighting."

"I wasn't planning on going to the general store with you," he told Bertha.

"Good," Miranda stated.

"To tell the truth, there's not a thing in that store that interests me—except when you go there," he whispered to

Bertha. "Anyway, I don't think people would be wanting to buy too much stuff there if Arthur's blood was all over it."

She nodded hesitantly. "That would cause a lot of people to pretty much avoid the place. Except maybe Miranda."

"Naw, it was just Sam's blood I was interested in," Miranda said.

"Of course, I think the more *you* stay away from the owner of that store, the better, too."

"Don't worry." Then she leaned a bit closer to Sam and whispered, "Do you think we'll be safe?"

He only hesitated a moment. "Sure. Like you said, it's me he's after. And you've got a whole townful of people watching out for you."

Bertha gave a skeptical little laugh. "I don't think Widow Crenshaw or Miss Barber would exactly come running to my aid."

Sam raised a knowing finger. "But Lester Martin will always help you sue the fellow."

Bertha shook her head. "I don't want to have anything to do with that man ever again, either."

"Don't worry. Pops is always there. He's a good lookout."

Bertha laughed again, this time with a little more humor.

"I'll be over at the sheriff's office, seeing what can be done."

"Just be careful."

"Yeah, stay out of saloons and alleys," Miranda warned.

Sam might not have had any intention of going into the General Store, but as he pulled the wagon up to the hitching post out front, it was pretty clear Sheriff Duncan had other plans. He stepped up to meet him.

"Hey, Sam." He waved, signaling for him to come over. "I need to talk to you."

"I need to talk to you, too," Sam said as he jumped down from the wagon seat. "Somebody was creeping around in the bushes around our house last night. He even came up on the front porch again. I saw a pair of boots."

The sheriff looked over at Bertha. His belly shook with laughter.

"Did you think it was Sam?"

"No—"

Before she could finish, he turned to Sam. Still laughing, he asked, "Did you think it was her?" He nodded toward Bertha.

"No, it was the fairies!" Sam snapped. "I don't know for sure, but I got a good idea who's been prowling around my house both times."

"Is that so?"

"Yeah."

"Are you going to tell me who it is?"

Sam looked around. "Not in the middle of Main Street."

"Why? Don't you want the town to know you're being stalked by the big, bad giant?" His belly bounced up and down.

"Sheriff, are you going to talk seriously with us or do I have to run for sheriff next election just to see that something gets done around this town?"

Sheriff Duncan's eyebrows drew down into a ferocious frown. "I like being sheriff, boy."

"I'm sure you do. Now act like one." Sam's eyes were just as dark with anger—and with frustration—at this increasingly puzzling problem that wouldn't allow itself to be solved.

The sheriff tucked in both his chins and said, "Why don't you come on in here and I'll show you what I been up to as sheriff while you been out on your farm playing with the fairies."

Sam threw Bertha a surprised glance.

"In the General Store?" Sam asked. "Is that such a good idea, considering—?"

"Considering what?"

Sam was reluctant to accuse Arthur without having any kind of real evidence against the man. He couldn't even check Arthur's boots because he hadn't gotten that good a look at the pair in the dark.

"Why don't we go to your office, instead?"

"'Cause I got somebody in here I think you'd be real happy to meet—again."

Sam followed the sheriff into the General Store. Bertha grabbed for Miranda's hand to lead her in, but the little girl was too quick.

"Hey, Sam, wait for me!" she called as she ran on ahead to catch up to Sam.

"I don't want to miss the blood this time," she called back. She caught up with Sam and grabbed his hand as she walked with him into the store.

"There's not going to be any blood this time," Sam said.

"Oh, rats! I hate being a kid. I always miss the good stuff."

Bertha followed them into the store.

"Hey, Pops," Sam greeted.

"Hey, young feller. How're you doing?"

"Real fine."

"Told you so." Pops grinned broadly.

"Mr. Hamilton." Arthur Quinn, scowling, and with arms crossed defensively over his chest, acknowledged Sam from behind his counter.

"Mr. Quinn." Sam just nodded.

"Now, what we got here, Sam," the sheriff said as he leaned his bulk on the back of the chair across from Pops, "is the young fellow who's been in such demand."

He moved aside.

Sure enough, Max Douglas turned his freckled face up to Sam. The sheriff still kept his heavy hand on the boy's shoulder.

"I'm sorry, mister. I'm real, real sorry," the boy started babbling. "I didn't know what was going to happen. Really I didn't!"

Ignoring the boy's plaintive outburst, Sam asked, "Where'd you find him?"

"Back in my woodshed," Pops answered. "It seems the little coyote has been hiding out there ever since."

"I was scared, mister. I really was," the boy pleaded. "I was only told to get you back in that alley. I only did it for the money. I didn't know he was going to bash you like that. I was so afraid you was dead, with all that blood and everything."

"Sissy," Miranda said, her lip curling disdainfully.

"I was awful glad to hear you was alive, mister."

"Me, too."

"Then I was afraid they'd all think I did it, 'cause they all know me and my brothers ain't got such a good reputation in this town. They always like to blame us when something turns up missing, or somebody gets beat up."

"Nine times out of ten it *is* you Douglases. You're a whole nest of polecats out there." Sheriff Duncan grabbed the boy's freckled ear and tugged.

"Ow! I wasn't me this time, sheriff. I swear!" He raised his right hand as if he were in court. "I swear it, as Lord Jesus is my witness."

The sheriff tugged again.

"Ow!"

"Don't blaspheme, boy. You're already in enough trouble in this life. I wouldn't risk losing points in the next."

Sam reached out and moved the sheriff's hand from the boy's ear.

"Frankly, Sheriff, I don't blame the kid for not wanting to get caught."

Sam stooped down to be on eye level with Max.

"I don't blame you for hiding out, Max. I don't even blame you for getting me into that alley. We weren't looking for you to punish you."

Max shot the sheriff a dark look. "Yeah?"

"Yeah. I'll make sure of that. We were looking for you because we believe you're the only one who saw the man who really did hit me, and you can tell me who it is."

"Yeah, sure, I saw him. I took his money. Although the

lousy two bits wasn't worth the trouble I been through to get it."

"Well, maybe you'll learn a valuable lesson about ill-gotten gains from this, son," Pops said.

Max just raised his eyes to the ceiling.

"Maybe not," Pops finished.

"Who was he, Max?" Sam asked. "What did he look like?"

He was glad Quinn was here. Then the sheriff wouldn't have to complain about having to go so far to arrest his culprit. And Sam would be right there when Quinn got his come-uppance.

Bertha held her breath, waiting. She shot a glance over to Arthur. If he was slowly making his way toward the back exit, that could be a good sign of his guilt. But he just stood there, arms crossed over his chest, waiting, just like the rest of them.

"You really won't punish me? Promise?" Max pleaded.

"I promise, Max," Sam answered.

Max raised his hand and pointed his finger at Arthur Quinn. "About like him."

"What!" Arthur's arms sprang apart and he grasped the counter tightly.

Sam sprang to his feet and stood poised to pounce on Quinn at the slightest provocation.

Bertha's heart nearly stopped with shock. Her head began to spin. Little white stars started to fall through the darkness at the corners of her vision. She clung to one of the counters to support her failing knees.

"Did you and the kid set this up, Hamilton?" Arthur bellowed.

"No, no!" Max shot up from his seat and was shouting frantically. "No, no! I said about like him—not just like him. It wasn't him."

The sheriff strode across the floor between Quinn and Sam. "Now, now, folks, settle down. Settle down or we'll never get anything done."

"Geez," Max complained. "Did you all think I was so dumb I'd pick out the feller right under his own nose? I don't want to end up dead or nothing."

The sheriff passed by Bertha, who was still clinging to the counter. Jabbing a thick thumb in her direction, he ordered, "Do something for her."

Sam opened a bottle of vinegar, tapped a few drops onto his pocket handkerchief, and stuck it under Bertha's nose.

"I'm fine, I'm fine," she repeated, pushing his hand away. "I don't need that."

"You were surprised to think it was me?" Arthur asked hopefully.

"No, I was horrified," she stated as she regained her composure.

"Are you glad it's not me?"

"Yes. But I'd be horrified to find out it was anybody I knew who would try to kill my husband."

"Now, just go back behind your counter and shut up, Arthur," the sheriff said. Turning back to Max, he asked, "What did he look like, boy? And this time, try to be a bit more specific."

"Like I was saying, he looked kind of like Mr. Quinn, about as tall, only a little skinnier. Same color hair, only a little grayer on the sides, with a bald patch about the size of your fist right in the back."

Max thumped his fist down on top of his own hand to illustrate the location.

"Don't know what color eyes, 'cause they was kind of beady-like—like little pig eyes, you know?"

Sam, kneeling again by the boy's side, nodded slowly.

Bertha knew it couldn't be impaired vision from her earlier shock. She knew she'd recovered from her partial faint, so she knew she couldn't be seeing things that weren't there. Sam had a funny look on his face, almost as if each time the boy mentioned another feature of the man who had hit him, Sam knew what the boy was going to say in advance. Almost as if he already knew this man.

"Weirdest part was, he was missing a tooth."

"Not too uncommon around here," the sheriff said with a chuckle. "Just one?"

"Near as I could tell," Max answered. "I wasn't about to go diving in like Mr. Carter does."

"Which tooth was it? Do you remember?" Sam asked.

Bertha could almost have said he asked eagerly. She had a sneaking suspicion Sam could have told the boy which tooth was missing.

"This one."

Max opened his mouth and drew back his lips, exposing teeth and gums. With a grimy finger he tapped his left front tooth.

"Thanks, Max," Sam said, rising again.

"Is there anything else you can remember about him, boy?" the sheriff asked.

"No. Can I go now, mister? Please."

"Not yet, boy," the sheriff answered. He placed his hand on the boy's shoulder again, but avoided his ear. "Have you seen this fellow before?"

"Nope."

"He doesn't sound like anybody in town I've ever seen," Pope said.

"He's new in town?"

"I never seen him before, 'til about a couple of days ago," Max answered. "Then I only seen him hanging around Miss Sadie's or Miss Rosie's, and a couple of the different saloons."

"Would anybody there know who he is?"

"Maybe. Folks don't always give their names 'round there—leastwise not their right names. And it ain't polite to ask."

"I could ask around Miss Sadie's or Miss Rosie's," the sheriff offered with a grin. "See, Sam, there's a couple of advantages to being sheriff that I really don't want to give up."

"I can see that. You're welcome to them."

"You mean you ain't coming with me to get the feller, Sam?"

"Nope, the pleasure's all yours, Sheriff."

Sam headed out the door.

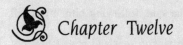

Chapter Twelve

"Sam, Sam, where are you going?" Bertha called, hurrying to follow him. Miranda trailed right behind.

Once outside the store, Sam stopped.

"What was that all about?" Bertha asked.

"I just needed some fresh air. I'll bet you do, too." He placed his hand under her elbow, giving her support. "I'm sorry you had such a shock back there with Quinn."

"Forget Quinn. You know that man, don't you?" she demanded. "The man who hit you?"

Sam just looked at her. His face was impassive and his eyes were cold and blank.

"How could I know him?" He gave a hollow laugh. "I didn't even see him. I told you, he hit me from behind."

Suddenly Max tore out the door and past them, heading down the street back to his end of town.

"I guess the sheriff's finally done with him," Sam said with a little chuckle.

"You knew that man from Max's description of him, didn't you, Sam?"

"Geez, you are persistent, aren't you? What makes you think that?"

"Because you're a lousy liar," she answered. "Because I'm your wife and I can read every thought that plays across your face. How do you know that man? Where did you meet him? Why on earth would he try to hurt you? Kill you?" Her voice was rising.

"Calm down, sweetheart," he told her, patting her patronizingly on the shoulder. "We're in the middle of the street." He turned and headed for the wagon. "Why would I lie to you?"

"I don't know, Sam," she said, following him. "You tell me."

He climbed up onto the wagon seat and rested his foot against the splashboard. He nodded toward the store.

"You forgot your coffee."

"Oh. Is it any wonder?"

"I think I'll wait out here for you."

"Can I get a candy, Mommy, please?" Miranda pleaded as Bertha entered the store once again.

Sam sat there, pondering his predicament. It had been a whole lot easier and probably a whole lot safer when he suspected Arthur. This new wrinkle opened the door to a lot of new problems he'd rather have left behind.

"Why, Mr. Hamilton," Widow Crenshaw called to him from the sidewalk. "How good to see you up and around. I do hope your restored locomotion has improved your disposition."

Miss Barber just waved. If Widow Crenshaw hadn't mentioned his name, she could have been waving to a scarecrow propped up in his seat, for all she knew.

Sam nodded. He didn't need these two interfering in his thoughts. Right now, he had to figure out what he was going to do, and how to keep Bertha and Miranda safe in the meantime.

"We noticed the little Douglas urchin traveling down the street mighty quick," Widow Crenshaw said, coming up to stand beside the wagon.

"I suppose Pops finally found him in his woodshed," Miss Barber said, following her.

Sam blinked. Those two really did know everything that went on in this town. Then why didn't they know who had hit him? Maybe it was just as well for their sakes, too. This fellow was a whole lot more dangerous than Max in a woodshed.

"We're really glad to hear it wasn't Arthur Quinn after all. Although we could have told you that." Widow Crenshaw grinned smugly.

"How do you know? What were you two doing, hiding in the flour bin?"

"The storeroom," Miss Barber said.

"Hush, Catherine. After all, Mr. Quinn is quite a pillar in the community, even if he doesn't bother to lock his back door, so we really wouldn't want to see him swinging from the gallows. Not to mention, if he was the one who tried to kill you, we'd have to go to all the trouble of finding a new storekeeper again. It was such a bother after Mr. Finnerty passed away. Good honest ones are so hard to come by."

"I suppose you've got some opinions about it not being Bertha, as well," Sam prompted.

Widow Crenshaw pressed her lips together and shook her head. "Quite disappointing, actually. We were so sure . . ."

"We'll have to study up on where we went wrong," Miss Barber told her.

"Yes, indeed." He supposed MacKenzie and Sons Bookstore could be expecting a rush on volumes of Poe and Collins.

"I don't suppose you'd know anything about the man Max was talking about, would you?" Sam asked.

Their nosiness and wild suppositions had almost helped him out of his marriage. But they liked to talk, and oddly enough, they sometimes even knew what they were talking about. Maybe they could be more help to him if they didn't actually know they were doing it.

Widow Crenshaw drew herself up and harrumphed. "We rarely travel to *that* side of town," she informed him. Lowering her voice, and taking a step closer to the wagon, she continued, "However, Catherine's cousin is rather taken with the drink, and he says the fellow's been here since the day after you arrived—near as he can reckon."

"What's his name?"

"We still can't get a name, yet, but Chauncey never was much of a one for remembering things like that."

"Much obliged, ladies," Sam said, tipping an imaginary hat.

"Of course, if you're so obliged, Mr. Hamilton, we'd be pleased to know why this man hit you."

"Right now, I'd rather not say," Sam repeated their own words back to them.

Widow Crenshaw gave a disgusted snort.

"However, it does have something to do with the attempted robbery."

"Well, we knew that!" Miss Barber protested as Widow Crenshaw led her away.

Miranda had her nosed pressed tightly against the display of penny candy.

Bertha found it difficult to raise her eyes above the edge of the counter. "I need a pound of coffee, please, and a candy for Miranda."

"Certainly, Mrs. Hamilton," Arthur replied.

"Don't be so formal, Arthur. We're still friends. I never really thought it was you who tried to hurt Sam."

"But you didn't do much to try to talk Sam out of it."

Bertha smiled. She couldn't tell him she had agreed with Sam. Instead, she told him, "If you knew Sam better, you'd know he can't be talked out of anything."

Arthur grimaced. "Yeah, I sort of figured that. Well, if anything should happen to change your mind, I'll still be waiting for you, Bertha."

She shook her head. "Don't wait for me, Arthur. I plan to be spending a lot of time—for a long, long time—with my husband."

"I know."

"I want that one," Miranda told him, pointing to a whip of black licorice.

Arthur handed it out to her. Like a skinny little snake, it slithered into her cupped hand.

"Thanks."

Taking great care to hold it by the top so that he wouldn't risk touching her, he placed the small, fragrant sack of dark beans in Bertha's hand. She slid her coins toward him across the counter. He waited until she let them go before he picked them up.

"But I'll still be here if you ever need me."

"Thanks."

Bertha slipped her apron over her head, then tied the apron strings around her waist to protect her dress. She wrapped the kerchief around her head to protect her hair. She grabbed the broom and the feather duster and prepared for battle.

First she tackled the parlor, an easy enough job, since it was rarely used, especially now that Arthur no longer came for his weekly game of dominoes. As she flicked the feather duster over Great-aunt Sophie's precious lamp, she decided she was very glad he didn't.

Now Sam and Miranda sat at the brightly lit kitchen table, playing their own special version of the game. It wasn't that she didn't like dominoes, but they always reminded her of the mistake she'd almost made. She didn't mind watching Sam and Miranda play, but she wouldn't mind if she herself never played another game again.

She usually sat with the mending, or knitting socks for the winter. It had seemed ordinary enough to knit a bigger size each year for Miranda. It was funny now to be knitting big socks again for Sam. It was also very good. She liked his big warm feet next to hers in bed at night. She was really looking forward to this winter when, cuddling next to him, she never had to suffer cold feet ever again.

She bypassed Miranda's room. Picking up her toys and clothes, as well as keeping her furniture dusted, was one of her chores.

She brought her cleaning things into their bedroom. Sam had brought his own special feeling to the place. He left his brushes and hair tonic, his razor and soap, on the bureau. He left his trousers hung over the back of the single chair in the room. At night he left his shoes under their bed.

To her, this was no longer just a room to sleep in. It was a haven where she and Sam could forget the problems the rest of the world brought to their doorstep. Here they could love each other as if the past seven years had never come between them. It was a room where they could love each other with their bodies and hearts for as long as they lived. It was a place where, for them and them alone, time stood still.

Bertha did her best to keep the room as clean as possible. She was feeling so good and so full of life and energy this morning that she decided to sweep behind the furniture.

That's when she remembered Sam's carpetbag.

It was the worn-out, empty-looking carpetbag that she had first noticed as Sam's only possession when he returned. It was the carpetbag that he had pulled the gun out of.

She couldn't remember if he had unloaded the darned thing when he'd come back to bed that night. They'd both been in such a state of nervous excitement that it was hard to remember what they'd done.

What if he hadn't unloaded the gun? What if he'd been as upset as she'd been, and had just tossed it back in the bag? What if Miranda, with all her childish curiosity, went rooting around and found the darned thing?

Bertha had to make sure the gun was safely unloaded and put away.

Bending down, she tried to pull the carpetbag out from behind the chest of drawers. For an empty bag, it shouldn't be that hard to move. Was it caught on something back there? she wondered.

Getting down on her hands and knees, she felt around behind it. It wasn't caught on anything. She gave the handle one more tug. The bag came sliding out, sending her sprawling back on her bottom.

"What in the world do you have in there?" she asked the air.

Only one way to find out, came the response.

"Well, I really do need to make sure that gun is put away properly," she told the air.

Yes, you do.

"It's for Miranda's own good."

Of course it is.

"I'm not really all that curious."

Not *you*, my dear!

She knelt by the side of the bag and untied the clasp. She felt just a moment's hesitation. Was she as bad as Widow Crenshaw and Miss Barber, sticking her nose in business where it didn't belong?

Of course not. She was in her own home, not nosing through someone else's. It was her husband's carpetbag. Her responsibility as a good homemaker obligated her to open it. The safety of her child was at issue. Her duty as a devoted mother mandated that she open it. She had every right to open it, almost a moral obligation.

Slowly she separated the two halves and peered inside.

She blinked and looked again, harder. It must be a trick of the light, she decided. She needed better light.

She carried the carpetbag over to the bed and lifted it toward the window. Beams of sunlight lit the interior. Now she'd see for sure.

Yep, she'd been right the first time.

She plopped down in a stupefied heap on the side of the bed.

Money. Lots and lots of paper money. Stacks and stacks bound with little paper tabs. She reached in a shaking hand and lifted one out. She ruffled through the edges. Fifty-dollar bills, each and every one of them, she discovered as she lifted out more. Stacks and stacks of fifty-dollar bills.

She placed some on the bed beside her and some in her lap, just to get some idea of what that much money felt like.

She liked it.

"Where in heaven's name did you get this money, Sam?" she asked aloud.

She wished someone could have given her an answer.

She'd ask Sam, she decided. As soon as he came in from the field this evening, she'd ask him. She'd find out where this came from.

A chill feeling swept through her. There was a darn good chance this was what the man who hit Sam over the head was *really* after. He hadn't gotten it the day he'd hit him. Suppose he tried again? For this amount of money, she'd be darned surprised if he didn't.

The man with the missing tooth hadn't managed to get what he wanted in town. But he knew where Sam lived. He knew he had a wife and a daughter, too.

It was also a darn good chance this was the same man who'd been prowling around their house, looking for ways to get to this. He was probably also the same man who'd ransacked their house, searching for this. While Sam was lying there bleeding in that alley, and also being seen to in Doc Marsh's office, the man would've had more than enough time to get from the saloon alley to their farm and do all that damage.

How had Sam come by all this money? Why was the other man so intent on getting it back? Had Sam stolen it from him? He must have; otherwise, why hadn't he told her about it as soon as he came home? Why hadn't he put it in the bank? Why hadn't he spent some of it?

Suppose he had stolen it? That could explain his reluctance to spend any of it yet, until the law stopped looking for him. That would explain him having a revolver and telling her he knew how to use it.

Suppose Sam was a notorious bank robber out there in Nevada? What if he'd only come back to her now to hide out until the law stopped following him?

What if the man with the missing tooth wasn't a robber? What if he was some kind of renegade lawman or bounty hunter or a Pinkerton man from the railroad? What if Sam went looking for him and killed him? Or if he killed Sam? What if they arrested her for helping Sam hide out? What would happen to Miranda?

Why had Sam done this to her?

Frantically brushing the falling tears from her eyes, she began to pack all the money back into the bag.

Damn it! she cursed as she slammed the last bundle back in. Why hadn't he sent some of this to her?

She couldn't wait for Sam to come home.

She tried to keep her temper under control. She tried to keep the tears of hurt from falling. She managed to wait until Miranda was tucked in bed and she was pretty sure the child was asleep.

"Sam," she began tentatively, "I have a little question to ask you."

"Sure. What is it?"

"I . . . I need to see you in the bedroom about it."

"Aha!" Sam exclaimed, springing up from the rocking chair. "My favorite kind of question."

Eagerly he followed her into the bedroom. He closed the door behind him and stood there, hands behind his back, rocking on his heels, and grinning at her like a possum.

"Now, what kind of question can I help you with, my dear?"

Sam's grin fell a little as Bertha turned away from him. When she reached behind the chest of drawers, his grin turned into a worried frown.

When she plopped the carpetbag onto the bed, he gulped.

"What is this?"

"My carpetbag."

"What's in it?"

"My stuff."

"And what exactly would that be?"

"Well, you saw my gun."

"Yes, yes. That doesn't alarm me half as much as it used to. Go on."

"I've taken my clothes out and put them in the drawers."

"I know that very well. What else?"

Sam didn't say anything.

She picked up the carpetbag again and gave it a little shake. The money inside clunked against the lining. She held her ear to the side of the bag.

"Did you hear that?"

"Yep."

"Now, that would sort of tell me that this bag is not completely empty. What could possibly still be in this bag that you brought all the way from Nevada?"

"Sweetheart, I meant to tell you—"

She held up her hand to stop him. "Don't sweetheart me again, Sam. Tell me the truth."

"Would you believe me?"

"Yes," she answered without hesitation. She *would* believe him. She *had* to. "And remember," she warned, "you're a bad liar."

"It's my money—it's *part* of my money."

"You didn't steal it, did you?"

"Of course not! Whatever else you may think of me, Bertha, I'm not a thief."

"Then why were you hiding it?"

"Would *you* walk around and let everybody know you had that much money on you?" he countered.

"How much money?" she asked slowly.

"Twenty thousand dollars."

Bertha felt her head spinning again. She sat on the edge of the bed and held on to the handle of the carpetbag.

"The rest of it—well, the rest of what's in cash—is in a bank in Carson City," he explained.

"Where's the rest of what's not in cash?"

"Still in the ground."

"The ground?" She started taking in big gulps of air,

trying to help her poor brain make sense of all this very strange and startling new information.

"Well, do you remember we sent me out to Nevada to find work?"

"Uh-huh" was all she would manage to mumble.

"Most of the work out there is in the silver mines. And once a fellow works enough in somebody else's mine, and sees a lot of folks getting rich but him, he sort of gets to thinking he'd like to find and work a mine of his own."

"So you did."

Sam grinned at her triumphantly and wiggled his eyebrows up and down. "You ding-dong, double-darned right I did!"

Bertha still hadn't managed a smile. "You found a silver mine?"

"I found a *big* silver mine."

"How big?"

"We're rich."

"You're rich?" she asked.

"*We're* rich," he corrected.

"We're rich," she repeated. "How . . . how rich?"

"Close to six hundred thousand, I guess."

Bertha tried to talk, but choked on her own saliva.

"Of course, that's just what's in the bank right now."

"In . . . the bank," she burbled.

"There's a lot more in that mine to be brought up," he said proudly. "We'll be working that vein for a long, long time."

"How . . . how long have *we* been rich?" she finally managed to ask in a complete, coherent sentence.

"Well, I worked the claim without much luck for about a year and a half. But about ten months ago, I guess, I hit a motherlode of silver. It's kind of hard to keep track of time when you're working in a mine and don't see much daylight."

Bertha felt her fingers tightening on the handle of the carpetbag. She could feel her face and ears growing hot and her heart begin to pound as anger surged through her body.

She rose from the bed and slowly turned to face him.

Very slowly, as if each syllable were the last she might pronounce—or the last that Sam might hear—she said, "Do you mean to tell me we've been filthy, stinking shamelessly, prodigiously, light-your-cigar-with-twenty-dollars-bills rich for two whole years?"

"Well, for the first year, we were just modestly rich," he corrected, still grinning from ear to ear. "*Now* we're filthy, stinking—"

"Don't try to be funny, Sam," she warned. "Call me crazy, but I'm not seeing anything funny in any of this. For almost a year, you've been out there, rich as Croesus, enjoying yourself—"

"I wouldn't exactly call digging in the mine enjoying myself." He held out his hands to her. "I've got the scars to prove it."

"You'll have even more scars when I'm done with you. How could you not have told me—sent us some money— something?"

"I did. I tried," he stammered. "I wired you a hundred dollars."

"I never got one penny."

"I told . . . Oh, my God . . . !"

He stood there, his mouth hanging open, staring into space. Then he blinked quickly and shook his head.

"I should have known," he murmured, as if thinking aloud. "I should've known better than to trust that lying, thieving polecat!"

"Who? What?"

"No one," he answered quickly. "No one you need to know. I'll take care of him myself—if I ever get hold of him again. Never you mind."

"I can't never mind," she told him. "It's all that's been on my mind."

"Just . . . just someone who worked in my office. Someone I thought I could trust."

"Office! You've got an office?"

"Yeah. I've got a couple of dozen men doing the actual digging now," he admitted. "I work in the office, and that's no Sunday-School picnic, either. Employees, wages, miners' lamps, and safety equipment. I barely have time to eat anymore."

"Is that why you were so thin?"

"Yeah."

"You polecat! And all this time I was feeling sorry for you, thinking you were too poor to buy a good meal!"

He grimaced.

"An office. Is that why you need that fancy suit?"

He nodded.

"I haven't had a dress in a year. Every extra penny I had went to clothe Miranda, who's growing like a weed, and you're buying yourself a fancy suit!"

"I have a few more I left back at the boardinghouse where I stay. I figured I'd only need one here."

"You're right you'll need only one. You're going to need it for them to bury you in!" she exclaimed, flinging her arms out in anger. "Why in hell did you come home looking like some kind of saddle tramp with leprosy? When I found that money, I thought you'd stolen it!"

"Talk about trust!"

"I thought that man who hit you was the one you stole it from, or some kind of bounty hunter."

"No. Just leave him out of this, Bertha."

"What's he got to do with this money?"

"Nothing. I didn't steal it from him or anybody else. The money's mine—ours—fair and square. Now just leave him out of this," he repeated more sternly.

She backed up on that topic, but she wasn't done venting all the explosive anger pent up inside her, not at all. She had a lot more bones to pick with Sam.

"I thought there weren't going to be any secrets between us, Sam," she told him. "I told you all about Arthur, even though there wasn't that much to tell. Hell, this makes Arthur look like peanuts! Why in hell didn't you tell me you had this money as soon as you came home?" she demanded.

"Because I wanted to know you'd take me back because I was your husband, not because I was rich."

"Well, it didn't work, did it?" she yelled.

"I guess not."

"I didn't welcome you back with open arms right away because you looked so awful. I thought you'd only come back because this was the only place that would take you in all penniless and dirty." She was fairly screaming now. "It's pretty damn insulting to be somebody's last resort."

Sam's face was turning red and he was rapidly losing his grin. "So, if I had come to your door all dressed up in my suit and tie, you'd have welcomed me with open arms?"

"Welcomed you? Open arms?" She threw her hands up in the air. "Hell, I'd have had a parade and a great big, gol-dang brass band. I'd have made the Centennial Celebration look like a Temperance Meeting. I'd have been plum delighted to see a husband who could do his share of the work and pay the bills on this farm!"

She could see all the warning signs of his increasing anger and didn't care. Him and his blasted secrets, and thinking it was all so very funny to have fooled her like this for all these years! She was about to give him that piece of her mind to choke on, and she'd make sure it was really salty.

"Even if you didn't come home, why in hell didn't you send me some money in those two years?"

"So you don't really give a damn whether I came home or not as long as you get money. All you really want is a rich husband, is that it, Bertha?" he countered. "Is that why you were keeping company with Quinn, 'cause he's almost as rich as Henry Richardson and a lot easier to get to see?"

"I'll give you rich husband!" she cried. "I'll give you Quinn right on your head. Maybe this time I'll do the job that some stupid, toothless man couldn't get right!"

Bertha picked up the pillow and flung it at his head. He

bounced it off his arm and onto the floor. She picked up the other pillow and flung it at him with no more success.

"Oh, you think you're so smart, Mr. Samuel I-Know-How-to-Use-a-Revolver Hamilton. Let's see you try this!"

She picked up the carpetbag and tried to fling it at him, too. It was a good bit heavier than the pillows and didn't go as far or as high. It struck him in the groin, sending him, doubled over and moaning, onto the bed.

"Bertha, wait . . ." he groaned, rolling on the mattress.

She stomped past him, almost shaking the floor with her anger. She had half a mind to turn and kick him in the butt that still stuck up in the air. No, that would really be adding insult to injury.

Instead, in order to vent her seething anger, she pulled the bedroom door open with such force that it hit the wall behind. The doorknob made a big dent in the plaster, sending cracks up the wall.

She stood in the middle of the kitchen and yelled, "Get out of here!"

"It's the middle of the night."

"I don't care if it's Doomsday! Get out of here now!"

"I will not."

She paced the kitchen floor.

"You're so damn rich, you can just go into town and rent yourself a big fancy room and fill it with all of Miss Sadie's *and* Miss Rosie's girls, and I hope they give you the pox and your nose rots off—not to mention anything else. And you can eat steak and white bread and oysters, and I hope you choke on them!"

He stood in the doorway, feet planted stubbornly apart. Very calmly he stated, "This is my house and I'm not leaving it."

"Fine. Fine. You just stay here all alone like I've been." She headed toward the front door. "*I'll* leave."

Sam swallowed hard before he said what he had to say.

He'd sworn he'd never do this, but this was a pretty drastic time.

"If you leave, you can't take Miranda with you."

She whirled around. "What?"

He glared at her sternly. "You heard me. She's my daughter. Any woman who deserts her husband has no right to his property or his children."

"You bastard!"

He just stood there and watched her. He tried to keep his face a mask of stone, but inside his heart was aching.

"You've been listening to that weasel Martin again, and those two old crows."

Cautiously he stepped toward her across the kitchen floor. There weren't any pillows in here, and he didn't want to get hit with anything harder than she might be able to get her hands on.

"You know I really don't want to do that, Bertha," he told her in a much gentler tone of voice.

He placed one arm about her shoulder and tried to guide her back toward the bedroom.

"Now, just come back to bed and we'll settle all this in the morning. I promise, once you've had the chance to think about this, you won't be nearly so angry."

"No." She wiggled out of his grasp. "I'll sleep with Miranda."

He tried to hold her again. "You wouldn't want to wake her."

Once more she slipped out of his embrace. "Then I'll sleep on the sofa."

Bertha headed toward the parlor when, out of the corner of her eye, she noticed Miranda's bedroom door was open.

"Oh, my." Feeling the chill of fear and apprehension creeping up her arms, she cautiously approached the door. "Don't let happen what I think has happened."

"What is it?" Sam hurried to her side.

She gave the door a gentle push inward. The covers on

Miranda's bed were thrown back, as if she'd left the bed in a hurry.

"She ran away again," Bertha said. Then she looked up at Sam, her eyes brimming with tears. "Oh, dear God, I hope it's only that she's run away again."

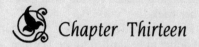 Chapter Thirteen

"She must've heard us arguing," Sam said.

"It's all your fault for not telling me the truth in the first place," Bertha snapped.

"Me?" Sam jabbed his finger at his chest. Then he pointed it directly at Bertha. "You were the one who was shouting and throwing things."

"I threw a pillow! How noisy is a pillow?"

"Two pillows."

"Okay, so it was twice as noisy. And we were *both* shouting," she reminded him.

"You're right," he replied more softly.

"Of course I am." Her voice lowered in volume, too, in response to his soothing words, not to mention in surprise that he would admit he'd been wrong, too.

"We shouldn't have yelled at each other, and I should've told you we were rich a long time ago," he admitted.

"Yes, you should have."

He placed his arm around her shoulder and drew her to him. This time she didn't pull away. Instead, she laid her head against the hollow of his shoulder. He placed a kiss on the top of her head.

"Come on, sweetheart, don't worry," he said comfortingly. "Miranda's probably on her way to the Picketts right now."

"In the dark?"

"She could probably go there and back twenty times

blindfolded. She's got her own little path worn through the field. She'll be safe as long as she follows the path."

Bertha looked up at him skeptically.

Sam released his embrace and headed for the front door. "Okay, I'll go bring her back."

He gave a little chuckle as he pulled on his shoes. "I'll bet Tom and the missus are going to be thrilled to see her turn up on their doorstep at this hour of the night."

"They're going to be really thrilled to see us, too."

"Us?"

Bertha grabbed the shawl she kept hanging on a peg by the door and swirled it over her shoulders.

"I'm going with you. I . . . I just couldn't bear to sit around here with nothing to do but wait."

"Me, neither. Come on."

He held the door open for her as they both set off into the night.

Sam kept the lantern shining on the little worn path as they traveled across the field.

Bertha kept looking from side to side, just in case Miranda had veered off the path and gotten lost. She held her breath as each hillock and mound of grass came into view, until she could see clearly that it wasn't Miranda, fallen and hurt. Then she felt relieved until she spotted the next indistinguishable mound in the distance.

She brushed her hand through the bushes at the front of the Picketts' house, just in case Miranda had lost her nerve about knocking on their door in the middle of the night and had decided to hide in the bushes until morning.

Sam knocked insistently on the door.

"Yoo-hoo! Tom! Yoo-hoo!"

Bertha came to stand behind him. She cuddled up close so as not to get in his way as he knocked on the door, and so her skirt wouldn't brush against the lantern. She wrapped both arms around him, as if he could keep her safe from her fears for their daughter.

"Oh, my gosh, you must be really worried," she mumbled into the comforting warmth of his strong back.

"Of course I am."

"I mean *really* worried. You've done the unthinkable— something you absolutely hate."

"What's that?"

"You yelled 'yoo-hoo.' "

"You're absolutely right," he agreed. "I really hate that, and I am really worried about Miranda." He started rapping on the door again. Throwing his head back, one more time he howled, "Yoo-hoo! Tom!"

Finally, through the window, the flickering light of a candle could be seen coming closer to the door.

Tom rubbed his eyes in the light of the lantern.

"Sam!" His eyes were still half closed. He was too sleepy even to smile a greeting. "You know you're the only man I'd let knock on my door at this hour and not punch in the face."

"We can't find Miranda."

Suddenly Tom looked much more awake. "Did she run away again? She doesn't usually run off in the middle of the night."

"Well," —Sam looked back at Bertha—"we had a bit of an argument. Miranda must've overheard us shouting and run away."

"Must've been a whale of an argument," Tom said, running his whole hand down over his sleepy face.

Sam just nodded.

"We were kind of hoping, being as it was dark out, that she'd come to your house where there are folks she likes, instead of going to her hiding place," Sam explained.

"Nope," Tom answered with a big yawn. "I haven't seen her. If she's here, she didn't come to the house. I'm awful sorry."

"Sorry we bothered you," Sam apologized. He and Bertha turned to go.

"No, wait," Tom said through another yawn. He was managing to speak a little faster. He must actually have been waking up. "I'll get dressed. I'll get Del up, and we'll help you search for her."

"She's probably already home, asleep in bed." Sam gave a laugh, but it didn't hold any humor.

"Maybe. No sense taking a chance in the dark. And with all the weird happenings that've been going on lately around here, you might be able to use a few more sets of eyes and ears," Tom offered.

"I sure appreciate it."

Sam tried to sound appreciative, and he was, for all their efforts. But he wasn't too happy Tom had to bring up the weird happenings that had been going on. He didn't want Miranda or Bertha involved in any of it. The worst part was, it didn't look as if he was going to be able to keep them out of it after all.

Within minutes Del was up and pulling on his shoes and socks in the kitchen.

"Doggone little pest," he muttered between gigantic yawns. "Getting a body up this time of night. I'll bet she's home, all snug and warm in bed, laughing her fool head off at us, thinking we're the biggest bunch of idiots on the face of the earth. And we are, too, falling for all her dirty tricks."

He gulped down a cup of coffee.

"Rotten little runt, getting everybody all riled up for nothing. When I get my hands on her, I'm really going to give her what-for!"

He might have been grumbling, but Bertha noticed Del was ready and standing at the doorway, with his lantern in hand, before anyone else was.

"If she falls down a well or out the loft window, and gets herself killed, I swear, I'm going to wring her scrawny little neck!"

Del shifted nervously from one foot to the other.

"Hey, c'mon. What's keeping you all?" he called to them. "I want to find the little pipsqueak and get home and get a little sleep before I have to be up again with the chores."

"Easy, Del, easy," Tom said. "You know I'd let you sleep in for just one day, but them cows are hard taskmasters."

Del just grinned, but he scuffed his feet restlessly against the floor.

"Now, Tom," Sam suggested, "I figure you should go looking through the barn, because the animals are all used to you coming in there anyway and won't be alarmed."

"Sure." He nodded and headed out the door.

Sam cautiously eyed Rachel. She was standing by the kitchen table, coffeepot in hand, and watching eagerly for the next step in the plan to find his missing child. He could hardly ask her to go tramping through the clumps of trees along the riverbank, or climbing through the outbuildings in her delicate condition. On the other hand, she'd been so supportive, he couldn't leave her out entirely, either.

"Mrs. Pickett, do you think you could you'd stay here just in case Miranda shows up?" he offered.

"Oh, definitely," she answered eagerly.

"I . . . I really don't think we'll take too long." Geez, Sam, he chided himself. How could you lie to them all like this? "But, just in case, if you could keep the coffee on."

"Oh, yes. And . . . and some warm milk for Miranda when you find her."

He nodded. "That would be mighty good of you, ma'am."

He turned to Bertha. She was sniffing and dabbing at her nose with her handkerchief. It didn't take a genius to see she was awful upset. He wasn't sure how much good she would be at searching in her condition, either. But it would be all the worse for her if she had to sit still, waiting with nothing to do for news of their daughter.

"Bertha," he asked gently, "do you think you're up to looking through the outbuildings, the toolshed and all?"

Quickly she tucked her handkerchief away and nodded vigorously.

"I know you can do it," he told her encouragingly.

She might be crying now—who wouldn't with a missing child? But she was a strong woman, he knew. She'd managed seven years on her own. She could find the strength still hidden within her to search for their child.

"How about me?" Del asked. "I sure hope you didn't get me up for nothing."

"You take the chicken coop and the outhouse."

His eyes grew wide and his upper lip curled in disgust.

"Geez! Not only do I not get to sleep because of the little botheration, now I got to search the two smelliest places on the farm."

He slapped his arms helplessly at his sides.

"I'll be sure not to forget the pigpen, either, Mr. Hamilton."

Del headed out the door, muttering, "You owe me, Miranda. Boy, do you owe me big this time."

He wandered off into the darkness.

Chicken coop and outhouse, my foot, he complained to himself as he kicked at the clumps of grass. Outbuildings, barn, springhouse. What did grown-ups know? They were all off track, way off track.

There was only one place Miranda could be. Her special hiding place. The one that used to be *his* special hiding place, Del thought with a wry twist of his lips. That was, until the pesky little pipsqueak had stolen it from him.

He'd never needed a hiding place before Ma married Tom Pickett and started having all those little Picketts. Once they started overrunning the house, even overflowing into his own bedroom, he decided he needed some time to himself, and a special place he could go to be alone to do some thinking.

He'd found this really swell place about as far from the pesky little Picketts as he could possibly get in a short space of time. He hadn't known then how slick Miranda was at snooping around, or what a pain in the neck she could be.

As he headed out over the field, he shut all but one panel on the lantern so the others wouldn't be able to see where he was going. Miranda might be a big pest, but he'd promised never to give away her secret, and he never broke his promises.

He cut across the field, heading toward the Hamiltons' farm. He really liked Mr. Hamilton—he still did, no matter what Mrs. Hamilton might have said about him earlier. He was glad to see them getting along again.

It seemed the best place to look for a hiding place was someplace a person felt safe. He'd always felt good over at the Hamiltons', until Miranda started tailing him like a lovesick puppy.

That Miranda was a clever little vixen for only six.

Sometimes Del didn't think she was a kid at all, even though he'd seen her, all pink and squalling and ugly, right after she was born. He'd watched her grow up this far, although, at this rate, he wondered if she'd make it to seven.

She was really a midget masquerading as a kid, or some kind of pixie from another world, some sort of changeling child like in his little sisters' fairy-tale books, come to play tricks on mere mortals like him. No kid could come up with some of the stuff she did.

Whenever she came to play at his house—or more likely to pester him—she'd run across the field from her house, heading for the Picketts. She'd worn her own little path across the field.

But whenever she wanted to run away to her own special place, she'd cut across the field just as if she were heading for the Picketts, only until she'd made it over the rise of the hill. That way she'd fooled them all into thinking her hiding place was at the Pickett farm.

But then she'd cut sideways along the ridge, always making sure never to walk the same exact way twice in a row so she wouldn't wear a path. Then she'd double back to her own farm.

There was a small, unused room behind the tack room in the barn. It hadn't been used in so long, probably everybody forgot it was even there. That was where she could sit and think, or sit and fume about what had made her angry, until she'd calmed down and decided to go back home.

She'd fitted up the place with an old pillow and an old horse blanket no one would miss. Usually she only went there during the daytime, so she hadn't put any candles in there—thank goodness! It would be just like Miranda to burn down her own barn.

Del headed there now. She'd probably be sleeping. Good. He'd take a great deal of pleasure in waking up the little stinker and hauling her all the way back to her parents, who were probably out of their minds with worry, still searching for her on his parents' farm.

Del walked through the quiet barn, smelling the hay and manure, and listening to the quiet snuffling of the animals in their stalls. He opened the door to the tack room and passed through the bridles, harnesses, and saddles hanging on the walls, and the bits of leather, buckram, and sinew meant to repair them laid out on shelves beneath. He pushed open the little door on the other side of the room and stuck his lantern in.

"Geez! Turn that light down," Miranda commanded. She pulled her rough horse blanket up over her head. "I'm trying to sleep in here."

Del moved into the room.

"Yeah? Well, ain't that just too bad."

He pulled the blanket down, exposing her face. He held the lantern up so it would shine right on her. She raised her arm to shield her eyes.

"I'd be home asleep in my own comfortable bed right now if it wasn't for you, Miss Pain-in-the-Butt."

"Del?" Tossing the blanket down over her lap, she sat up and started brushing at the bits of straw that clung to her nightgown. "What are you doing here? I thought you swore you'd never set foot—"

"Your parents are worried sick about you," Del scolded. "What the heck is wrong with you? What are you doing running away this time of night?"

Now that she'd removed the thick blanket and lowered her arm, he could see her whole face. In the brighter light he could see little white trickles down her smudged cheeks.

"You've been crying," he accused.

"I have not!"

"Yes, you have."

Roughly she wiped at her cheeks with the back of her hand. Then, with all the evidence of her weakness erased, she glared at him defiantly.

"So what if I have? What's it to you?"

"I . . . I don't like to see little kids cry."

"I'm not a little kid," she protested.

"I didn't think so." He put the lantern down on top of a wooden box and sat down beside her. "But you don't usually cry, either. What happened this time?"

She pressed her lips together and kicked at the straw and the blanket for a while. She picked at a knothole in the wood beside her head. Del just waited.

At least she said, "Oh, Del. They were fighting something awful this time!"

Her red-rimmed eyes were big with fright and horror.

"I was really scared. I didn't know what to do. I heard them both yelling real loud. And Mommy even saying *swear words* which she *never* does, unless she's *really, really* mad! I heard them throwing things. I heard Sam groaning something awful, so she must've hurt him. Then something almost went through the wall into my bedroom. Then Mommy ran out into the kitchen and told Sam to go away. When he said he wouldn't, she said she would. And he told her she could."

Suddenly she left off picking at the wood. She threw her arms around Del's neck, holding on so hard he almost couldn't breathe, and sobbed uncontrollably.

"Whoa, whoa," he managed to croak. He managed to untangle her and sit her down again beside him instead of practically on top of him.

"Oh, Del!" she wailed pathetically. "I thought they loved

each other. I thought they'd finally made up. I thought, finally, for once, I'd have a whole family, like the other kids."

"Some of the other kids don't have mothers and fathers, and they still have a whole family. My real dad died—I mean *really* died—before I was born, but Ma and I were still a whole family, even before Tom came along. Now we're a whole lot of family," he added with a chuckle.

He didn't feel like laughing. Sometimes it wasn't anything to laugh about. But he couldn't stand seeing Miranda so upset, or seeing her cry. He had to do something to cheer her up.

Miranda tried to smile, but her eyebrows kept pulling down into a frown and pushing her mouth in the same direction.

"Sam said if Mommy left, she couldn't have me. I want my Mommy. I love her. She's my mommy. Why would Sam want to take me away from her?"

"I guess because he loves you, too."

"How could he love me? He didn't even know he had a kid."

"I think it's got something to do with as soon as a man and wife start thinking about having a kid, they love it already, just like my mom and dad love this baby already, without even knowing if it's a boy or a girl or what its name is going to be. I think your mom and dad really wanted kids a long time ago. So they've been loving you for a long time."

"But how could he love me and not want me to be with my mommy? Is he trying to hurt mommy? Or me?"

"No. I think sometimes when people want something real bad, they're not very good at sharing, and sometimes they don't stop to think about anybody else."

"I wish they could learn. I want my mommy, and I want Sam, too. I like him. I could love him, too, if he was my father."

"He *is* your father, stupid."

"I know. I just can't make myself call him Daddy. I guess it's 'cause I didn't have one for so long."

"Maybe. I don't know. I didn't mind calling Tom 'Dad' right away."

"Why?"

"I don't know. Maybe 'cause I knew my real dad was really dead, and Tom was the only father I'd ever have."

"Sam's the only dad I ever had, and I thought he was dead, too. Except maybe Mr. Quinn might've been my dad, but he doesn't count 'cause I don't think Mommy ever really liked him all that much anyway. I didn't like him at all."

"Why not?"

She shrugged. "I guess 'cause he was always patting me on the head."

"Yeah, I used to hate it when people did that. I guess that's one of the good things about getting tall and growing hair. People stop patting you on the head. Mr. Richardson always did that to me."

"You *saw* Mr. Richardson?" she demanded, eyes wide with shock.

Del shrugged. "Sure."

"He *touched* you?" Her eyes grew wider.

He shrugged again. He'd never thought it was that big a deal. "He patted my head. I hated it."

"Is he really as old and ugly as they say?"

"Naw, not really."

"Were you ever in his house?"

"Nope."

"Oh."

Del could tell she was very disappointed.

"I love that house," she said with a sigh.

He curled up his lip. "Yuck! Are you crazy? That monstrosity?"

"Yep. Wouldn't it be great to have Mommy and Sam and me all living in that house together?"

"No, it would be awful."

"Yep. That's what I want. I want Mommy and Sam living together happy with me. Now they only yell and throw things, and try to kick each other out of the house. I hate it when they fight. I hate it! I hate it!"

She started kicking her feet in frustration. Del was afraid she'd plant one of those hard shoes right on his shin bone. Or worse yet, that she'd kick the box and knock the lantern over. It wouldn't be easy to get out of the tack room through a fire.

"Whoa, stop! Don't worry, Miranda," he said quickly. "Really, really, there's nothing to worry about."

What made him do this, he never could rightly tell, but it seemed the proper thing to do at the time. He'd seen Tom do it when Sally or Willy got all upset. Alice would only let Ma hold her. It seemed a grown-up kind of thing to do to comfort a kid. Well, he had his doubts about Miranda being just a kid, but he was almost all grown-up.

He reached out and put his arm around her shoulders. He pulled her closer to him and reached up and started stroking her hair, trying to calm her.

"Moms and dads always fight," he tried to tell her. "Even my mom and dad. Heck, my mom almost tried to shoot my dad once."

Miranda stopped kicking. Del breathed a sigh of relief.

"She *did*?" She gave a little giggle.

"Yeah, but she missed."

"Oh, rats! No blood."

"You are weird! Anyway, the important thing is that they kiss and make up afterward. When your parents came to my house looking for you, they'd already kissed and made up. They weren't fighting any more. But they really are worried about you. You have to go back."

"I know." She breathed a sigh of resignation.

Then Del saw a light coming into her eyes that made him worry even more.

"Can't I just stay here until morning?"

"Are you listening? I just told you they were out of their minds worrying for you."

"But I have a plan."

"Oh, no." Feelings of dread were already creeping up his back. He started shaking his head.

Miranda sprang excitedly to her knees, ready to explain.

"No, no. Listen. It's a really good plan."

"*Nothing* involving you is a good plan, you little trouble-maker!"

"You don't have to tell them you found me, Del. I'll just stay here long enough to get them to promise they'll stop fighting and live together happy with me."

Del grimaced. "I don't think that's going to work. I think you'd better go right home."

"Why not? Have you ever tried running away?"

"No."

Thinking back to what a little sissy he'd been at this age, he'd never really tried much of anything until Tom taught him how to fight.

"But I still don't think it's a good idea. I can't lie and tell them I didn't find you."

"You could for me, Del," she said sweetly, leaning against him.

"Nope," he stated firmly. Then, under his breath, he muttered, "Geez, where do you come up with these things?"

She sat up straight.

"I won't let your parents be worried out of their skulls any longer than they have to. They're good parents, and they're good to you. Sometimes better than you deserve, you little pest."

Miranda humphed, crossed her arms over her chest, and turned her back to him.

"You're so darned smart about everything else," he continued. "Why can't you understand what I'm talking about now?"

She uncrossed her arms. "Yeah, I guess I understand."

"So don't be so darned stubborn."

He rose and picked up the lantern.

"Let's go back now, Miranda. I'll tell them I found you in the outhouse."

"I would *not* hide there!"

"It's that or the chicken coop."

"Yick!"

"Do you want me to tell them where I really found you? All about your special place?"

"Nope. But I hate outhouses. When I grow up, I'm going to have a house with a bathroom inside."

"I don't know if Mr. Richardson has a bathroom inside or not."

"Why don't you just tell them you found me wandering around out in the field?" she suggested.

"'Cause they're not so dumb they'd believe you were out wandering around for this long in the dark."

"Okay, how about if you go back first, tell them you didn't see me, and then I—?"

"And have them so worried their hair turns gray? No way!"

"Okay, how about if *I* go back first? They'll be making so much fuss over me, they won't even bother to question you. They probably won't even notice when you come in."

"Thanks." Del frowned, thinking hard. At last he said, "Okay. It's really against my better judgment, but—"

"You're thirteen," she reminded him with a little sneer. "You don't have any better judgment."

"What makes you think you're so smart? I found you this time."

Miranda threw a laugh back at him as she started to run out of the tack room. "Ha! You won't find me next time, Del."

He waited through two verses of "Amazing Grace," which was all he could remember, and all the verses of

"Yankee Doodle Dandy," even some of the dirty lyrics Jimmy Walters and Allen Douglas had made up. He wondered if Jimmy and Allen could be tried for treason for doing that to a patriotic song?

Finally he figured Miranda ought to have had enough time to get back to his house, have her parents make a big fuss about her, and then he could come strolling in and they'd all ignore him. Maybe he could even manage to get a little more sleep before he had to get up and milk the cows.

He headed toward his house with longing thoughts of his comfortable bed. He noticed he was starting to cast a shadow as the sun came up behind him. The lights in the kitchen were dimmer in the increasing dawn.

He extinguished his lantern and left it in a corner on the porch. He hoped he wouldn't need it again anytime soon, until it was time for a sleigh ride in the dark. He hoped he *never* needed it again to hunt for Miranda.

When he opened the door, the kitchen was silent.

"Ma! Ma!"

He hadn't noticed Rachel, dozing by the fire. She looked up at him and sighed.

"Del?" She stretched and shrugged, trying to rouse herself.

"Oh, Ma. I'm sorry I woke you up."

"That's okay." She looked toward the window that was lightening from the dawn. "I'll need to be getting up soon anyway."

He looked around the empty kitchen. "Why are you still up? Where is everybody? Did they all go home?"

He knew he should've stuck to just the two verses of "Amazing Grace."

"They're not back yet."

"Not . . ."

Don't say too much, Del, he warned himself. Don't give yourself away.

He had a bad feeling he was in a heap of trouble. He had

an even worse feeling that Miranda was in an even bigger heap of trouble—if they could find her.

"Not back? Haven't they found Miranda yet?" He sat down on the floor at her feet.

"No."

"Geez! Where could she be?"

"Isn't that what you were supposed to find out?" Tom asked from the doorway.

Del turned around with a start. "Well, yeah, sure. We all were."

He just knew he had guilt written all over his face, in big bold red letters that nobody could miss. He just hoped Tom was too tired to notice them right now.

Tom hung his hat on the hat rack by the door. Sam and Bertha followed him inside.

Bertha held a big handkerchief up to her face and her shoulders were heaving up and down real quick, like she was crying very hard. Sam had his arm wrapped around her shoulder and was holding her real close to him, like he was trying to hold her up to keep from falling as she walked.

Boy, he was feeling bad enough already, Del thought. If ever any two people had deliberately intended to look miserable and pathetic trying to make him feel more guilty, they couldn't beat Sam and Bertha right now.

"I don't know where she could be," Bertha wailed.

Sam tried to settle her in a seat at the table.

Rachel had already gotten out of the rocking chair and was pouring cups of coffee for everyone.

Sam swirled the contents of his cup around and glanced over to Tom. "I could sure use something with a bit more bite to it."

Tom motioned with his head for Sam to follow him into the parlor.

Bertha hadn't even touched her cup. She just kept sitting there, dabbing at her eyes and sniffing. Rachel stood behind her, patting her on the shoulder comfortingly.

"I checked all through the barn, woke the hired hands and put them to searching the hayloft," Tom was saying as he and Sam emerged from the parlor. "They didn't find anything, either."

"I checked out the springhouse," Sam said. "I even moved crocks of butter just to see if she'd somehow managed to squeeze herself onto a shelf. She'd have to be the size of one of her dolls to hide there."

Sam took a hearty swig from his cup. He rubbed his hand backward along his forehead, pushing his hair out of his eyes.

"I peered down that well 'til I thought I'd fall in myself. But at least I know she's not down there, thank goodness."

Tom nodded to Bertha, still sitting at the table. "Did Mrs. Hamilton search the outbuildings?"

"She managed to do the corncrib. But she's so upset, she really isn't much good. So afterward, I got to looking through the tool shed and the smoke house, too. Miranda would have to be hanging from the ceiling to hide in the smokehouse—and I really think I could tell my daughter from a smoked ham or links of sausage any day."

Tom clapped Sam on the back. "That's good. Keep your sense of humor. It might be all you two have to get you through this."

"Oh, sweet Jesus, Tom," Sam moaned. "Tell me it ain't going to get that bad."

Tom took a sip from his cup and walked over to where Del was still sitting by the fire.

"How about you, Del? Did you check the outhouse?"

Geez! Why did he have to ask hard questions?

"Um . . . She wasn't in the outhouse," he answered.

It *was* the truth that Miranda wasn't in the outhouse, he told himself as he fiddled with the tail of his shirt. And he hadn't exactly said he *had* checked the place. So he wasn't exactly lying, he figured. Not exactly.

"How about the chicken coop?"

He shook his head. "She wasn't in the chicken coop."

He wasn't really stretching the truth, or embellishing the truth. Then why did he still feel so awful? Why did his guts feel about as twisted as the cloth he held in his hand?

"Pigpen?"

"Heck, no." He gave nervous laugh. "Do you really think Miranda would hide in the pigpen?"

"I guess not," Tom said. "Well, son, it seems that Miranda wasn't in any of those places, and you know, I discovered a sort of funny thing myself."

"What's that?" he asked.

Even though he could hear little alarms of warning that he shouldn't be asking that question, he knew Tom was going to tell him the answer whether he wanted to hear it or not.

"I noticed that you weren't in any of those places, either."

"I . . . how . . . but . . ."

"It's a little hard to miss when I've got a big overview of the barnyard from the hayloft."

"Oh, botheration," Del muttered. He hung his head and twisted the tail of his shirt even harder. He was done for now.

"I know you don't lie, Del," Tom said. "So would you please tell me why you were lollygagging around—"

"I *wasn't*!"

"When you were supposed to be searching?"

"I *was*!"

"Then will you please tell me where you went?"

"I . . . I can't tell you."

"Why not?" Tom gestured toward Sam and Bertha. "When you can see how heartsick the Hamiltons are, why didn't you do as you were told?"

"I . . . I went to Miranda's special hiding place, and she told me not to tell where it is, and I promised I wouldn't, so I can't tell you where I went."

Tom released a deep breath. "I'm very disappointed in you, Del."

"Why? Because instead of doing as I was told I went and did what I knew was right?"

Ordinarily he'd *never* talk to Tom that way, but his nerves were stretched to the limit, and at times like these, some things just come shooting out of a person's mouth that never would have come out if he was calm.

Tom backed up. Very quietly he responded, "You've got a point there, son."

"I . . . I didn't mean any disrespect—"

"That's not important now, anyway, Del," Sam said, coming quickly to stand beside him. "Miranda's what's important. Was she there?"

Oh, consarnation! Oh, hell and damnation heaped upon his soul for all eternity! Oh, double horse puckies! He was really in for it now!

"Don't ask dumb questions, Sam," Bertha said.

Reprieved! Oh, bless you, Mrs. Hamilton!

"Of course she wasn't there," she continued. "Del's a good, responsible boy. If she were there, he would've brought her home to us."

She brought the handkerchief up to her face and started sniffing again.

Doggone, Miranda! Where was she? If she'd come here like she'd told him, he wouldn't be going through all this now. He'd be in his bed already.

Now he was probably going to get the punishment of his life. Maybe Reverend Knutson would denounce him right from the pulpit in church next Sunday. Maybe the congregation would get so riled, they'd even try to lynch him. That is, if he survived his parents and the Hamiltons first. But he didn't care. He couldn't take it! He just couldn't take the guilt and the pressure anymore!

"Yes, ma'am, she was there," he answered.

Slowly Bertha lowered the handkerchief and stared at him. Tom and Sam turned and stared at him. Rachel dropped the coffeepot with a loud clank.

"She was there and you *didn't* bring her home?" Bertha

said in a low, shaking voice that was still hoarse from crying.

"What in tarnation is wrong with you, boy?" Tom demanded.

"She was there," Bertha repeated very softly, almost as if she were repeating it for her own benefit instead of to ask Del again. "But you *didn't* bring her home."

"Why on earth not?" Sam demanded. "What did you do, just leave her there?"

"Don't get mad at me, sir, please," Del pleaded. "I tried to talk her into coming straight here. Really, I did. She *told* me she was coming straight here."

"You let her come alone? In the dark?" Sam demanded, eyes growing wide with disbelief.

Darn you, Miranda! You've gotten me in more trouble than you'll ever be worth.

"It . . . she . . . she made it sound like a good idea at the time," Del offered by way of excuse. "Honest, Mr. Hamilton, you've got no idea how that girl can twist a guy around her little finger and make it sound like you want to do everything she says, exactly the way she says to do it."

Sam turned his lips into a wry grin. "Oh, yes, I do."

"She said if she came home first, you'd be so happy to see her, you wouldn't question me about where she'd been, and that way I wouldn't have to give away her hiding place. Honest, she said she was coming right here."

"And that was it?"

Del was twisting his shirttail so hard, the seams were about to rip.

"She tried to tell me she was going right to your house, but I told her you were all here. Then she got some wild idea into her head about hiding again and swearing not to come out until you two promised to stop fighting. I told her that was dumb, because parents always fight, but they make up again, too."

"Do you think she ran away to another hiding place?" Sam asked. "Just to scare us?"

"I hope not," Del answered. "If she does, I couldn't imagine where else she'd go around here."

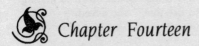 Chapter Fourteen

"Do you think she went back to our house anyway?" Bertha asked.

Del shrugged. "I . . . I don't know."

He'd always figured Miranda wasn't the kind to go home to an empty house where there was no one to make a fuss over her. Of course, he couldn't tell Mrs. Hamilton something like that now, although, being a mom, she'd probably already figured Miranda out.

"Well, it's getting light out," Sam said, placing his empty coffee cup on the kitchen table. "It'll be easier to go look for her. Why don't we wake up the hands and see if we can't scare her up?"

"We've already looked everywhere," Bertha said, shaking her head with hopelessness.

"We'll look again, one more time," Sam told her.

"And if we still don't find her?"

"Then we'll go into town. Maybe the sheriff can help. There's just one more thing I have to do."

"What's that?"

But Sam was already heading toward the door.

"I've got to go home first. C'mon, Bertha. Tom, I'll meet you there."

Bertha nearly ran into their house. "Miranda! Miranda!" she called as she ran through the house. She even ducked to look under the sofa in the parlor and under each bed.

Sobbing, she sank into the rocking chair and waited.

257

Sam headed directly for the bedroom. When he came out again, Bertha stifled a gasp. He had his revolver and a gunbelt fastened around his waist. The holster hung lower than the other side. He'd tied the holster down to his leg.

"Do you know how to use that?" she asked.

"Yep."

"Are you sure?"

"Of course I'm sure, woman. What kind of idiot do you think I am, strapping on a gun and not knowing how to use it? That's not just dangerous—it's plum stupid!"

"How . . . how . . . ?" She couldn't even manage to ask him the rest of the question that plagued her. How could her gentle husband have learned how to wield a revolver like that? "I . . . I guess you'd need to know how to use a gun to protect yourself going through the woods in the mountains," she offered.

"Sometimes," she answered with a nod. "It's also not just dangerous, but plum stupid, to walk into a mining camp without knowing how to protect yourself."

Whether Sam knew how to use it or not, he sure *looked* as if he did, Bertha thought.

For his sake, and the sake of their child, she just prayed he really did.

"I'll stay here at your house, just in case she shows up here," Rachel offered. "Del and the other children are at our house, just in case she shows up there."

"Thanks, Rachel," Bertha said as Sam helped her up to the seat of the buckboard.

Sam's very touch, the strength of his hand, helped her to keep her own strength of heart. Together they could get through this. But she knew she could only do it if Sam was there.

After a night of searching, she had fallen into an exhausted sleep just before dawn. She hadn't even bothered to take off her clothing. She was lucky to have gotten off her shoes.

She'd managed to control her terror for her missing daughter enough not to need a handkerchief constantly, but she still kept one tucked up her sleeve, just in case.

"I don't know what we'd do without you," she told her friend.

"You'd find somebody else to wait here," Rachel told her. "You've got lots of friends, Bertha. Everyone will be willing to help you as much as they can."

Bertha just nodded as Sam slapped the reins over the horse's back and they took off.

She couldn't believe the horse ever traveled that slowly. Were the wheels actually turning backward? Had someone just picked up the town in the middle of the night and moved it about ten miles to the east? Or maybe somebody had moved her farm about ten miles to the west? She'd never imagined the town was so far away until she was in a hurry to get there.

Sam pulled the wagon to a halt directly in front of the sheriff's office. He bounded down from the seat, then rushed around to help Bertha down.

She was already trying to move as fast as she could, but Sam practically dragged her up to the fat man who was sitting in front of his building.

"Sheriff, we need your help right away," Sam declared.

The sheriff looked up at him and belched. He pounded a hammy fist on his chest.

"Oops, sorry. The wife made cabbage last night."

Was it the speed of the wagon as Sam had taken it careening through town? Was it the loud noise Sam had made as he yelled for the sheriff? Was it some kind of vulture's instinct that drew people to them because they were in trouble? Whatever it was, Bertha was dismayed to see a crowd already growing around them.

"We need your help," Sam repeated.

"What? Did the fairies carry off your house last night?" Sheriff Duncan snickered.

"No, my daughter!"

"The fairies took your daughter?" he repeated, his bleary eyes growing wide. "Wait a minute, Sam. I was just teasing." He squinted at him. "You haven't been drinking this early in the morning, have you?"

"No, Sheriff. Have you?"

"I'm a lawman, son." He raised his chest proudly and tried to suck in his rotund gut. "I don't drink on duty."

Bertha had to admire him for not drinking, but he sure did a lot of eating to make up for it instead.

"Miranda ran away," Sam announced.

Most of the people surrounding them made little noises of disappointment. All that speed and noise and fuss when Widow Crenshaw and Miss Barber had let them all know not too long ago that Miranda Hamilton was in the habit of running away every time she didn't get her way.

"Again?" Widow Crenshaw demanded.

"I don't know why you're bothering me with this," Sheriff Duncan complained. "Seems to me a good spanking would put a stop to all that nonsense right quick."

"I swear, Sheriff," Widow Crenshaw declared. "If this doesn't prove that Bertha Hamilton isn't a fit mother, I don't know what does!"

"There's nothing wrong with my mothering," Bertha said with a deep warning tone in her voice.

"But none of the other mothers in town seem to have any trouble at all with their children running away."

"Sometimes I wonder if Mrs. Douglas wouldn't be happy to see some of that brood of hers take off," Miss Barber mumbled.

Widow Crenshaw glared at Miss Barber.

"The Douglas boys and that Jimmy kid are in all sorts of trouble," Bertha reminded them. "All Miranda does is go off to have a little time by herself now and then. Del Williams used to do the same thing."

"But she shouldn't be wandering around," Widow Crenshaw protested. "She's a girl."

"Does it make it any easier when the child is a boy?"

Bertha asked. After everything she'd been through, she saw no need to put on kid gloves. She dropped all pretense of civility. "What about Eustace, Janet?"

Widow Crenshaw looked flustered for only a moment. Then she lifted her chin and haughtily inquired, "Eustace who?"

"It seems to me, since you didn't have much luck with your own son, you've been itching to have my daughter taken away from me for a long time, and it's gotten worse since Sam returned."

"The child needs to be with her father and . . . and with a responsible woman who can care for her."

"Like you, Janet?"

Widow Crenshaw lifted her head proudly. "I think I would be an excellent mother to a little girl."

"But . . . but, Janet," Miss Barber mumbled. "I thought *I* was going to—"

"Oh, do hush, Catherine!"

"But, I *am* younger—"

"Oh, Catherine, I never expected a mutiny from you!"

"Miranda needs her parents, Janet," Bertha continued. "Both of them. And as far as being responsible, I never had all your money, Janet. I had to work by myself for everything I have. I'm pretty pleased with what I've got and I intend to keep it. Sam and I are staying together, with our daughter."

"If you can find where she's run off to," Widow Crenshaw reminded her with a sneer.

"We'll find her. And you can go . . ." Bertha shuddered with the indecision of exactly how to finish her sentence. She decided to be at least a little polite. "Go find somebody else's life to ruin. Or better yet, mind your own business for a change."

"The welfare of this town is my—"

"Shut up, Janet!"

Widow Crenshaw gasped. Miss Barber giggled.

Bertha placed both fists on her hips and glared at the

women who had been making so much trouble for her for so long. She'd tried being polite. Now it was time to resort to plain and simple honesty.

"I've had enough of your meddling, and I've been through so much tonight, one more word out of you, and I think I just might forget I'm a lady and punch you right in your big, busy nose."

"Oh, oh," Widow Crenshaw flustered. "Sheriff, did you hear her threatening me with bodily harm?"

"Yeah. And if you don't shut up, I just might decide to turn a blind eye to that one." When Widow Crenshaw stared at him in outrage, he amended his decision. "On the other hand, I think I might rope off an area out back and charge admission."

"You'd be a rich man, Sheriff!" someone yelled from the back of the crowd. His remark was met with resounding cheers and at least a dozen offers to be the first to buy a ticket.

Widow Crenshaw seized Miss Barber by the wrist, shouldered her way through the crowd, and stomped off.

"Now what's all this about Miranda?" the sheriff asked. "If she's in the habit of doing this, why are you coming to me now? Why're you riling up the whole town?"

"Because she's been gone since last night," Sam explained. "She isn't in all her usual hiding places. We've searched the Picketts' farm and can't find her."

The sheriff scratched his several chins. "You've searched the Picketts' place. Did it ever occur to you to search your own place?"

Sam stared at the sheriff. "Well, she'd never hide out on her own farm."

"I don't care if she's hiding on the moon," Bertha interjected. "I can't find my daughter. We've searched all night until we've run out of places to look."

Sam stepped up onto the bench outside the sheriff's office. From his perch, he could look out over the crowd that had gathered.

"Look, folks," he started to explain. "I know I've been gone a long time. I don't even know some of you folks new to town. You all got no reason to be beholden to me. But my wife and I, and the Picketts, have been searching all night and we still can't find our little girl. All we're asking is some help."

"Well, shoot! Why didn't you say so, Sam?" someone called.

"Yeah, we thought you was accusing us."

"Thunderation, no!" Sam exclaimed. "I . . . we never thought that for a second!"

"We wouldn't take your kid, Sam."

"Heck, no. I already got six of my own."

Sam chuckled. He was relieved that no one held any grudges over imagined wrongs.

"Just tell us what we got to do," someone offered.

Sam looked out over the crowd.

"Charlie, Charlie Carter," he called, pointing him out. "You still got that swell hunting dog?"

"Sure. I'll go get her and meet you at your house." Charlie headed off for the dog pen he kept behind his house.

"Ian, Ian MacKenzie." Sam singled him out of the crowd. "Weren't you a scout or something during the war?"

Ian nodded. "Something like that."

"Think you could still do it?"

"Heck, yeah."

"Meet us at my house, too."

"Sure thing."

Sam spotted the blacksmith. "Fred, we're going to need you, too."

Fred just nodded and started heading for his horse.

In the sea of faces that confronted him, Sam noticed one in particular was missing.

"Quinn? Arthur Quinn?" he called.

No one responded.

"Where's Quinn?"

The crowd murmured and searched amongst themselves, but Arthur wasn't there. Sam hadn't thought he would be.

Bertha had been watching Sam with growing admiration. He had stepped in and immediately taken charge of the situation when she knew she'd never be able to handle it. He was her husband, and she was darned proud of him.

But now she felt cold chills of apprehension shivering in her stomach. Miranda was missing and Arthur wasn't here. Worse yet, Sam had drawn specific attention to the fact.

She'd known that Sam hated Arthur, and Arthur hated Sam. She knew Sam suspected Arthur of spying on them. She hadn't been able to prevent herself from speculating that Arthur might even be trying to hurt Sam. But hurt her daughter? Would Arthur be crazy enough to hold Miranda until she agreed to divorce Sam and marry him? How could Arthur stoop that low?

"Hey, Max!" the sheriff shouted. He bobbed his head back and forth, trying to spot the elusive boy. "Yeah, you, you nosy little whippersnapper. Don't try to duck behind anybody," he ordered, pointing his stubby finger in the boy's general direction. "I see you hanging around the back of folks there. You're probably trying to pick their pockets."

Max poked his head through a gap in the crowd. "Am not!"

"Yeah, well, instead of sticking your spotty little nose into other folks' business, why don't you get out here and make yourself useful for a change?"

Max eyed the sheriff cautiously. Sam didn't blame him. If it were him, he'd have his ears covered, just in case.

"What d'ya want?" the boy asked.

"Go run and get Mr. Quinn," Sheriff Duncan ordered.

"What for?" someone asked as Max took off at a run.

"Yeah, what do we need him for?"

"I want him here," Sam insisted.

"We might need some things from his store before we're through," the sheriff explained. Bertha hadn't thought he'd be sharp enough to figure out those kinds of things.

"Like what?"

"Like lanterns if we're searching 'til dark." The crowd started calling out suggestions.

"Picks in case she fell down a well."

"Ropes and pulleys."

"Block and tackle."

"Whiskey."

"She's a kid, for crying out loud!"

"But I'm grown up."

"Medical stuff."

"Hey, yeah, somebody ought to go wake Doc."

"Do you think we ought to set Reverend Knutson to praying?"

Sheriff Duncan rubbed his chins. "That might not be a bad idea."

Sam stepped off the bench and come to Bertha's side.

"Why do you want Arthur here?" she asked quietly, so no one else in the crowd could hear her suspicions.

"I just do."

"What if Max can't find him?" she asked cautiously. "Do you think he—"

"Look, we can't think anything of the sort right now," he said. "Let's just concentrate on finding Miranda."

Bertha frowned as she digested what he'd just said. She looked at him, puzzled.

"I thought you were the one who hated Arthur, and now you're defending him?"

"No. I'm not that forgiving," Sam said with a bitter laugh. "I just . . . let's just say I've got a different feeling about this."

"Sam? What are you talking about?"

She wanted an answer, but at the same time she was almost afraid of what he might tell her. If Miranda wasn't still hiding just to be cantankerous, and if Arthur hadn't actually taken her, then what had happened to their daughter? And what did Sam know that would make him think anything different?

Bertha gave a sigh of relief when Arthur finally showed up, straightening his shirt collar.

"I can't believe I overslept." He smiled sheepishly. "What in the world's going on here? That little rascal Max was banging on my door, wouldn't go away 'til I'd opened the store."

"Miranda Hamilton—the little girl—is missing," Sheriff Duncan explained.

"I *know* who she is," Arthur replied gravely.

He shot a quick glance toward Bertha. She could hardly bare to meet his gaze, after the horrible things she'd just been thinking about him.

"We need you to open the store now and keep it opened till we find her—just in case we need anything."

"Yeah, sure, help yourself, but I won't be there."

"Arthur!" Bertha couldn't help but exclaim.

"Pops can sit there and keep track of what you take."

"Yeah, sure," Pops replied with a nod. "I'd go with you myself if I could."

"Yeah, we know. Thanks, Pops," Sam said. Then he turned to Arthur and demanded, "But why won't you be there, Quinn?"

Arthur focused his gaze directly at Bertha and didn't change.

"Because I'm going to be searching with you. And *I'm* going to find her," he asserted. "I'm going to find her for you, Bertha."

"Don't say that, Arthur," she told him.

She could feel her face growing hot with embarrassment. How could he still bring this up after all the times she'd told him he'd never be her husband? How could he bring this up in front of all these people?

There was only one way she could manage to forgive him, she decided. If he could actually manage to find her daughter.

* * *

"Oh, come on, Sally, please."

"Don't whine, Del," Sally scolded. "It makes you sound like a baby."

"Look, you little thief, what more do you want?" he demanded. He pulled out the linings of his pockets, revealing how empty they were. Then he gestured toward the objects sitting on the kitchen table. "You've already got my pocketknife, my tin whistle, and two whole dollars I was saving up for when the traveling show comes through town in September."

Sally sat down at the table and began to sort through the things. Now and then she'd pick one up and turn it over and over in her hand, examining its worth.

"Now, as I see it—"

"Doggone it, Sally! Hurry up, would you?" He began pacing back and forth across the floor. "Miranda's missing and I'm going to miss all the excitement if you take much longer deciding."

"Now, as I see it—" she repeated a little more slowly, just to let him know she wasn't happy being interrupted. "You want me to stay here with Willy and Alice while you go out."

"Sitting home waiting is women's work," Del complained.

"Bertha's out looking, too."

Del shook his head. "She's a mother. That doesn't count. I'm a man."

Sally laughed.

"Nearly," Del asserted. "I want to be out doing what the men are doing."

"Peedling against trees?"

"No! C'mon, Sally. What else do you want?" He held out his hand, wrist up. "My blood?"

"Your bed."

"My bed?"

"You've got that really wonderful bed with the big high

wooden headboard, and I've got to sleep on that nickel bed."

"It's a wonder you don't get your pointy little head stuck between two of the poles," Del grumbled.

"How come you got a girl-looking bed, and I got a boy-looking bed?" Sally complained. "I think they're mixed up. So when you come back from hunting for Miranda—whether you find the spoilt little brat or not—I want you to move that nice big bed into my room and you take the nickel bed."

Del grimaced. "Geez, I don't know what Ma and Dad will say."

"I don't, either." Then she gave him a smug grin. "But I can pretty much tell you what they'll say if they find out you disobeyed Pa again and just left us here. And you're in enough trouble already," she warned. "I wouldn't risk it, if I was you."

"Geez! You're not seven. You're a midget, too," he grumbled under his breath.

"What?"

"You're a pain, Sally."

She just grinned at him. "Yes, but I've got a really nice bed. Now, go on, get out of here!" A little more softly she added, "I hope you find Miranda."

"I can't believe it." Sam slammed his hat down on the floor as soon as he walked in the door.

"I don't understand," Bertha murmured. "I just don't understand where she could be!"

She wasn't crying anymore. She felt drained of tears, as if she'd never be able to cry anymore. She hoped she'd never have to.

She collapsed into the rocking chair. She leaned forward, her head in her hands. Sam rested his hand gently on her shoulder. Just maintaining the physical contact between them seemed to be helping them to remain strong until Miranda could be found.

"We've searched every square inch of both farms," Tom said as he entered the Hamiltons' house.

The rest of the men in the search party filed in after him.

"She hasn't been back here," Rachel said. "I never left the house. . . . Well, just that once . . . or twice or so when I had to . . . well, use the facilities."

The men just milled around and harrumphed. Bertha understood perfectly well how frequent the use of the facilities was when a woman was in a certain condition, like Rachel.

"But if she'd shown up then," Rachel continued, "even if I wasn't here, I think she would've stayed."

"Could she have tried to reach one of the other farms?" Charlie Carter asked.

"I don't think she knows the way."

"She's pretty sharp. Wouldn't she just follow the road?"

"But why would she go anywhere else?" Bertha asked.

"Maybe this has something to do with it," Fred said, reaching up to the crumpled piece of paper stuck in the edge of the frame of the mirror hung over the mantel.

Bertha perked up immediately. As long as there was any new hope, even if it was as slim as a piece of paper, she was determined to see it followed to the end.

Fred handed the paper to Sam. He took it. He knew his hand wanted to tremble with nervousness, and anticipation that the news might be good. But he held his hand steady as a rock. It was a far, far chance the note bore good news, and he was going to need all his strength and courage to overcome it when it was not.

Slowly Sam began to unfold the paper.

"What is it?" everyone wanted to know.

"Oh, God, Sam. What is it?" Bertha gasped. She ran to his side and held on to his shoulder, strengthening the contact between them.

Sam laid the note on the kitchen table and tried to smooth out the wrinkles.

"What does it say?" she asked in a whisper.

"Should I read it aloud, Bertha?" Sam asked.

"Of course," she answered. "They're all our friends here. They've helped us so much, they deserve to know. Maybe they can help us even more." She gave a shuddering sigh. "By tomorrow everyone in town will know what's happened anyway."

Sam held the paper up to the light first and gave it a quick glancing over.

His jaw dropped open and his fingers jerked spasmodically around the paper. Bertha could see he was trying very hard not to destroy the note completely.

"Oh, my God," he gasped.

"Sam? Sam, what's the matter?" Bertha asked. Her voice grew increasingly strident. "Sam, for Pete's sake, read the letter!"

"I was afraid, but . . . but I never thought it would come to this," he moaned.

"What?"

The men were all urging Sam to read the letter. But right now he only seemed capable of staring and gaping.

"Want me to read it for you?" Tom asked.

Sam nodded and handed him the letter. Then he sat down beside Bertha. She reached across and held his hand firmly.

Tom began to read: " 'Sam, you lousy, two-faced, double-crossing bastard.' "

"Quite a love note you got there, Sam," the sheriff said with a snicker.

"Shut up, Amos," Sam groaned.

Tom continued to read. " 'I've got your kid. If you don't give me all your money, I'll kill her. Roy.' "

Tom extended the letter back to Sam, but he refused to touch it. Tom tossed it onto the table.

"Short and to the point, wouldn't you say?" Tom asked.

"Someone kidnapped Miranda?" Bertha gasped hoarsely. "Roy." She looked to Sam, puzzled. "Who's Roy?"

"You mean the person who kidnapped Miranda, this Roy

person, left that note in the house while I was right here?"
Rachel said.

"How?" Bertha asked. "How?"

"I never saw anyone come in. I . . . I only left a few
times, for only a few minutes," Rachel said. Her white
fingers grasped the edge of the table for support. "I swear.
As God is my witness, I . . ."

She started to shake. She reached for the chair and barely
made it there in time to collapse into her seat. Tom rushed
to her side.

"Oh, my goodness. Does that mean whoever left it was
watching me the whole time you were all gone . . . and I
was here . . . all alone?" She placed her hand protectively
over her stomach.

"It's not your fault, Rachel," Bertha assured her. "It's
probably good you weren't here."

"I don't think he'd harm you anyway," Sam said. "It's me
he's after."

"He *did* wait until you were out of the house," Bertha
reminded her.

"But he was watching me the whole time." Rachel was
definitely pale.

"Who's this skunk called Roy?" some of the men
demanded.

"I don't rightly know, but I'll bet I can tell you pretty
much what he looks like," Sheriff Duncan said. "Bald spot
right about here." He placed his fist on the top of his head.
"Missing a tooth right about here." He tapped his left front
tooth. He looked toward Sam. "Tell me if I'm scoring any
points with this, Sam."

Sam nodded. "You're absolutely right, sheriff. That's Roy
Kiley."

"That's the man who hit you."

"The same."

"Never heard of him. I haven't seen his name on any
wanted posters."

"You won't. He's not an outlaw."

"Well, I'd say after this, he definitely could be considered one."

"No," Sam said very seriously. "After this he'll be considered dead."

"What does he want with you? Why'd he take Miranda instead?" the crowd demanded to know.

"Who is he?" Bertha pleaded. Her grip on his hand was tightening. "Why didn't you tell me any of this before, damn it? Why does he want you?"

"He wants our money," he corrected very quietly.

"Oh, who cares?" She released her grasp on him and threw her hands up in the air. "It can be *his* money—he can eat it if he wants. Give it to him—all of it—if he'll just give us Miranda back."

Sheriff Duncan was chuckling again, so hard his stomach was bouncing once more. "The man's a dang fool if he's still thinking of robbing you, Sam. He ought to go after Quinn or Richardson, maybe even Widow Crenshaw or Miss Barber, but not you."

"No, Sheriff," Sam said. "It's me he wants. It's my money he wants."

"You don't have any money."

"Yes, I do."

The crowd began to laugh.

Sam threw a glance at Bertha. He figured he might as well tell them now. Sooner or later the whole town would find out anyway. Between Miranda's kidnapping and Sam's wealth, the Hamiltons would be giving the folks in Grasonville something to gab about for months to come.

Bertha nodded her consent.

"I was out in Nevada," Sam began.

"We knew that, Sam," one of the men responded.

"I worked the mines for a while. I wanted to claim a stake of my own, but I didn't have enough to go it alone. I met this fellow, Roy Kiley. He said he was from Sacramento and knew all about mining. We went in as partners. He knew his stuff, all right. But after about a year of not coming up with anything but rocks and dirt and only little bits of silver, he said he got tired of waiting. Said the mine was worthless, said he was going home."

"Was it worthless?"

Sam ignored that question and continued with his tale. "If I'd had a lick of sense, I would've believed him and come home, too. But I just couldn't."

"Why not?"

"Just a feeling in my gut, I guess. I'd managed to save a little. I paid him back what he'd originally invested, and I just kept on digging—like some kind of fool. About a year later I hit the motherlode. I guess that mine's worth about a million or two today."

The men started hooting and shouting in celebration. Tom and Rachel blinked and stared. Del just groaned.

"What's the matter?" Rachel asked.

"Miranda's rich. If we thought she was rotten before, just wait," he predicted ominously and shook his lowered head. "Just wait."

The Reverend Knutson quietly and humble approached Sam and whispered, "Do you think your first act of charity as a wealthy man might be to donate a new organ to the church?"

"Buy a new organist, too, while you're at it," some called.

"Roy never could accept the fact that he didn't still own part of that mine," Sam went on. "He accused me of holding out on him—but, heck, he was the man with all the experience. He should've known. I even offered him a job in the office for a while."

Bertha laid her hand on his arm. "Is he the one . . . ?"

Slowly he nodded. "Roy's the man I thought I could trust to send you the money. How could I have been so stupid! I'm so sorry, sweetheart."

"It doesn't matter now. I just want Miranda back."

"Roy's been after me for a long time now. We even went to court over it. The judge upheld my claim. But Roy's a stubborn cuss. He just wouldn't stop."

"He ain't too bright on a lot of other things, either," Sheriff Duncan said. "He didn't even tell you how to get the money to him."

Sam nodded. "That figures. Roy never did think things out completely. I just . . . Oh, God, I just hope he *does* think about not hurting Miranda."

"Well, why on earth didn't you tell us you were rich before?" someone else demanded.

"Why didn't you put it in the bank?" another man asked. Then he gave a little chuckle. "Richardson'll have an apoplectic fit when he hears this!"

Everyone was chatting amongst themselves, probably making sure they got the story right—or close enough— before taking it home to their families and the friends who hadn't managed to come out.

Rachel quietly approached Bertha.

"I know it's your kitchen, but you don't look up to doing a lot of cooking. I'll cook up some dinner for these fellows—"

"Oh, yes," Bertha answered vaguely, struggling to her feet. "They've worked so hard. They've got to be fed. But I'll do it, Rachel. You shouldn't—"

"I'm fine—a lot better off than you are, I think," she insisted. "If you'll just go out and get the milk or buttermilk, or whatever you've got in the springhouse, that would be a big help."

"Yeah, sure. Thanks, Rachel."

Bertha knew she was heading in the direction of her springhouse. She'd been there enough times she could walk the path at midnight on a new moon. The blades of grass blurred into vague clumps as she walked. She just didn't seem to have much heart in seeing anything else. The call of the birds blended into silence under the beating of her own heart in her ears. All the budding trees and green blades of grass sprouting, the tiny spring flowers peeking out from under the low leaves, the birds singing as they built their nests, weren't anywhere near as beautiful without Miranda to be sharing them with.

"Bertha?"

She turned. She hadn't expected anyone to be fool enough to bother her with questions at a time like this. She hadn't counted on Arthur.

"Did you come to help me carry in the milk?" she asked.

Of course not, she knew down in her bones. But maybe if she distracted him, she could get him to do that, and he'd forget he'd come to pester her. It didn't matter what he came to talk to her about. Right now he was a pest. He was worse than a pest. He was a blasted botheration she kept thinking she'd gotten rid of, and he just kept coming back!

"No. I . . . I didn't know what you were going outside for," he stammered. "I . . . I just wanted to be with you."

"Thank you, Arthur. But, just in case you need reminding, you've been with us all morning."

"No, Bertha. You know I just want to be with *you*."

With a heavy sigh she stopped in her tracks and turned to him.

"Look, Arthur. I've been through enough for *days* now. I've just about reached the end of my rope. I've already nearly punched Widow Crenshaw in the nose." She scowled at him fiercely. "Don't make me go through the same thing with you, Arthur," she warned.

Arthur took a step backward.

She really didn't want to scare him. She was already scared enough and didn't like the feeling, so she sure wouldn't want anyone else to feel that way. But right about now, if it got rid of Arthur, she'd try anything.

"I don't want you to get so riled you punch me, Bertha. I just wanted to . . . to let you know I'm here."

"I see you, Arthur. I know you're here. Half the whole darn town is here. And you know what? Not a one of them is doing me any darn good. And right now neither are you."

She turned her back to him and continued on her way to

the small springhouse that Sam had built in a little hollow along the bank of the stream.

She heard Arthur's footsteps following her. How thick-headed could a man get? Maybe Fred should use Arthur's head instead of his anvil.

"Bertha, if it's his money that makes you—"

"I seem to recall telling you I was staying with Sam a long time before anything about this money ever came to light."

"You'd never need for money again with me, either."

"I don't love you, Arthur," she reminded him, not even bothering to be subtle or tactful. "And how dare you suggest I'd be the kind of woman who would choose a man just because he had money!"

"Even if Sam's rich, he's not dependable," Arthur continued his argument.

She didn't even bother to answer him.

"Who knows when he'll take off again, leaving you penniless once more?"

Finally she stopped. Her fists were balled tightly at her sides.

"Who knows when he'll catch pneumonia and die? Who knows when he'll get kicked in the head by a mule and die?" she exclaimed. "I've been penniless a lot longer than I've been rich. I think I'd manage. But let me tell you, I'd rather be penniless with Sam than rich with anyone else."

She turned away and practically ran to the springhouse. Once inside the cool darkness, she drew in deep breaths, trying to calm down. Finally alone, she felt the tears returning. This time they weren't for Miranda.

Why did Arthur have to bring up Sam leaving again? She had enough uncertainty wondering where her daughter was. Why should she have to worry about Sam staying or leaving anymore? Didn't she have more faith in him than that?

Why should she let a few snide remarks by Arthur ruin the trust she'd come to place in Sam again?

She shouldn't. But she did.

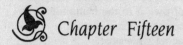 Chapter Fifteen

It was nearly dark. Most of the men had gone home. Sam and Bertha really hadn't expected everyone to stay around until Miranda was found. They all had jobs and families. They were lucky to still have their families.

Anyway, they'd already searched everywhere they could. There was no sense in everyone just hanging around uselessly, waiting for Roy to send them another message.

"You really need to get home and check on the children," Bertha told Rachel.

"I . . . I hate to leave you at a time like this."

"I'll be fine. I have Sam," she said, tucking her arm through his.

"Look, if you need me, fire a gunshot or something," Tom offered. Then he said, "Heck, Sam. If I hear a gunshot, you know I'll come running."

"Thanks."

"Go home, Rachel. Feed the children and have a good night's sleep," Bertha urged. Heaven knew *she* wouldn't until Miranda was found.

Tom took Rachel's elbow. "Yeah, come on," he said as he urged her toward the door. "There's really not much we can do now but wait. For your own good, and the good of the baby, you need to be waiting in your own home in your own bed."

"Go on, Rachel," Bertha insisted. "You've really done more than enough."

Reluctantly Rachel allowed Tom to lead her toward the door.

"I . . . I'm staying here, all right?" Del asked.

"Why?" Tom asked.

"I . . . I guess I kind of owe it to the Hamiltons," Del admitted with a blush.

"Let him stay, Tom," Rachel whispered.

"Well, then, you can come running if the Hamiltons need anything," Tom ordered.

"Yes, sir."

"Yeah, I'm staying, too," Max said.

"How long have you been here, Max?" Sam asked.

Max just shrugged. "Don't know. Can't tell time."

"What are you doing here anyway?"

Max shrugged again. "Ain't got no place else to be."

"Nobody else to lure into alleys?"

"Shucks, mister. I said I was sorry."

"Just teasing, Max."

The four of them each found someplace to sit. They sat and they waited.

The creaking of the rocker as Bertha moved back and forth kept time with the ticking of the camelback clock on the mantel.

Sam sat in the ladderback chair by the fireplace. His elbows were propped up on his knees and his head hung down in his hands. He started shaking his head again for about the fiftieth time that evening.

"I don't know. I just don't know," he murmured forlornly.

"Where could she be?" Bertha asked. She sat there, shredding a damp handkerchief. "We've searched every inch of this place several times. Different people have searched, so it's not like only one person missed something."

"What I can't figure out is why Roy hasn't sent another note. How the heck does he expect me to give him the darn money if he doesn't tell me where to meet him?"

"There's only one place we haven't looked," Bertha said.

"The outhouse?"

"No, Rachel's been there enough times," she said with a weak little laugh.

"Where?"

"Miranda's hiding place."

Sam sat up and threw his arms down by his side in a gesture of disgust.

"For Pete's sake, Bertha. We've been all over this farm. If we haven't hit Miranda's hiding place by now, we never will."

"We still haven't found it, have we, Del?" she asked.

Del jumped. Darn, he knew he shouldn't have stayed around. He'd only wanted to make sure Miranda was all right.

"Have we?" she insisted.

Darn, how did she know that kind of stuff? She wasn't *his* mother.

"No, ma'am."

"What have we missed, Del?"

"I . . . I . . ."

"If we don't find Miranda, that Roy fellow might kill her. He might've already killed her, and we wouldn't even be able to give her body a Christian burial if we don't find her."

"Oh, I think you'd find her after a couple of days," Max said, holding his nose.

"Shut up, Max," Bertha scolded.

"If Miranda's still alive, she's going to kill me for giving away her secret place," Del complained.

Bertha jumped up from her chair and glared at Del.

"If you don't take us right there, right now, I just might forget I'm a lady and strangle you myself!"

"Yes, ma'am. Yes, ma'am," Del repeated again and again, ducking and dodging his head the way Tom had taught him years ago to avoid Jimmy's and Allen's punches. "Come with me."

* * *

"Just sit down and shut up!" Roy roared. He waved his gun back and forth between Miranda and the horse blanket folded in the corner.

"I can't sit down. I got to go to the outhouse!" Miranda declared. She couldn't do much with her hands tied together in front of her and her feet hobbled. But she had managed to stand up and was hopping around the floor of the little room behind the tack room.

"You went an hour ago."

"I got to go again," she insisted. "I'm a little girl. Little girls have to go a lot. Don't you know anything about little girls, you big dummy?" she asked with a sneer.

"No, I don't have any kids."

"Geez, I'll bet everybody's really glad of that." She sneered at him again.

"Why? What do you mean by that?"

"Well, the kids might be just as dumb as you."

"I'm not dumb!"

"Then how come I'm only in the second grade and I had to help you spell *double* and *bastard*?"

Roy starting grumbling under his breath. "Little girls shouldn't know how to spell words like *bastard*."

"Little girls shouldn't have to go to the outhouse, either, according to you. Shows what you know, you big dummy."

"Sit down."

"Nope, you definitely shouldn't have kids," Miranda continued. "You're so ugly, they might look like you, and that would be horrifying."

"Shut up."

"You're so ugly, if ugly was bricks, you'd be Mr. Richardson's mansion."

"What? Who? Oh, shut up."

"You're so ugly, when you were born, the doctor slapped your mother."

"Shut up. I don't even know who my ma was."

"You're so ugly, when you were born, your ma ran away when she saw you."

"Just sit down and shut up," Roy repeated.

"You're so ugly, when you were born the doctor thought your face was your butt and told your mom she had twins."

"Will you stop it!" he roared.

Miranda hopped closer to him and examined the top of his head.

"What happened to your hair?"

"What about my hair?" he asked, reaching up and patting the bald spot.

"Did you run into Indians who tried to scalp you and somebody stopped them in the middle? Did you go to a really bad barber?"

"Just shut up about my hair, too."

"How come it's gray on the sides?"

"Too much hard work," Roy snapped.

"Did you work too hard? Did you get tired of working? Is that why you stopped and became a kidnapper?"

"No," Roy snapped again. "It was worry."

Miranda clucked her tongue. "You know, if you didn't go around kidnapping little kids, you wouldn't have to worry so much."

"Just shut up about that and sit down."

She bent down and peered closely at his mouth.

"What happened to your tooth?"

"I lost it."

"How? Did it just fall out one day while you were walking along the street? Did you bend down and try to put it back in again? My mom won't let me put anything from the ground in my mouth. Did yours?"

"I told you, I don't know who my mother is. Now sit down and shut up!"

"Did you eat too much candy and it sort of rotted out? Did it taste rotten? Did you have really bad breath for a while?"

"Shut up."

"You know, it's not so great now, either."

"Shut up."

"Did somebody punch you in the face and knock it out?"

"Yeah, I was in a fight."

"Do you lose all your fights?"

"Kid, I'm warning you—"

She made a horrible face and stuck her tongue out at him.

"I hope your face freezes that way, you little brat."

"Nope, Sam already told me, it's too warm out for that to happen."

Her face would freeze that way, Miranda repeated to herself as she continued to hop around. Sam had teased her about her face freezing that way.

For Pete's sake, where was Sam? Why hadn't they found her by now? Why hadn't they found that stupid note Roy had written and brought the darned money to him?

Why hadn't they grabbed Del and squeezed the location of her hiding place out of him? If their places were switched, she'd sure have wrung all the information he had out of Del by now.

"I'm hungry," she said.

"You can't be hungry. You have to use the outhouse."

"I used the outhouse an hour ago. But I haven't eaten *all day*!" she wailed. "I'm so hungry!"

"Look kid, I'm risking enough just letting you out to peedle in one of the stalls. I'm sure as hell not going to take you to the local hotel for a meal."

"Well, I sure can't go into one of the stalls and eat hay."

"Then sit down and be hungry. Your father's got to come along soon with that money."

"If I faint from hunger, and Sam comes in and sees me lying on the floor, he's going to think I'm dead, and he'll kill you."

"He ain't gonna kill me, kid. Remember, I'm the one with the gun." He lifted the revolver he held, just so she'd notice it more.

She'd been very aware of the gun all along. Mommy

never used a gun. She didn't like to go hunting. If somebody gave Mr. Quinn a gun, he'd probably shoot himself in the foot.

Did Sam have a gun? She'd never seen him with one. She wasn't sure if he knew how to use a gun or not. He'd been out West, with bears and wolves and Mexican bandits and wild Indians. Maybe he did. But was he a better shot than Roy?

Of course he was, she tried to reassure herself. Sam was handsomer than Roy, and a whole heck of a lot smarter. She'd bet Sam knew how to spell *bastard*. He just *had* to be a better shot.

Now if Sam would just find her!

"You might be the one with the gun, but Sam's the one with the brains."

"I got brains, too," he declared proudly.

"If brains were ink, you couldn't make an *X*."

"Don't start that," he warned.

"If brains were gunpowder, you couldn't blow your nose."

"Geez, kid, are you sure you're not a midget or something? I only knowed adults had as nasty a mouth as you."

"Thank you." She paused a moment. "See. I *can* be polite."

"Shush!"

Roy didn't yell this time. He whispered. Why would he be whispering?

"What are you whispering for?" Miranda demanded loudly. "You were really happy yelling a while ago."

"Hush! I'm trying to listen."

"What for? You haven't been listening to me, and I've been trying to tell you some real interesting stuff so this kidnapping wouldn't be so darn boring."

"Shut up!"

Roy held the gun up and crept closer to the door of the tack room. Miranda figured he wasn't just trying to shut her up because she bothered him. He'd been trying that all day and it hadn't worked. He must really hear something.

It must be Sam! Oh, she knew he'd come rescue her.

"What do you hear?" she asked. "Can I listen, too?"

She tried to hop over to the door, but bumped into Roy, sending him grunting against the door. He gave her a push that sent her tumbling backward onto her blanket.

"Geez, kid. Watch it!"

"It's not my fault. I tried to tell you I couldn't walk if you tied my feet together."

"You're not supposed to be walking around. You're supposed to sit still and shut up and whine and cry like other little girls."

"I'm not like other little girls," Miranda protested.

"I've noticed."

Roy listened again at the door.

"What is it?"

"Naw, nothing. I don't hear nothing now."

"Maybe it was Sam. Maybe you ought to go out and check."

"What, and have you try to sneak away again?"

Miranda just shrugged.

The door slammed inward with a thunderous crash.

"Come out, Roy!" Sam commanded.

"Daddy!" Miranda exclaimed. "It's about time you got here!"

"Come out now, Roy, you slimy scum!" Sam ordered. "Leave Miranda in there. I just want you now."

Miranda had thought Roy was slow and stupid. But before she could scramble away, he grabbed her by the waist and hoisted her up in front of him. She wasn't prepared for him to move that fast.

She felt the cold barrel of the gun touching her forehead.

She screamed. Out in the barn she heard her mother scream, too.

"I've got your kid, Sam."

"Don't hurt my daughter, Roy," he warned.

"Where's my money?"

"It's out here. You have to come out here to get it."

"Back up. Back way, way up. I'm coming out. And I want my money."

Sam kept his gunsight trained on the doorway as he backed up.

"Bertha," he called, never taking his eyes from Roy.

He had left her standing by the door, waiting to take Miranda as soon as Roy let her go. He didn't hear her feet moving across the barn on the soft padding of straw on the floor. He couldn't hear her make any other sound. He could only hope his stubborn wife had actually listened to him for once.

At last Roy stepped out of the tack room. Sam's heart lurched when he saw the gun pointing at Miranda's head. He heard Bertha scream again, but he tried to ignore her. He could only hope Del and Max could keep her from making a dash for their daughter. Roy was nervous—and crazy. Nobody knew what a man in that state of mind could do if a woman started screaming.

"I told you, back up, Sam."

"I am backing up."

"Where's my money?"

"It's here."

"I didn't track you this far just to lose it now."

"It's here, Roy." He tried to keep his voice low, so the man wouldn't get any more riled and do something really stupid. "Come on out and get it."

He had to keep Roy's attention centered on him. He had to keep the man calm, he had to keep him believing he'd get his money.

Sam kept his gun trained on Roy while the man moved into the center of the barn.

"Del!" Miranda shouted.

Oh, geez, Miranda, Sam silently moaned. How can I keep your mother calm when you're yelling?

"Yeah?" Del responded.

"Del, you big dummy!" Miranda scolded. "Thanks for giving away my hiding place, you tattletale! If I die, I swear, I'm coming back to haunt you."

"What the hell is she talking about?" Roy demanded, bewildered.

"You better not kill me, mister," Miranda threatened, "or I'll come back and haunt you, too."

"Shut up, kid." He gave Miranda a shake. "Criminy, Sam. She's a pest. Does she always talk that much?"

"Yeah."

Roy shook his head. "I'm looking for my money and I don't see it, Sam," he said, looking around. "Don't turn into the lying, cheating bastard you were in Nevada."

"I didn't cheat you, Roy," Sam said. "You wanted out. I gave you exactly the same amount of money you put into that mine. I paid you fair and square."

"It wasn't fair when you struck silver after I left."

"No, it wasn't fair, but that's the way it is."

"I'm here to make it all fair again."

"Fine, Roy. Fine. Just don't hurt my daughter."

"Then where's my money?"

"Max."

Max came forward slowly, holding the carpetbag out in front of him to show that he had nothing else, in his hands or in the bag. He placed the bag at Sam's feet and scampered away.

"Okay, back up," Roy ordered.

Sam moved a pace or two from the bag.

"Let Miranda go, Roy," he said. "You've got the money."

"And you've got a gun. That was really dumb bringing it out here for me to see. I know as soon as I let the girl go, you're going to kill me. I ain't as stupid as I look."

"Yes, you are," Miranda said.

He gave her a shake and pressed the gun closer against her head.

"I've had about enough of your mouth, too, miss," he said

without ever taking his eyes off Sam. "I can't let her go now. You understand. She's my protection."

"You can't hurt her."

"I really don't want to. You know I ain't really a bad guy. You make sure you tell your missus that." Without taking his eyes off Sam, he nodded toward Bertha. "I'm just a poor one, that wants his fair share of the mine—his *real* fair share—that you and the court cheated me out of."

"Let the girl go. You don't need her now. You've got the money and you've got me."

Roy studied him silently. Sam figured he was starting to weaken. Thinking straight never had been Roy's long suit.

"I'm really the one you want, aren't I, Roy? Not some helpless little girl. It wasn't some little kid who cheated you. It was me, a grown-up man. What's the point in taking it out on a kid when it's bigger game you're really after? Where's the success in hurting a little kid—a little girl—when it's really me—a big, strong, adult man who's your adversary?"

Roy remained silent. Sam guessed the man couldn't think and talk and make sense all at the same time. Maybe he didn't even know what the word *adversary* meant? Sam couldn't waste time letting Roy figure it out. He had to get Miranda out of there soon before Roy lost his patience and started shooting just because he could.

"That's what you were really trying to do in that alley, weren't you, Roy? Come for me?"

"Yeah."

"That's what you were really doing prowling around my house late at night both times, wasn't it?"

"Yeah."

"Then why stop short of your goal now? You came for me and the money. You got your money. Are you going to settle for a job half done?"

"Nope."

"Then what're you going to do, Roy? Are you going to let the little girl go?"

Sam waited for his answer. Roy was slow. Sam didn't think he was ever going to decide.

Finally Roy said, "Throw the gun away."

"What?"

"You heard me. First get rid of the gun."

Sam drew in a deep breath. There really wasn't much choice but to do what Roy said. He'd sort of figured he wouldn't be able to keep the gun.

He gave the revolver a toss into a mound of straw near one of the stalls. He only hoped he'd be able to find it again fast if he had the opportunity.

Roy gave a wicked laugh. "You really are dumber than me! Now I got the only gun. Five of you and six bullets."

"Big deal," Miranda muttered. "You can count, but you can't spell worth a darn."

"I . . . I could shoot everyone of you," Roy declared angrily, "and walk out of here with the money and nobody'd ever know."

"Don't you kill my daddy, you dirty, rotten, low-down, sidewinder, polecat—"

He gave Miranda another shake. "Where'd she learn language like that?"

"She just sort of came that way. Now let her go."

Roy just stood there staring at him.

"Let her go." Sam's voice took on a stern, threatening quality.

"No, no, no." Roy waved the gun under Sam's nose. "Don't get feisty with me. Remember, I've got the gun." He pointed it at his own chest.

"Please, let her go." Sam's voice was soft now. "I'll get down on my hands and knees and kiss your boots if you want me to. I'm not proud, Roy. I just want my daughter to be safe."

"I'm such a soft-hearted fool," Roy said with a chuckle.

He released his grip on Miranda. She thumped to the ground. She struggled to get up. Sam reached up to help her. He felt the gun barrel, cold and hard against his temple.

"Slowly, Sam," Roy warned.

Cautiously, so nothing he did could be seen by Roy as the least bit threatening, Sam untied Miranda's feet and helped her to rise.

She took off at a run, heading for Bertha, who was standing in the doorway.

"You've got me. You've got the money. Let them go now," Sam said, jerking his head toward the four people standing in the doorway of the barn.

"Let my daddy go, you miserable poop head!" Miranda yelled from the safety of the doorway.

"Real handful, huh?" Roy observed.

"Come on, Miranda," Bertha said, dragging her by the hand. "Let's get out of here."

"No! No! I want to stay." She started pulling against Bertha's grasp as she tried to untie her, and kicking and stamping her feet.

Sam had never seen Miranda put on such a show. From the look on Bertha's face, neither had she.

"I want to make sure Mr. Chicken-Hearted Lily-livered Pig-poop doesn't shoot my daddy."

"I'll tell you, Sam," Roy said. "It was a sore trial not to shoot her."

Sam could hear the exasperation in his former partner's voice. How could he really make Miranda understand right now that it wasn't a good idea to offend a man with a loaded gun?

Roy raised his gun and aimed it directly at the middle of Sam's forehead.

"Time to pay the piper, Sam. This is where I get even for the dirty tricks you played on me. I never did like dirty tricks."

"Me, neither."

Roy pulled back the hammer.

Bertha screamed. "Don't! Not . . . not in front of the children. Please, don't!"

"Go on then. Get out of here. Fast," Roy warned, "or I'll kill him anyway."

"I'm not leaving! I'm not leaving my daddy!" Miranda dug her heels into the straw and screamed. She was still stamping her feet and kicking up straw and dust.

"Get her out of here!"

All the while Miranda had been screaming and fussing, she'd been pointing with her bound hands. She was hoping her mother would see what she was pointing to and understand.

At last Bertha looked up. The rope attached to the hook in the doorway led upward to support a bale of hay that the hired hands must have been hauling up when they were interrupted in their work to come look for Miranda. Bertha would have to remember to cook something special for them. Now she could only hope what Miranda had been trying to show her would really work.

"Here, here!" Max was frantically pushing Sam's discarded gun into her hand.

"I can't," Bertha protested. "I don't know how to use one of those."

"Take it, take it!" Max insisted. "While Miranda's pitching a fit has the weasel distracted."

"Where'd you get this? No, I know." She was terrified Roy would stop bragging about how clever he was to fool Sam, and notice that she was fiddling with farm equipment and now a gun. "How'd you get this without being seen?"

Max shrugged and admitted, "I'm a thief. I'm sneaky."

"Hold it for me. I have something else to do first."

Slowly she reached up to begin unwinding the rope. Two loops should have done it. Why did it seem to be taking twenty or thirty?

The bale was heavy. If her judgment was only a foot or two off, Sam would be the one crushed under the bale, not Roy.

She shut her eyes and released the rope.

The bale only glanced off Roy's shoulder, sending him

sideways into the straw. As he rolled, he came up shooting. Sam ducked and dived beside the carpetbag for what little protection it could give. He began crawling toward the mound of hay where he had discarded his gun.

Del grabbed Miranda, dumped her down into the straw, and threw himself over top of her.

"Get off, you big dummy!" she mumbled. "You're heavy."

"What gratitude."

"This straw tastes like horse poop! When I get up—"

"Just shut up, Miranda."

Max shoved the gun into Bertha's hands.

She fired. What else could she do? Two shaking hands clasped around the gun, she lined her index fingers up with the barrel, pointed her fingers at Roy, and pulled the trigger.

Once, twice. Roy was still shooting at Sam. She stepped closer all the while she fired.

Three, four. Roy turned and started shooting at her.

Five, six. The gun just kept clicking as she bore down on Roy, still pulling the trigger with each measured step. She had to tread stiffly, to keep from collapsing completely.

But Roy was lying face up, eyes open, staring blankly. His hand hung limp at his side. A dark red spot was starting to spread over his chest.

Sam cautiously lifted his head. Slowly everyone converged on the body.

"Yick! Blood!" Miranda exclaimed. She promptly turned around and vomited.

"Where'd you get the gun?" Sam asked.

"It's yours. Max got it from where you threw it."

"So that's where it went."

With hands that still shook, Bertha held it out to him. "Take it! Take it! I don't want it anymore."

Sam stood and looked around him. "What'd you do here?"

"I . . . I think I shot him."

He looked down at the still body and all around. There

was a bullet hole in the carpetbag precariously close to where his head had been.

"Yep. I think so, too."

"Oh, no. I shot the money," Bertha wailed.

"Don't worry. I think we can spare a couple hundred dollars."

There were two bullet holes in the dirt around Roy's head. There was a bullet hole sunk into the wooden stall door about two feet above Roy's head. There was even a bullet hole in the stirrup strap of a saddle perched on the stall door. There was one single bullet hole in Roy—directly in his heart.

"Is . . . is he dead?" Tears were already beginning to stream down Bertha's face—tears for a man she didn't know who had caused her so much pain.

Sam nudged the body with the toe of his boot. "Appears to be."

"I . . . I guess my aim got better as I went along."

"Guess so."

"I . . . I had to do it, you know."

"I know."

"I didn't want to. I'm sorry. But . . . but I had to. He'd taken my daughter. He'd scared Rachel. He was going to kill you. I couldn't let him do that."

"I'm glad you didn't."

She sniffed back her tears and wiped the last ones away. She took one last, unbearable look at the body before she turned away, never to look back.

"I don't think I like blood too much anymore," Miranda said as she clung to her mother. "I think I want to go home."

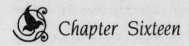# Chapter Sixteen

Max went running back to town for the sheriff and the undertaker.

"Oh, Del," Miranda said, taking his hand as they headed back toward the house.

Del grimaced, but it was pretty obvious he had enough manners to know that pulling his hand away was not quite the thing to do right now.

She stared up at him adoringly. "You saved my life."

"Oh, geez!"

"You're almost as wonderful as my daddy."

Del finally managed to tactfully untangle his hand from Miranda's grasp.

"I think I better go tell my ma and dad you all are safe," he offered.

Before Bertha or Sam could respond, Del took off over the rise at a run.

At last Bertha, Sam, and Miranda were alone again, as a family. The sun was setting. Bertha went around, lighting a lamp or two. At last she settled into her rocking chair. Miranda climbed up on her lap.

"The last time we were together, you two were fighting," Miranda said.

"We're not going to fight anymore," Sam promised.

"Don't lie to the child," Bertha scolded playfully. "The truth is, sometimes mothers and fathers argue, Miranda. A lot. But the important thing is that they kiss and make up afterward."

"I know," Miranda answered. "Del told me all about it. When I grow up, I'm going to marry him. Remember?"

"All too well," Bertha replied in resignation. Right about now she was so glad to have her daughter cradled in her lap in their big rocking chair, she'd have agreed with Miranda if she'd said the moon was made of green cheese.

"Miranda, you know you did something back in the barn that you swore you'd never do," Sam reminded her.

"Oh, well, if it's about that mess in the one stall, it's not my fault! It's the only place that stupid rattlesnake would let me—"

"No, no. Not that."

"Oh, what then? I can't remember any other mess—"

"You called me daddy."

"Well, that's who you are, isn't it?"

"If you want me to be."

Miranda eyed him warily for a few moments. "So, you're really leaving the choice up to me?"

"That's right," Sam said with an emphatic nod.

"Okay. I think I'd really like for you to be my daddy, which is really good, 'cause you already are."

"Then you've got to do one more thing before you go to bed."

"What's that?"

"Come here and give Daddy a good-night hug."

Sam held his arms out wide for Miranda. She jumped from Bertha's lap and dived into his arms. She wrapped her little arms around his neck in a loving choke hold. Strangulation had never felt so good.

"I love you, my little girl."

"I love you, Daddy. I'm glad you're all right and Roy didn't shoot you."

"Thanks for saving my life, Miranda."

"Thanks for saving mine. I did it because I love you."

"I know."

"You're a pretty clever little girl, you know."

"Yeah, I know."

Miranda gave him one more big squeeze, then hopped off to bed.

Sam came and sat on the floor at Bertha's feet.

"I love you, too," he told her.

"I think you're the bravest man in the world. All along I've been so afraid you'd just up and leave again for another seven years. I was never sure I could depend on you. Now I am."

"You can depend on me, sweetheart. But I will be leaving here again from time to time."

"What?"

"Remember, we have a silver mine to work."

"Oh, my goodness, yes. Can I . . . can I . . . do you think I could buy a new dress?"

"New dress? Thunderation, woman! You can buy the whole dang dress shop!"

Bertha laughed. "I think one will do for now."

"But wherever I go, I'll have my wife and daughter with me. I never want to be away from you again for as long as I live."

She grew serious. "I'm glad Roy didn't shoot you, too."

"I'm glad *you* didn't shoot me."

"Okay, so I need some practice."

"I know something else I need a lot of practice on."

He stood and took her hand. He helped her to rise, then slowly led her into their bedroom. Bertha would always look forward to entering this room now.

He shut the door behind him and took her into his arms. He bent his head to nuzzle her neck, then pressed his cheek against hers.

"It's good just to hold you, to know you're mine, all mine."

"It's good to have you home again with me."

His lips descended to meet hers. She held him tightly to

her, savoring his strong masculinity, enjoying the strength of his body and heart.

"I'll never leave you."

He kissed the edges of her mouth, then the tip of her chin. Tilting her head upward, he ran his lips down her smooth neck, lingering to place a kiss in the small indentation at the base of her throat.

"I'll always welcome you back again."

"No. You know at our wedding when the preacher said, ''Til death do us part'?" he asked.

"I didn't think you were listening."

"Well, I was. And that's about what it's going to take to get me away from you ever again."

She held him more tightly to her, wanting never to release him ever again. "Welcome home, my love."

FREE
Romance

(a $4.50 value)

Send in the Coupon Below

To get your FREE historical romance and start saving, fill out the coupon below and mail it today. As soon as we receive it we'll send you your FREE Book along with your first month's selections.

Mail To: **True Value Home Subscription Services, Inc. P.O. Box 5235**
120 Brighton Road, Clifton, New Jersey 07015-5235

YES! I want to start previewing the very best historical romances being published today. Send me my FREE book along with the first month's selections. I understand that I may look them over FREE for 10 days. If I'm not absolutely delighted I may return them and owe nothing. Otherwise I will pay the low price of just $4.00 each: a total $16.00 (at *least* an $18.00 value) and save at least $2.00. Then each month I will receive four brand new novels to preview as soon as they are published for the same low price. I can always return a shipment and I may cancel this subscription at any time with no obligation to buy even a single book. In any event the FREE book is mine to keep regardless.

Name
_____

Street Address _____ Apt. No. _____

City _____ State _____ Zip Code _____

Telephone _____

Signature _____
(if under 18 parent or guardian must sign)

Terms and prices subject to change. Orders subject
to acceptance by True Value Home Subscription
Services, Inc.

11881-8

Our Town

...where love is always right around the corner!

All Books Available in July 1996

__Take Heart__ by Lisa Higdon
$$0-515-11898-2/\$5.99$$

In Wilder, Wyoming...a penniless socialite learns a lesson in frontier life—and love.

__Harbor Lights__ by Linda Kreisel
$$0-515-11899-0/\$5.99$$

On Maryland's Silchester Island...the perfect summer holiday sparks a perfect summer fling.

__Humble Pie__ by Deborah Lawrence
$$0-515-11900-8/\$5.99$$

In Moose Gulch, Montana...a waitress with a secret meets a stranger with a heart.